Stay TOGETHER

NEW YORK TIMES BESTSELLING AUTHOR

KAYLEE RYAN

Cover Design: Book Cover Boutique
Cover Photography: Sara Eirew
Editing: Hot Tree Editing
Proofreading: Deaton Author Services. Editing 4 Indies,
Jo Thompson, Jess Hodge
Paperback Formatting: Integrity Formatting

WILLOW RIVER, GA · HOME OF THE KINCAID BROTHERS · WILLOW RIVER, GA · HOME OF THE KINCAID BROTHERS · WILLOW RIVER, GA · HOME OF THE KINCAID BROTHERS · WILLOW RIVER, GA · HOME OF THE KINCAID BROTHERS ·

Willow River
Georgia

WWW.KAYLEERYAN.COM

Stay
TOGETHER

NEW YORK TIMES BESTSELLING AUTHOR
KAYLEE RYAN

Chapter 1

RUSHTON

I'M PUTTING ON MY SHOES to head out when my phone rings. When I see Sterling's name on the screen, I laugh. "I'm on my way," I answer.

"Can you stop and get some fishing line?"

"Are we going fishing and someone forgot to tell me?" I know that's not why he needs it, but as his brother, it's my job to fuck with him.

"It's for the pictures, Rush." He sighs. "Just hurry. I want everything done before she gets here."

Since I can hear the stress in his voice, I cut him some slack. "I'm putting my shoes on now." I glance down at said shoes.

"Thanks, man."

"Anything else you need?"

"Nah. The twins are here, and everyone else is on their way."

"Got it. Fishing line coming right up." I end the call, not bothering to say goodbye. Not that Sterling notices. He's so wrapped up in what he's about to do later this evening and the surprise he has for his best friend turned live-in girlfriend to call me out on my lack of telephone etiquette.

I finish with my shoes, grab my phone from the cushion next to me, and head for the garage. My keys are on the hook next to the door, and in no time, I'm on the road, heading to Gunderson's hardware for some fishing line.

Gunderson's is the place in Willow River for anything you might need. From road trip snacks to small tools to bolts and zip ties. They even have homemade baked goods that a few locals drop off for sale. It truly is the place to be if you need something in this town.

The drive is short, and that's with me taking my time. I know it will annoy Sterling. I can't hide my smile when I think about his huff of irritation that I'm sure he's going to direct my way. I get it. He's making moves, big moves, and he wants his surprise to be perfect, but Alyssa is going to be occupied all day. The other Kincaid ladies will make sure of it. He needs to just relax. It's not like she's going to turn him down.

Pulling open the door to Gunderson's, I'm hit with nostalgia. I don't know how many trips we made here as kids with Dad. He was always tinkering with something or working on his honey-do list for our mom. Gunderson's has been a staple not only in the town of Willow River but in my life as well.

"Rushton Kincaid," George Gunderson announces as I step inside.

"George, good to see you." I nod at him. George is a third-generation Gunderson, and it's always his smiling face behind the counter with each visit. His son, George the fourth, is sure to take his place one day.

I'm glad our parents gave us our own names and identities. I couldn't imagine any of us being Raymond Kincaid the second. Besides, with nine boys, they needed more options.

I know this place probably as well as George himself, so I turn left and head toward the back wall, where I'll find a selection of a fishing line. When I reach the wall, I encounter something so much better than what I came here for.

A beautiful woman.

She's got dark, straight shoulder-length hair, and from the looks of her ass in those jeans, a tight little body. She's reaching for the top shelf, standing on her tiptoes, and making no headway.

"Need some help?" I ask, shoving my hands in my pockets to keep from reaching out for her. I'm nervous she's going to topple over with the way she's balancing on her toes and reaching over her head.

The beauty falls to her feet and turns to face me. She blows out a breath, causing her hair to fly out of her eyes. "Yes, please." She smiles kindly.

Her smile is meant to be kind, but it hits me in the chest. I don't know if I've ever seen a more beautiful woman. I've seen many—my momma for one—and my brothers' wives and girlfriends are all beautiful, but this woman, she's breathtaking.

"What do you need?" There is a huskiness to my voice that surprises me.

"Fishing line."

"You fish?" I ask, not making a move to grab the line.

She chuckles. "No, well, I mean, I have, but that's not why I need it. I'm a teacher, and I plan to use it to hang my students' crafts from the ceiling in my classroom."

My mind is suddenly riddled with a naughty student-teacher scene that is definitely not safe for work.

"A teacher," I repeat, because apparently, in the presence of this beauty, my mind stops working.

She nods, a smile lifting her lips. I know because I'm staring at them, imagining how they would feel wrapped around my cock. "Kindergarten."

"Y'all need some help?" George's voice breaks me out of my fantasy.

"Nah, we're all set," I call back to him. I turn to look, and he nods, heading back to his spot behind the counter. "Which one?" I ask the woman turning me into my teenage self. I point to the fishing line.

"Any of them." She shrugs. "It's just for decorations."

"That's why I'm here too," I tell her. "My brother, well, one of them, is planning a surprise for his girlfriend and asked me to stop and pick some up."

"That's sweet." I can tell by the tone of her voice she truly thinks so. I'm not sure if it's me picking up the fishing line or Sterling's surprise that she thinks is sweet, but I'm going to pretend it's the former.

Reaching up, I grab us both what we need, handing one of the packages to her. She opens her palm to accept, but I pull it back. "I'm Rushton. Rush. My family and friends call me Rush," I amend.

Again with that smile. "Crosby. It's nice to meet you, Rush."

Even her name is sexy. How is that possible? "You as well, Crosby," I say, just to hear her name on my lips.

"Are you from here? Willow River?" she inquires.

"Born and raised. Where are you from?" I'm certain if she grew up here, I'd have already met her.

"How do you know I'm not from Willow River?" She tilts her head to the side, waiting for my reply, and it reminds me of a baby kitten.

"I know everyone in this town, or at least recognize them. I would have remembered you." My eyes trail over her body.

"Small-town living." She chuckles. "I'm from Atlanta. I just accepted a teaching position at Willow River Elementary."

"My old stomping grounds."

This gets a full-blown laugh out of her, and it causes a weird flutter in my chest. "Stomping grounds in elementary school?"

"I have eight brothers. Four older and four younger. We're all close in age, so yeah." I shrug.

"Nine boys?" Her eyes widen. "Your parents are rock stars."

"That they are," I agree. Carol and Raymond Kincaid are not only great parents but the best humans I know. I'm not just saying that because they're my parents.

"Well, Rush, thank you for the assist." She holds her hand out for the fishing line, and I place it in her palm.

"You're welcome, Crosby."

With a smile and a wave, she walks away. I force myself to stand still and watch her go. It's not until I hear her tell George thank you, and the chime on the door, that I make my way to the front, placing my own fishing line onto the counter before pulling my wallet out of my back pocket.

"This all for ya?" George asks.

"Yep."

"She's a looker," he says, nodding to the door Crosby just walked out of.

"Harriette know you're looking to replace her?" I tease. Well, I'm half teasing and half irritated. He could be her grandfather.

George lets loose with a belly laugh. When I say belly, I mean his belly is shaking beneath the suspenders he uses to keep his pants held up. "Son, my Harriette knows she's the love of my life and has been for over forty years. Just because I recognize beauty doesn't mean I'd ever replace the love of my life. One day you'll understand."

I don't tell him that I know what love looks like. I grew up with parents who adore one another, and I've watched my cousin and four older brothers fall madly in love. It's not that I don't understand. No, the issue is that I'm jealous as fuck of a man twice my age over a woman I just met minutes before.

"Thanks for this," I say, sliding my card back into my wallet and picking up the fishing line.

"Thanks for stopping by." I can hear the smugness in his voice. He and I both know why I smarted off at him. It's not that I think he wants to replace his wife. It's because the dark-haired beauty, also known as Crosby, has me tied up in knots after one very brief conversation.

Pushing through the door, I move my sunglasses from the top of my head to cover my eyes as I make my way to my truck. I scan the lot, looking for her, even though I'm sure she's already gone, when I spot her.

Crosby.

She's got her head inside the trunk of her car, ass in the air, tempting as hell, and dangerous as fuck. Sure, Willow River is a safe town, but that doesn't mean it's okay to take unnecessary risks. I stop right behind her, and she doesn't even notice that I'm there.

"Shoot," she mumbles.

"Need some help?" I ask.

She startles, lifts her head, which she smacks on the trunk, and turns to face me. Her face is scrunched up in pain as she rubs the spot she just whacked on the back of her skull.

"Let me see." I step closer and replace her hand with mine, checking her over. Gently, I run my fingers over the back of her head, checking for injuries. "No bleeding," I tell her, stepping away.

"Thanks."

"What's going on?"

"That." She points to the right rear tire that's flat as a pancake. "I was trying to get to the spare to change it."

"Do you know how to change a tire?"

"What? Because I'm a woman, I don't know how?"

I shrug. "Just asking. Do you?"

"No, but I have my cell phone, and I'm sure the internet will help me."

"Or you could let me do it for you."

"I can't ask you to do that."

"You didn't."

"I—" She quickly clamps her mouth shut. I can see her internal battle. "Thank you."

"You're welcome." I give her what I hope is a reassuring smile. "Can you hold this for me?" I offer her my reel of fishing line.

"That's the least I can do. I really appreciate you doing this, Rushton." I don't miss the way she uses my full name, when moments before I was Rush.

"It's no problem. I'll have you out of here in no time." As I say the words, my phone begins to ring in my pocket. I don't bother pulling it out to look at the screen. I know that it's Sterling, and he's wondering where in the hell I am. It doesn't take this long to stop and pick up some fishing line. When the ringing halts and immediately starts again, I know he's not going to stop unless I give him something.

"Am I keeping you from something?" she asks.

"Nah, I was picking up that"—I point to the fishing line in her hand—"for my brother. He's just wondering where I am." Instead of calling Sterling or answering his call, I send it to voice mail and type out a quick message.

Me:	At Gunderson's. Lady with a flat tire. I'm changing it, and I'll be there.
Sterling:	Of all the days for you to be a Good Samaritan.
Me:	Ha! You know damn good and well, you would have done the same thing. Even today.
Sterling:	Just hurry.
Sterling:	But be safe. Mom will never forgive me if something happens to you because you were rushing to bring me fishing line.
Me:	I'll be there soon, and we'll knock this out. There are nine of us, bro. We've got this.

I don't wait for his reply as I slide my phone back into my pocket and get to work. In no time at all, I have the spare swapped out for the flat, and I'm tightening the lug nuts. "This isn't meant for long-term driving," I tell her. "You need to get a new tire to replace it."

"Right. And do you happen to have suggestions for where I might do that?"

I glance up at her. She's staring down at me. Her big brown eyes are filled with concern as she bites down on her bottom lip.

"Yeah, I do, actually." I finish with the lug nuts, ensure they're tight, and stand with the jack in my hand. "My brother, well, one of them has an auto body shop in town. He sells tires and will be able to put it on for you. Kincaid's Auto Repair," I say, moving to the trunk to replace the jack. Once I have it back in its rightful spot, I place the flat tire in the back as well.

"It's here in town?"

"Yes. They're open today. Why don't you follow me over there?"

"Oh, I've imposed enough. You don't need to do that."

"I insist. In fact, let me give you my number. You're new in town, so if you ever need anything, you can call me."

She shakes her head, but there is a tiny trace of a smile pulling at her lips. "That's sly. I'll give you that."

"What?" I feign innocence. Sure, I meant what I said. If she needs me, I'll be there, but I won't lie and say I didn't have an ulterior motive. Sterling is probably losing his mind right now, and he's depending on me; otherwise, I'd be taking her to coffee or dinner, maybe. I just don't know how long this is going to take today, and I promised my brother I would be there for him. I don't ever go back on a promise.

"Are you a player, Rushton Kincaid?" she asks.

I'm impressed she picked up on my last name from telling her the name of Declan's shop. "Nah, not a player. Just a man who sees a beautiful woman he'd like to spend more time with."

Her fucking smile could light up New York City on New Year's Eve. "Your momma had her hands full with you, didn't she?" she teases.

"We were perfect angels."

Her head falls back in laughter, and it's a sound I could listen to every single day. Deep, yet feminine all at the same time. Uninhibited.

"Maybe I should roll my jeans up. Shit is starting to get deep out here," she jokes.

"Or you could take them off." I bat my eyelashes at her, and another round of laughter ensues.

"You're relentless." She steps forward and hands me my fishing line. "Thank you for your assistance today, both with my purchase and with the tire. I appreciate you taking the time out of your day to help me."

"If that doesn't deserve digits, I don't know what does." It's a corny line, but I have a feeling she's going to walk away from me, or drive rather. And something tells me that letting her go without her number will be a huge mistake. However, Willow River is a small town, and I already know she's a teacher at the elementary school. It's not like I can't track her down. It would just be easier if I didn't have to.

She shakes her head. "Thank you, Rushton. Enjoy your day with your brothers." With that, she climbs into her car, and I have to watch her drive away.

I stand in the parking lot, staring after her until I can no longer see her. Once her taillights are out of sight, I move to my truck and climb behind the wheel, tossing the fishing line on the seat. It looks like Miss Crosby is going to make me work for it. Too bad for her, she doesn't realize the Kincaids aren't afraid of a little hard work. I'll get that date.

The drive to Sterling's place is filled with thoughts of the dark-haired beauty. I'm the last to arrive by the looks of his driveway, and I push all thoughts of Crosby out of my mind. If I go in there thinking about her, my brothers are going to catch on and start spouting shit about me settling down.

I want to settle down one day. I just haven't found a woman who I can see myself waking up next to every day of forever. I can only hope that I'm as lucky as my older brothers and our cousin Ramsey. My girl is out there. I just need to find her.

Chapter 2

CROSBY

I'M NERVOUS. SINCE GRADUATING FROM college and getting my teaching degree, I've been a substitute. This is the first year where I have my own classroom. These are my students, and I'm equal amounts excited and anxious.

Moving to Willow River from Atlanta was an easy decision. I was living in a rundown shithole apartment, and I have no family, and the only friend I did let get close slept with my boyfriend. That was my senior year of college. I've kept to myself since then. Sure, I met up with other teachers when I got the invite after a subbing gig, but I never let them in. I kept my guard up. It's still up. I learned at an early age to never depend on anyone but myself. When Shonda, my ex-best friend turned boyfriend seducer, betrayed me, I knew more than ever that my walls needed to stay up. No matter the cost.

I spent the majority of the weekend setting up my classroom, thinking about the handsome stranger who came to my rescue, not once but twice on Saturday. Rushton Kincaid has taken more of my headspace than I feel comfortable admitting. It's all that dark hair, those blue eyes, and the obvious muscles that his tight black T-shirt did nothing to hide.

I found his brother's shop easily, but by the time I got there, they were already closed. I was kicking myself for not giving in and exchanging numbers with Rushton to see if he could pull some strings. Even though the thought of owing him sent me into panic mode. Instead, I drove back to the school and returned to work. My plan is to stop today on my way home.

It's not just Rushton Kincaid that's been on my mind all weekend. I was making name tags for desks yesterday, and low and behold, one Blakely Kincaid is on my list of students this year. Sure, it could be a coincidence. However, Willow River is a small town, and with eight brothers, he's bound to have some nieces and nephews, or hell, she could be his daughter for all I know. I'm pretty certain that he's single. I didn't see a ring, and he was flirting. Not that that stops some men, but something tells me that Rushton isn't like most men. He's in a league all on his own.

The pitter-patter of feet and the voices of young minds start to fill the halls, so I shake out of my thoughts and smile at my students and parents as they make their way into the classroom.

I watch as each student, with the help of their parents, searches for their name on the tables we use as desks and then rushes to find their cubby where they will store their personal items each day.

The next twenty minutes are a flurry of activity. Now, here I stand in front of a room of nineteen five-year-olds, all staring at me with wide eyes. "Good morning." I smile. "My name is Miss Greene."

"Oh! That's my favorite color," one of the boys announces.

"Green is a very cool color," I tell him. "Today, we're going to get to know each other. We're going to take this." I hold up the small squishy light-up ball that I bought over the weekend. "When you have the ball, it's your turn to talk. I'll start. My name is Miss Greene, and my favorite thing to do is read." I smile at them. "Let's start here." I move to the left of the classroom and start with the little girl with the cutest pigtails. I hand her the ball. "Tell us your name and something about you. Favorite toy or color. Anything you want to tell us."

"Macie is my name," she tells us. "I don't like the color green." She wrinkles up her little nose. "Yellow is the bestest." She hands the ball back to me.

"Yellow is a great color. It is the best," I correct, but I know she doesn't realize that's what I'm doing. I move on down the line and eventually reach the little boy whose favorite color is green.

"My name is Finn, and I'm going to be a superhero when I grow up. A green one." He pumps his little fist in the air, making the boys cheer and the girls giggle.

"Very ambitious, Finn." I smile at him. He hands me the ball, and I move to the next in line. It's a little girl with dark hair and big blue eyes.

"My name is Blakely Kincaid, but you can call me Blake. I have a new baby cousin, a new mommy, and I'm getting a baby brother!" Her eyes are sparkling with excitement. "Oh, and I have a gazillion uncles who like to buy me things and take me for ice cream to get me to tell them I'm their favorite."

I have to bite down on my cheek to keep from laughing. There is no way that this little girl isn't related to Rushton. "Wow," I say when I realize she's gazing up at me, waiting for a reply. "You had a busy summer."

She nods. "So busy."

She talks like she's fifteen, not five. I move on down the line, letting each of them tell us their name and something about themselves. I've learned more about their families than I'm sure their parents would like.

For example, Sadie told us how her older brother got in trouble for showering with his girlfriend, but she doesn't know why because she's taken lots of baths with her cousin Hannah who is not in school until next year.

Then Jacob told us that his mom has a statue of boy parts that she keeps in her dresser by her bed. But he told us not to tell because he wasn't supposed to be snooping. And if that wasn't bad enough, Kinzie shared that she has a new baby sister and that her mom's boobies have milk in them. It was an interesting day, to say the least.

I've bitten down on my cheek more in the last twenty minutes to keep from laughing than I have in my entire life. I love this age, which is why I chose kindergarten. The innocence of this age where the world has not yet tainted their young minds. It's a good time getting to see the world through their eyes.

The remainder of the day is more about learning classroom rules and structure. How to line up for restroom breaks, lunch, and recess. We also spend the afternoon doing an art project. Just a simple try-to-stay-in-the-lines coloring exercise to open their minds and work on their concentration. Some did very well, and others not so much, but they all seemed to enjoy it. They got to hang their pictures on the huge display board by the door, and I already had small name tags posted. They had the task of finding their name to match the name on the top of their papers that I put there. I'm happy to say that everyone passed that exercise with flying colors.

It's just after three, and I'm exhausted. I used my planning period to make some adjustments to the seating chart. There were a few students who liked to chat just a little too much, so I decided to try and separate them now to get a handle on it. Then it took me twenty minutes to get them in their new seating assignments. I probably shouldn't have made a move on day one, but I wanted to try and get the distractions under control as soon as possible.

I tidy up my classroom a little before grabbing my stuff and heading out. When I reach my car, I see the donut, and I can't help but smile when I think about Rushton, which reminds me that I need to go to his brother's shop today to get this tire handled. The last thing I need is to be stranded on the side of the road with another flat.

In my car, I navigate to Kincaid's Auto Repair without my GPS. Willow River is a small town, and I have a pretty good sense of direction. Ten minutes later, I'm pulling into the lot that's already quite full. I hope they're able to work me into their schedule at least one day this week.

Parking, I grab my keys and head inside. There's a woman sitting behind the counter who greets me with a wide smile. "Welcome to Kincaid Auto Repair. Can I help you?"

"Hi." I wave awkwardly. "I was referred here to replace a spare tire with a new one. Or maybe repair the old one, I'm not sure."

"Sure. How did you hear about us?" she asks as she types on the computer in front of her.

"Um, Rushton."

She stops typing and looks up at me. "Rushton Kincaid?"

"Yes, ma'am." I don't know why I called her ma'am. She appears to be close to my age.

"How do you know Rush?"

"Well, I don't really know him. He helped me change the flat in the parking lot of Gunderson's on Saturday. He said not to drive on the donut tire for long, but by the time I made it here on Saturday, you were already closed."

"Yeah, we close at noon on Saturdays. Let me grab one of the guys and have them take a look. I'm sure we can get you taken care of today. We had a brake line replacement cancel, so today is your lucky day." She smiles kindly, and the action instantly sets me at ease.

She scoots back in her chair and stands. I watch her as she walks to the garage service door and disappears into the work area. I glance around the room and smile when my gaze lands on a picture of Blakely and who I assume are her parents. The three of them are smiling. The man's hands are on the woman's baby bump while Blakely stands in front of them.

"That's Declan and his wife and daughter. He owns this fine establishment." The voice behind me sounds. I turn to smile at her. "I'm Alyssa, by the way. I'm engaged to Sterling Kincaid." She flashes me her engagement ring. It's sparkling in the light, and without getting close, I know it's beautiful. "The guys are going to pull your car around now. Can I have your keys?" she asks.

I hold my keys out to her. "It's the Ford Edge." I pause. "I'm Crosby by the way."

She smiles. "Nice to meet you. Your car sticks out like a sore thumb with that donut," she teases. "I'll give these to the guys and be right back. Help yourself to a refreshment." She points to the corner where a small refrigerator and one of those one-cup coffee makers sit. There's also a basket with snacks.

I open my mouth to thank her, but she's already gone. I make my way to the small refrigerator and grab a bottle of water. Moving to the front of the waiting area, I peer out the window as I watch a guy in blue overalls slide behind the wheel of my car and move it into the garage.

I'm lost in thought when I hear my name being called. "Crosby?" I turn and fight a grin when I see Rushton standing behind me. He's wearing worn blue jeans, work boots, and a black T-shirt. From the looks of it, he just got off work.

"Rushton, nice to see you."

"What are you doing here?" he asks, taking a step toward me.

"Getting my tire fixed."

His jaw ticks. "You were supposed to do that on Saturday."

"I tried. They were already closed," I counter.

"Shit. I forgot Dec changed the Saturday hours. I'm sorry. I should have made sure you got it taken care of. I could have opened the shop and fixed it for you." He runs his fingers through his dark hair that's longer on top and shorter on the sides.

"It's fine. I stayed close to home, just going to the school and back this weekend. No tire catastrophes." I smile, but he's still scowling.

"I'm sorry."

This time it's me who takes a step closer to him. He's obviously upset that I've been driving on my donut tire for a couple of days. "It's all good, Rushton," I assure him, placing my hand on his chest. I tell myself it's to calm him down, but if I'm being honest, I just want to touch him. His hard pecs flex beneath my palm. I don't know what's going on with me. I'm not this person. I'm never this forward.

He places his hand over mine, and we're locked in a stare. His gaze is so intense I want to look away, but I can't. I can't stop gawking into his deep blues as I try to work out what he's thinking. I'd give anything to know his thoughts right this minute.

A throat clears, causing him to drop his hand, and I do as well, taking a step back from him. My eyes move to glance behind Rushton to find the man in the picture. He has the same dark hair and blue eyes as Rushton.

"You must be Crosby," he says, walking around Rushton and offering me his hand.

"Yes. Nice to meet you…." I let my words hang in the air.

"Declan Kincaid."

"Ah, one of the many brothers," I tease.

"So you've heard of us?" Declan asks, a hint of a smile pulling at his lips.

"No, well, I mean, I guess so. Rushton explained there are nine of you."

"Oh, he did, did he? And how do you know my little brother?" Declan slings an arm around Rushton's shoulders, only for him to shrug him off and take a step closer to me. He's standing so close I can feel his body heat.

"We, uh, don't really know one another. Not really."

"We do," Rushton counters.

"We met briefly on Saturday. Rushton helped me in a jam with my flat tire."

"So you're the damsel in distress." Declan's smile widens.

I turn to look at Rushton. "Is that how you see me?"

"No." He's shaking his head even while saying the words. "Saturday was a big day for my brother Sterling. Remember I told you he had a surprise for his girlfriend?"

I nod.

"Well, that girlfriend is Alyssa." As if his saying her name summoned her, she walks back into the front office from somewhere in the back, and we all turn to look at her.

"Why do I get the feeling y'all were just talking about me?"

"We were," Rushton tells her. "I was just explaining to Crosby how Saturday was a big day for Sterling, and he was irritated that I was late. When I told him I helped someone with a flat, and he found out it was a woman, he referred to Crosby as a damsel in distress."

"Right." I laugh. "He's not wrong. I had no idea what I was doing, but I was bound and determined to figure it out." I hold up my phone. "I was depending on the ole interweb to show me how to change my tire."

"I'm going to teach you how," Rushton announces. "Just in case you are ever in a place where you need to know again. Wait, on second thought, just call me." He grabs my phone and swipes at the screen, and I curse the fact that I don't have a passcode on it. I watch as his fingers fly across the screen, adding his number, and then I hear a beep coming from his back pocket. "You find yourself in that situation again. You call me."

"And what if you're not around?" I take my phone from him. I don't plan on calling him in the future if I find myself in need of a tire change. I'm a grown woman and can take care of myself. I don't need to rely on a man to do it for me.

"I have eight brothers, and our dad lives close. One of us will come to help you." He's giving me a look that says his word is gospel. But what he doesn't realize is while the sentiment is nice, it's unnecessary. I might not know how to change a tire, but I know how to call a tow truck to get me somewhere that does, and I have the internet. I know how to take care of myself. I'm the only one who ever has. I don't need a man.

"That's very sweet of you, but I can take care of myself." I smile kindly, letting him know his demanding looks don't have an effect on me. Well, not the desired effect. They somehow make him even hotter.

"Crosby." Rushton's voice is low and growly.

Tingles race down my spine, not out of fear but of desire. I choose to ignore that feeling and square my shoulders and turn my attention toward Declan. "Thank you so much for working me into your schedule this afternoon. I really appreciate it."

"Anytime. I'll give you my card in case you have any trouble in the future," Declan says, reaching over to the desk and pulling a business card out of the small display, and handing it to me.

"She has my number," Rushton replies grumpily.

"She is new in town," Alyssa speaks up. "The more people she has in her arsenal, the better."

"She has me." Rushton glares at her.

Declan and Alyssa share a look, and both crack up laughing. "It was nice to meet you, Crosby. Your car is ready." He nods to where one of his employees is pulling my car into a spot in front of the building.

"Thank you again. How much do I owe you?"

"I've got it," Rushton says.

"Thank you, but that's not necessary," I tell him.

"Consider it a welcome to Willow River gift," he insists.

Shaking my head, I make eye contact with Alyssa. "Do I pay you?" I ask her.

"Yep. Come on. I'll ring you up."

"Family discount," Declan tells her.

"Got it, boss." Alyssa grins and takes her spot behind the counter and rings me up.

I can feel Rushton standing behind me. He's pouting, I'm sure, because I refused to let him pay, but the referral and helping me with the spare were plenty. He's done too much already. I don't like owing people, no matter how sexy they are.

"Thank you," I tell Alyssa when she hands my card back to me.

"You're welcome. It was nice to meet you." She gives me a warm smile, and I return it in earnest before turning to face Rushton.

"Thank you for the referral and for your help on Saturday."

"You're welcome. Are you heading home?"

"Yes. It's been a long day."

"Have dinner with me?"

"I really shouldn't."

"Come on. You have to eat."

"I have leftover pasta in the fridge. I'm going to heat it up, take a long hot bath, and read until I fall asleep."

"Read?" Alyssa says with interest from behind me.

I can feel my face heat. I'm not embarrassed, but talking about my sexy books in front of Rushton is causing me to blush. "Yeah, romance mostly."

"Yes!" Alyssa holds her hand up over the counter for a high-five, and I slap mine against hers. "I have a monthly book club. You have to come."

"Sure. That sounds fun."

"Here." She hands me a pad of paper with the Kincaid Auto Repair logo on it. "Write down your number. Is it okay if I text you the details?"

"Perfect." I quickly jot down my number and wave goodbye to both of them. I rush out of the building and into my car before Rushton has a chance to stop me. That man is trouble. Not in "he's going to jail" trouble. That's not the vibe I get. No, he's got heartbreaker written all over him.

Chapter 3

RUSHTON

"WHY ARE YOU SITTING ON my couch on Friday night holding my daughter?" Brooks grumps from the recliner.

I don't bother to look at my brother. Instead, I keep my eyes trained on my niece, who is wide awake, staring at me from her place in my arms. "Daddy's grouchy," I tell Remi. At just over two months old, she's starting to be awake more when I see her, and I know she's smiling at me even if Brooks insists that it's gas, and that she only smiles for him.

"You'd be grouchy too if someone was hogging your daughter," he tells me.

"You get her all the time. I haven't seen her in a few days. Besides, I'm not staying long. I promised Blakely we could go get pizza for dinner. I thought Declan and Kennedy might like the night off. I can take this little one with us if you want."

"Nah, we're good here," he says. When I look up, I see his gaze on his daughter.

"It's unreal how much I love her. And Palmer." He shakes his head. "I didn't think I could love her more than I already did, but seeing her bring our daughter into the world, watching her be a mother to the little girl that we created—" He pauses, clearing his throat. "I don't even have the words to tell you what that kind of love feels like. Dad did this nine times with Mom. And Declan, fuck, Rush, Declan missed out on this. I fucking hate that for him and for Blake."

"He's getting it all this time around," I remind him.

"Yeah." He nods. "Thanks for the offer to take her with you, but I already have dinner in the Crock-Pot since it was my day off. I plan to spend the night in with my girls."

Before I can comment, the sound of the garage door opening alerts us to the fact that Palmer is home from work. "That's my cue." I lift Remi to place a kiss on her forehead before standing from the couch and placing her in her daddy's arms. "Uncle Rush loves you," I tell my niece even though I know she doesn't understand yet, but she will.

"You don't have to leave on my account," Palmer says, walking into the room. She stops to hug me, and I kiss her cheek before she moves to Brooks and perches on his lap. She simultaneously kisses him while stroking her daughter's cheek.

"I have a date."

"Oh, someone we know?" she asks.

"Yep. She says I'm her favorite."

"We all know that title belongs to me." Brooks chuckles.

"Blake?" Palmer guesses.

"Who else?"

"Oh, I don't know. Someone closer to your age and not related to you, maybe?"

"Not tonight. I promised my first niece we could go out for pizza."

"That's sweet of you," Palmer says. "Once the baby gets here, alone time will be short-lived for a while."

"Hey, I offered to take Remi with me."

"You're an angel, but we're good. Thank you for the offer. I miss my girl." Brooks clears his throat. "And my husband. A quiet night in is exactly what we need."

"Well, if and when you're ready for that break, call me."

"You're going to have to compete with Mom and my mother-in-law," Brooks tells me.

I lift my arms and flex my muscles. "I can take them, and if these don't work"—I motion toward my biceps—"I have these." I bat my long eyelashes that frame my baby blue eyes. I've been told many times that my eyes are lady killers and I have been known to use that to my advantage a time or two. No shame in my game.

"You're too much." Palmer shakes her head and grins.

"I'll see you guys later." With a wave, I head out the door, and I'm off to pick up my date.

"How was your first week of school?" I ask my niece. She's sitting across from me in the booth because that's what big girls that go to kindergarten do. Her words, not mine.

"Uncle Rush, it was so much fun!" she exclaims. Her voice is loud, but this place is packed tonight, and no one even turns their head at her excited reply.

"Yeah? Did you make any friends?"

"So many friends. Except for Jacob." Her little nose scrunches up in distaste.

"What happened with Jacob?" I ask, already wondering what I'm going to have to do to get this kid to leave my niece alone.

"He pulled my hair at recess." She's appalled, and I have to clamp my mouth shut to keep from laughing. "Then, when we were in line to go to lunch, he tapped on my shoulder but moved to the other side." She rolls her eyes. "He was trying to trick me." She scowls.

"That's not cool," I say, feeding into her annoyance with this Jacob kid.

"Right?" she asks, sounding much older than her five years.

"Aside from Jacob, the meanie, what was your favorite part?"

She taps her index finger against her chin. "Miss Greene. She's so nice and so pretty, Uncle Rush." There are two kindergarten classes at Willow River Elementary. One of the teachers taught me, and the other has been the center of my thoughts over the last week.

My reply is halted when Blakely starts bouncing in her seat, waving her arms in the air. "Miss Greene!" she calls out.

I turn when I hear a soft feminine chuckle. "Blakely, how are you?" Crosby asks. Feeling my gaze, her eyes find mine. "Rushton."

"Are you having a dinner date too?" Blakely asks, and I make a mental note to pick her up something special for reading my thoughts and voicing the words.

"I'm going to order something to take home to eat."

"Alone?" Blakely asks, her brow furrowed.

"Yes."

"No. You can eat with us, right, Uncle Rush? Miss Greene can have some of our pizza. I gots pepperoni, we can share," she tells Crosby.

"Got," Crosby and I correct at the same time.

"That's what I said." Blakely scoots over in the booth and pats the spot next to her. "Sit."

"I really don't want to intrude."

"No intrusion. Blakely was just telling me about her first week of school. She's rather fond of you."

Crosby's eyes soften as they move to Blakely. "She's such a joy," she replies softly.

"Join us. I insist."

"What he said." Blakely is once again bouncing in her seat.

"You've already ordered." Crosby tries to protest.

"More food than we can eat. Breadsticks, a large pepperoni, and large meat lovers."

"For the two of you?" Crosby asks, her eyes wide.

I shrug. "I'll just box up the leftovers and send them home with Blake. My sister-in-law is expecting their second baby in a few short weeks. This way, she won't have to make lunch tomorrow, and it gives both her and my brother a break." Her eyes soften at my words.

"Then you should save it for them."

"Nah, there will be plenty left over. If I need to order another to pull off my plan, I will. Please. Join us."

"Please, Miss Greene." Blakely puffs out her bottom lip and bats those long Kincaid eyelashes, and I know Crosby is going to be joining us for dinner.

"Thank you." She slides into the booth next to Blakely.

It's hard as hell not to just stare at her, but I'm not that guy. This night was about my niece, and while she's with me, it will remain that way. I can sneak looks at her sexy teacher without her noticing.

"So, you told me about Jacob and Miss Greene." I flash Crosby a grin. "What else happened this week?"

"We got to color the letter A, and Miss Greene told us all kinds of words that start with the letter A. We had reading time, and recess, and lunch, and it's so much fun." She sits back against the booth as if her confession took all her energy. I'm not buying it. I've seen my niece in action. She's got more than that in her.

"So, you love kindergarten?" I ask.

"Yes. I love it so much, Uncle Rush."

"Here you go." The young waitress places our breadsticks on the table. "What can I get you to drink?" she asks Crosby.

"I'll have a root beer, please."

"Sure, your food will be out soon." She's gone from the table as quickly as she came.

I dive in, placing a breadstick on one of the plates and cutting it up into more manageable pieces before pouring some of the pizza sauce onto the plate and placing it in front of Blakely. I then add two more to another plate, with some sauce, and hand it to Crosby.

"What? I don't get mine cut up too. What kind of establishment is this?" she asks, humor lacing her tone.

"It's 'cause he wants me to tell him he's my favorite. I have lots of uncles, and they do nice things for me all the time."

"I do it because I love you and because I know it will be easier for you to eat," I tell my niece.

"And he wants to be my favorite." She looks across the table at me. "Miss Greene will be your favorite if you cut hers as well." She then looks back at her teacher and gives an exaggerated wink that causes Crosby to burst with laughter.

I still. Taking in the sound as it washes over me and memorizing the smile on her face. She's beautiful, but when she smiles like that, she gives all new meaning to the word breathtaking.

"I don't know," Crosby says, pretending to ponder the idea. "Do I want to be his favorite?" she asks Blakely.

"Sure, but I want them all to be my favorite. Do you know my other uncles?"

"No, just your daddy," I smile at her. "He fixed my car, and I met him at orientation, remember?"

She nods. "He's real good at that kind of stuff. I like going to work with him, but that usually means I have to wear my wiener pants, and I don't much like that."

Crosby's mouth falls open, and her wide eyes find mine. I was in the middle of taking a drink, and I have to beat on my chest as I sputter and cough as it goes down the wrong pipe. "They're jeans," I correct my niece.

"Yeah, those. They make me look like I have a wiener. Girls don't have wieners, do they, Miss Greene?"

"Um, no. No, they don't," Crosby says, a slight blush coating her cheeks.

"Eat your breadstick," I tell my niece, holding back my laughter. Declan and Kennedy have their hands full with this one.

Blakely shoves a bite of breadstick covered in pizza sauce into her mouth, mumbling something about wieners. My eyes find Crosby's, and she, too, is holding back her laughter.

Thankfully, both of the pizzas arrive, and we all dive in. Blakely tells us more about kindergarten, things I'm sure Crosby is already privy to, but she gives my niece her full attention, riddled with smiles and words of encouragement. In just one dinner, I can already tell she is an amazing teacher. She has patience, and there's a kindness inside her, a light that shines bright. It lights up her eyes when she talks and listens to Blakely.

"Wipe your mouth, squirt." I reach over and hand Blakely a napkin, but Crosby is already all over it. She helps her wipe her mouth.

"Thanks, Miss Greene. Wait, do you have a real name?" Blakely asks her.

"Miss Greene is her real name," I tell her.

"No. I mean, like, I'm Blakely and you're Uncle Rushton. What's your real name?" Blakely tilts her head to the side as she looks at Crosby with a question in her eyes.

"Greene is my last name," Crosby explains. "My first name is Crosby, but you can't call me that while we're in school."

"Why not?" Blakely asks.

"It's respect, kiddo." I'm not sure how I'm going to explain what that means to a five-year-old. Maybe I should just tell her to ask her parents. I'll toss this one back on Declan and Kennedy.

"Oh, my mommy said respect is when you're nice to people."

Crosby smiles at my niece and, to my surprise, places her arm around her shoulders and hugs her to her side. "Your mommy is right. Using last names is also professional, and being your teacher is my job, so we have to stay professional while at school."

"Okay, but when I see you not at school, do I call you Miss Crosby?" she asks.

A light chuckle falls from Crosby's lips. "No, sweetie. If we're not at the school or at a function for the school, you can just call me Crosby."

"Okay, Crosby," Blakely says, shoving another bite of pizza into her mouth.

Talking dies down after that while we all dive into our dinner. By the time we're all claiming to be full, we have half of the meat lovers and over half of the pepperoni left to take home.

"Here are some refills. Can I get you anything else?" our waitress asks.

"Two boxes, please."

"Sure thing. I'll be right back." She places the check on the table, and I'm quick to grab it up before Crosby can get any ideas about paying.

"Let me help." She reaches for her purse, but I cut her off.

"No. This was on me. We didn't order anything extra with you being here." I give her a pointed look, willing her to argue.

"Fine, thank you for dinner. I'll get the tip."

"Nope."

"You should just let him get his way," Blakely tells Crosby. "I heard my mommy tell my aunt Palmer that you have to pick your battles and that the Kincaid men are stubborn. I don't know what that means, but my mommy is really smart, so I'd let him win." She shrugs as if she didn't just dole out adult-level advice to an adult, her teacher no less, and finishes off her milk.

"Did I just get schooled?" Crosby asks. Her lips are tilted in a grin.

"Yep."

She shakes her head. "She's something else."

"My mommy says that too. You know what? Lots of people say that about me." Blakely smiles like it's a compliment, and it is. She's a handful, but I wouldn't have her any other way. Being the only grandchild for so long, she's spoiled but doesn't act like it, but she does talk and act well beyond her age.

"Thank you for dinner," Crosby says, then turns to Blakely and gives her a hug. "I'll see you at school on Monday."

"Okay, Miss Crosby. I mean Crosby." Blakely places the palm of her hand against her forehead. "I'm never gonna 'member that," she mumbles.

Crosby and I laugh. "You'll get it," Crosby assures her. When she looks across the table at me, I want to beg her to stay. To let me drop Blakely off, and then we can go grab a drink, or just... I don't know, hang out? I don't really hang out, so that thought is staggering. "Thank you, Rushton."

"Rush," I remind her.

"Rush." She smiles softly. "I'll see you around."

"You have that number I gave you," I tell her as she slides out of the booth.

"Emergencies only."

"It's an emergency."

She tilts her head to the side to study me. "I'm almost afraid to ask."

I grin up at her. "Use it."

"We'll see. Bye. Thank you again," she says with a wave before walking away.

"She's the coolest teacher ever," Blakely tells me.

"Yeah, kiddo. I think she is too." I stand and offer her my hand, and together we leave the restaurant. Blakely chatters on, but I'm barely listening. All I can think about is Crosby and how, for a non-date, it was the best one I've been on in, well... ever.

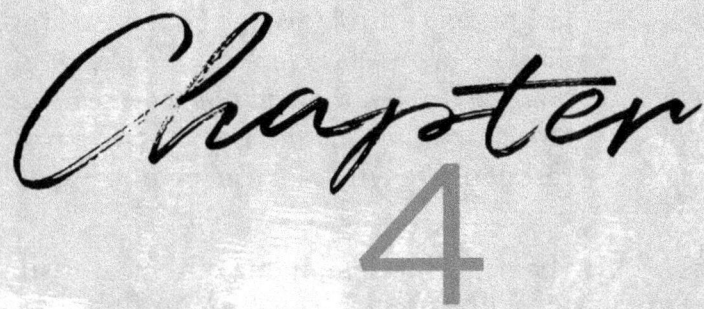

Chapter 4

CROSBY

I'M IN THE MIDDLE OF folding a load of laundry—how I have so much for one person is beyond me—when my phone alerts me to a new message. I've been packing my phone with me like it's an extra limb since having dinner with Rushton and Blakely last Friday night. He told me to use his number, and I've typed out about a hundred different messages only to delete them.

Rushton Kincaid is... a lot.

I mean that in the best way. He's sexy and brooding, sweet and funny, and he's not afraid to show any of those emotions, especially when it comes to his niece. He's unlike any man I've ever dated, and there's a reason for that. He's too much of everything, and that intimidates me.

Glancing at the screen, secretly hoping that it's him, I see an unknown number.

Unknown:	Girls' night at the Willow Tavern tomorrow evening.
Me:	Who is this?
Unknown:	Sorry. It's Alyssa from Kincaid's Auto Repair.
Me:	What exactly is entailed in girls' night?

I hit Reply and quickly add her number to my contacts. Her response is immediate.

Alyssa: Nothing too crazy. Most of the ladies are preggers, but we do have a few drinks, lots of laughs, and lots of talking about men. Mostly Kincaid men all except for Piper, who is married to Heath, and Ramsey, who is a Kincaid cousin but married to Deacon. The rest of us are either married to or engaged to a Kincaid.

Why is it just hearing his last name has heat rising to my cheeks? A night out with the girls does sound fun. I don't know them, but I've always been able to fit in with all kinds of personalities. That definitely comes in handy as a teacher with students, parents, and colleagues.

Me: I don't want to intrude.

Alyssa: Never. The more, the merrier, and I need someone who's not preggers to drink with.

She follows her text with a string of laughing emoji, and I can't help but smile. Alyssa, just from the short time I've been around her, seems like she would be fun to hang out with.

Me: Okay, if you're sure. Just tell me what time to be there. You said the Willow Tavern, right?

I remember passing the Willow Tavern in town, so it won't be hard to find my way back.

Alyssa: Yes! Tomorrow night at seven. We'll eat there.

She follows that with the address of the Willow Tavern, and just like that, I have plans for Friday night. I'm thankful because, without the invite, I would have spent the night at home, thinking about how I spent last Friday night. I definitely don't need another reason to be thinking about Rushton Kincaid.

Pulling open the door of the Willow Tavern, I'm immediately assaulted with country music and the smell of alcohol. Scanning the large room, I spot Alyssa waving her hands in the air and walking toward me.

"Hey." She greets me with a hug. "We have a table in the back." She links her arm with mine as if we've been besties our entire lives, immediately setting me at ease, and leads me to the table.

"Ladies," she greets. "This is Crosby. She's the new kindergarten teacher at Willow River Elementary. She came into the shop the other day to have her flat tire fixed."

"I feel like I already know you." One of the ladies smiles kindly. "Blakely Kincaid is my daughter. We met briefly on the first day of school, but there were a lot of us in your classroom." She gives me a welcoming smile.

"I remember, and she's a sweetheart," I tell her.

"She's rotten, is what she is," another of the women speaks up, making everyone at the table laugh.

"A rotten sweetheart," another amends.

"I'll go around the table," Alyssa says. "You know me, and I'm engaged to Sterling Kincaid. This is Ramsey Setty. She's married to Deacon. Ramsey is cousins to the Kincaid brood."

I nod in understanding, and she keeps going.

"Next, we have Palmer. She's married to Brooks Kincaid, and they have an adorable little girl named Remi. Beside Palmer is her sister, Piper. Piper is married to Heath. His brother owns this fine establishment. She's preggers, as you can see. Jade is next to Piper. She's married to Orrin Kincaid, and she's also preggers. Kennedy, Blakely's mom, married to Declan Kincaid, who you've met, and also preggers. Ladies, this is Crosby Greene."

I wave. "It's nice to meet you. I'm sure I'm going to forget your names, so bear with me. Thank you for letting me crash girls' night."

"You're not crashing," one of them says. I think it's Ramsey. "Ramsey." She grins, and I nod. "Sit. What are you drinking?" She nods toward the pitcher of beer on the table. "Grab a glass, or we can get you something else."

"No. The beer is perfect. Thank you."

"Well, now that we're all here, let's order. I'm starving," Jade says, rubbing her hands over her baby belly. "Eating for two is no joke." She chuckles.

"Do you all know what you're having?" I ask the table.

"Orrin and I are having a boy. Jade, by the way," she adds, and I smile in kind.

"Declan and I are having a boy too." Kennedy nods. I remember her, knowing she's Blakely's mom.

"Heath and I are waiting to be surprised. The pregnancy was a surprise, so we decided to just roll with it. My mother-in-law and this lot"—she points around the table—"are losing their minds saying they don't know how to shop, but the anticipation is part of the appeal."

"She's crazy," another woman speaks up. "I would have driven Brooks crazy had we not found out." She laughs, then smiles at me. "Palmer."

"Okay, I think I've got it." I start to point at each one of them. "Ramsey, Palmer, Piper, Jade, Kennedy, and Alyssa."

"Nailed it." Alyssa leans her shoulder into mine, smiling.

"I have you all, but not the men you're attached to."

Ramsey waves her hand in the air. "You'll figure it out soon enough. The only ones you might have issues with are the twins."

"Twins?"

"Yeah, the youngest of my nine cousins are identical twins. We all can tell them apart, but with you being new in town, you might struggle."

"I did at first, but you learn their personalities quickly, and Maverick is half an inch taller than Merrick. Oh, and Maverick is the more outgoing one. They're both full of life, but Mav is usually the instigator," Kennedy tells me.

"Got it." I nod. I kind of feel like I should have brought a notebook and should be jotting this down.

"Crosby is going to be joining us at book club. That's next weekend, by the way," Alyssa tells me.

"Oh, please tell me you read romance too?" Piper asks.

"I do." I smile at her.

"Perfect." She offers me a kind smile.

"So, Crosby, you have the rundown on us. Tell us about you," Ramsey says, grabbing her mug of beer and sitting back in her chair.

"Not much to tell. I'm from Atlanta. I was working as a substitute teacher within their system and waitressing at night or on my days off. When I got the job offer to have my own classroom, I jumped at the chance."

"It must be hard moving an hour away from all of your friends and family," Palmer speaks up. "Assuming you don't have connections to Willow River."

I shake my head. "No connections and no family." No friends either, but I keep that to myself. I hope that changes with these ladies sitting around the table.

"I'm sorry." Palmer's face falls. "I shouldn't have—" she starts, but I shake my head while holding up my hand to stop her apology.

"It's okay. You didn't offend me, and it's not a big deal. Just something that has been, and always will be." I shrug. I'm not lying. Sure, I'd love to have a big loving family, but I accepted long ago that's not how my life's going to play out. I have me, and I'm okay with that.

"So, how did the two of you meet?" Jade asks. There's a sparkle in her eyes that tells me she already knows.

"Rushton," I say, glancing over at Alyssa.

"Rush?" Ramsey asks.

"Yeah. I was at Gunderson's hardware, trying to reach the fishing line from the top shelf. He came up on me, needing the same thing, and helped me out."

"That's not all. She had a flat, and Rush changed it for her. He told her to come to the shop to have it fixed. She came in a couple of weeks ago, and we exchanged numbers."

All of the ladies seem to share a look. One that I don't quite understand. I start to ask them, but a large guy I've never seen before leans over and kisses Alyssa from upside down.

When he stands, he smiles at her as if she's his entire universe. "Just got here. Wanted to let you know I was here. Love you." He kisses her again, waves to the group, and heads to a table in the back corner. I want to turn to watch him leave, but I think better of it.

"That's Sterling, my fiancé." Alyssa holds up her hand, flashing her engagement ring.

"I thought this was girls' night?" I ask the table.

"It is, but we're married to protective men. We drink and laugh and eat all the greasy bar food we want, and then when we're ready to go, they make sure that we get home safe."

"They do this every time?" I ask them. "Do they get mad when you drink?"

"No. Not at all," Ramsey tells me. "They're here to make sure we have our fun but get home safely. It's the best of both worlds, really. We get to let loose knowing that we have someone here who's going to look out for us. All of our guys come, and usually, a few, if not all, of the remaining single brothers end up showing up as well. We basically have guys' night and girls' night at the same time and at the same place."

"Wow. I'm not really sure what to say about that. My ex would have flipped his lid if I had gone out drinking with friends. Now that I think about it, it's probably because he was sleeping with my best friend—excuse me, ex-best friend—behind my back." There's zero emotion in my voice. That's something else I learned to do. Keep my emotions in check. Never let them see what their actions do to you.

The table erupts with outrage on my behalf. The ladies are not worried about how loud they're being. They're firing off insults to my ex left and right, and I hide my smile behind my beer. As I lower my glass, I'm about to tell them I'm over it, and I am. I've written them off, and I moved on. However, before I get the chance, the table is surrounded by very large, very handsome men with concerned looks on their faces.

"What happened?" The one who is standing behind Jade with his hands on her shoulder leans over to make eye contact with her. "Is it the baby?"

Jade turns to face him, offers him a smile, and pats his cheek. "Everything is fine. The baby is fine. We were just reacting to some news that Crosby told us."

"Crosby?" His brow furrows.

"Hi." I wave. "I'm Crosby."

"Nice to meet you." He nods.

"Boys," Palmer speaks up. "Meet Crosby. Crosby, I'm going to point them out, but we don't expect you to remember them all. This one is Orrin, married to Jade. Beside him is Heath. He's not a Kincaid, but he is Piper's baby daddy. His brother owns this fine establishment. Deacon"—she points to another man—"also, not a Kincaid, but married to Ramsey. My husband, Brooks." She places her hand on her shoulder over his. "You've met Declan and Rushton." I nod as I try to keep up. "Then we have Ryder, Archer, Maverick, and Merrick, the twins. You're in luck that the gang's all here tonight."

I feel a body step in close behind me, and I turn to see Rushton standing there. His eyes immediately lock on mine. "I didn't know you'd be here," he says in greeting.

"Was I supposed to tell you?" I counter.

"She's been here a while, Rush. You could have come and said hi," Ramsey tells him.

He swallows hard. "Are you drinking?"

I hold up my almost empty glass of beer. "Yep," I say, tossing the rest of it back.

"How are you getting home?"

"We've got her covered," Jade speaks up.

Rushton's eyes never leave mine. "I've got her covered," he tells his sister-in-law.

"No can do, brother," she replies. "The arrangements have already been made. That is unless Crosby says it's okay."

I look away from Rushton, which is harder than it should be, and find Jade's gaze across the table. She gives me a sly grin, and I nod. I know what she's doing. She's giving me a choice that I wasn't sure I even had until she spoke up. I can choose to let Rushton take me home like he's demanding, or she and her husband will happily take me home as well. The choice is in my hands, and for someone who didn't get to choose until she turned eighteen, I appreciate that. These days, I don't allow myself to put my trust in someone else to let them make decisions for me.

"We'll see." That's the only reply I can come up with. On the one hand, I want to spend time with Rushton. I don't know that there's a single woman on the planet who wouldn't want time with him. On the other hand, I know that he's too much. The risk is too high to let myself get close to him. And I know that I will fall. The risk is far too great to my heart. I don't let people in, but with Rushton, there's this pull I've never in my life felt before. I'm usually a trust-your-gut kind of girl, but what happens when you don't recognize what your gut is telling you?

I feel his hands on my shoulders and his hot breath next to my ear. I shiver as he speaks the words. "Let it be me, Crosby. Let me take care of you."

Six words that I've longed to hear, and they come from a man I barely know. It's not that I need someone to take care of me. I'm an adult and am very capable. I've been proving that over and over since I turned eighteen and was released from the foster care system. That doesn't mean I don't think about what it would be like to have someone in my life to lean on. To carry some of the burdens.

"It's girls' night," Alyssa speaks up from her place beside me. "You guys are cramping our style."

Her fiancé whispers something that makes her laugh. He gives her a quick kiss on the lips and urges the others to leave us be. It's not until they all walk away that I realize I've been holding my breath when I pull a heavy inhale into my lungs.

"Damn." Palmer's eyes are wide as she pretends to fan her face with her hands.

"I thought you said you and Rush just met?" Kennedy asks.

"We did."

"That"—Ramsey points to where Rushton was just standing behind me—"did not seem like just meeting."

"I've seen him three times, counting tonight four."

"Gunderson's and the shop." Alyssa ticks off what they know. "What am I missing?"

"Last Friday, I went to Pizza Town to grab dinner. I ran into Rushton and Blakely. They insisted that I join them. Blakely looked so hopeful I couldn't say no."

The group turns to look at Kennedy. "You knew about this?"

She nods. "Blakely talked about it for days after. She really likes you." Kennedy smiles kindly.

"I really like her. She's a joy to have in class."

"Who paid?" Palmer asks.

"Uh, Rushton did. I tried, and he refused." Palmer nods.

"He's into you," Piper speaks up.

"He's being friendly. Besides, Blakely didn't give him much of a choice."

"Trust me, Crosby. The Kincaid men don't do a damn thing they don't want to do."

"Are you into him?" Ramsey asks.

"I don't know him."

"Are you going to let him take you home?" Alyssa asks.

"I... don't know. I hate to impose on anyone. I've only had one beer."

"You're not an imposition," Jade tells me. "I promise you that it's not a bother to drop you off at your place. I can also promise that there is no judgment if you want Rush to be the one to see you home."

"I'm—" I pause, wondering how much of myself I can let them see. Glancing around the table, all I see are kind eyes watching me patiently. "I'm used to being on my own," I finish.

Alyssa reaches over and places her hand on top of mine that's resting on the table. "You can trust us, and whatever is said between us stays between us."

"Nothing to tell. I've been on my own for a long time, and I'm not used to relying on anyone or having anyone to rely on."

"That changes here and now," Palmer tells me. "You have all of us. You plan to stay in Willow River?"

"I love what I've seen of the town so far. I signed a one-year contract with the school. So, I don't know that it matters if I want to stay. It will depend on if my contract gets renewed. Since this is my first full-time teaching position, they didn't want to risk more than a year until they saw me in action, I guess."

"My daughter is an excellent judge of character," Kennedy says. "Welcome to Willow River."

I nod and smile. Feeling tears prick my eyes, I remain silent, willing them not to fall. The other ladies give me similar words of welcome, and Jade once again comes to my rescue.

"Orrin and I can't decide on a name." And just like that, we spend the rest of the night talking about babies and bouncing around name ideas. For the first time in I don't know how long, I feel included. I feel seen, and most of all, I don't feel like an outsider.

I barely know these women, and I feel like I belong.

The night goes on, and it's Heath and Piper who end up giving me a ride home. Rushton didn't look impressed, but conceded that at least I was getting home safe. When they drop me off, Heath says something about the twins, but I'm too busy thinking about Rushton to comprehend what he says. I wave and thank them both, and let myself inside. I dream about a tall dark-haired blue-eyed man who saves me from the loneliness that sometimes threatens to swallow me whole.

WILLOW RIVER, GA · HOME OF THE KINCAID BROTHERS · WILLOW RIVER, GA · HOME OF THE KINCAID BROTHERS · WILLOW RIVER, GA · HOME OF THE KINCAID BROTHERS

Willow River
Georgia

WWW.KAYLEERYAN.COM

Chapter 5

RUSHTON

GUYS' NIGHT WITH MY BROTHERS hits a little differently these days. It used to be the twins would stay sober so that we all had rides home, or we would all just crash at the same place and let the twins drink. It's our right as their older brothers to get them drunk. However, these days, there's less drinking.

Take tonight, for example. The ladies are all gathered at Declan's house for book club. That leaves my married and engaged brothers and Deacon with nothing to do until their other half lets them know it's time to go home. So, here we are sitting at Sterling's home that he shares with Alyssa, sitting out back around the firepit. I know what you're thinking. Doesn't sound like a bad time. And it's not. Except for the bottles of beer we used to nurse are now bottles of water or glasses of sweet tea. It's not a bad thing. It's just different.

I can't even be mad about it. If I were them, and my wife or fiancée was out, I'd be sober too. I'd be the only man to bring her home. Add to it that Kennedy, Jade, and Piper are all pregnant, which heightens their need to stay sober. Hell, Heath didn't even come this time. Instead, he's at home with his brother, Hank, putting together a baby bed. We offered to help, but he insisted they had it under control.

We're pros at this by now. First Blakely, then Remi. We helped Declan a few weeks ago with his son and Orrin too. We're no strangers to putting together baby furniture. The thought brings a smile to my face. Our family is growing, and my brothers are happier than I've ever seen them. Well, the married or soon-to-be-married ones. We, single men, are still just taking life day by day. Maverick and Merrick are the babies of the family. Ryder, well, he's still hooked on his ex-girlfriend Jordyn. That leaves Archer and me, and while I'm not in a rush to settle, it's damn hard not to be jealous of our four older brothers. On the flip side of that jealousy is the knowledge that, like them, I'm not willing to settle.

When I find her, I want it to be all-consuming.

"Do you need us tonight?" Merrick asks as he shoves his phone back into his pocket.

"Hot date?" Ryder asks him. "Wait, don't tell me you finally asked your hot neighbor out?"

"Nah, but there is a group getting together at Old Man Gentry's field for a party," he answers. "As for the neighbor, she's like a ghost in the night. I've seen her getting into her car, and entering her house. I don't even really know what she looks like."

"She's hot," Maverick chimes in. "I mean from what we've seen of her, she's hot as hell. We're both trying to catch her to ask her for drinks."

"Both of you?" I ask.

They shrug. "One of us is bound to finally meet her. It's not like we're going to pull the old bait and switch."

"You better not," Brooks warns. "You little shits are going to end up pissing off the wrong girl."

"One time, B. One time." Maverick holds up his index finger.

"We learned our lesson," Merrick assures us.

What he doesn't say is they both ended up in a scuffle and got black eyes from the girl's older brother. That was their senior year of high school. The girl was from Harris. Her older brother stepped in, and although I hate that they were hurt, it could have been much worse. Hopefully, they learned their lesson.

"Does Old Man Gentry know about that?" Orrin asks, bringing the conversation back to the field party. Always the big brother making sure we all stay out of trouble. He's going to be a good dad. Hell, how can he not be when we were raised by the best man I know?

"He knows. He's cool with it as long as we clean up and keep the noise down."

"You going too?" Declan asks Merrick.

"Yep. No offense, but you all are old and boring," he teases.

"Call us if you need a ride." Brooks levels them each with a stare that gives zero room for them to argue.

"We're staying there. We'll sleep it off in the truck."

"Anyone else in?" Merrick asks as they stand to leave.

"Me." Archer also stands. "Someone has to keep you little shits out of trouble." He grins.

There's nothing little about our little brothers. They are both tall and physically fit, just like the rest of us. Our parents made some good-looking kids, if I do say so myself.

The twins say their goodbyes, and the rest of us remain as we wait for the ladies to tell us their book club meeting is over.

"Do they really talk books the entire time?" Ryder asks.

"Yep," Sterling says. "They really do."

"Are they all like the one that Alyssa's phone started playing that day?" I ask.

Sterling lowers his head, but his shoulders shake with his laughter. "Pretty much," he finally says once he maintains his composure. "Tink assures me that there is a love story and that the sex just enhances it."

"Before I fell ass over heels for Palmer and convinced her to be my wife, I would have called bullshit, but it makes sense," Brooks explains.

There's a murmur of agreement from every man in the room except for me. It's not that I don't believe them, but it's hard to agree when it's something I've never experienced. Sex has always just been sex for me. It's intimate, but there's never been this deep meaning to it. Two people seeking release in an intimate way. I've never been privy to the kind of meaning my brothers and Deacon insist is there.

"Rush, man, you don't know—" Declan starts, but he's cut off by the ringing of his phone. "Hello." He's smiling, and then his face goes pale. "Stay where you are. I'll be right there. I'm on my way, Kens, you hear me? I'm on my way." He's standing and rushing toward the door.

"Declan!" Orrin calls out as we're all on our feet, moving after him. "What's going on?" Orrin asks as he clamps his hand down on Declan's shoulder, keeping him from moving forward.

"Kens is in labor. Her water broke. I have to get there." His eyes are wide with panic, but the smile on his face is pure joy.

"I'm driving," Orrin says.

"We're all right behind you," Brooks tells him.

Orrin jumps behind the wheel of Declan's Tahoe, and they peel out of the driveway. The rest of us go to our respective vehicles and follow along behind him. As I'm driving, my phone rings. I see Ryder's name pop up on the screen. "What's up?"

"I'm going to Mom and Dad's to fill Dad in on what's going on and to help with Blakely. I'm sure Mom will end up at the hospital, and Dad will probably want to go be with her as well."

"Good call. I'll let Declan know what's going on."

"Thanks, man. Keep me updated, yeah?"

"You got it. Give Blake a kiss from her favorite uncle."

"I'm the favorite." He laughs, ending the call.

I'm sure tonight, he will be her favorite. She plays us all, and we're good with it. There's nothing that any one of us wouldn't do for that little girl.

When I get to Declan's place, I park my truck out of the way to ensure they can leave as soon as they get Kennedy loaded into the car. I'm not sure what I'm walking into, but I knock on the door and step inside.

Declan is standing in front of Kennedy. His forehead is leaning against hers, and both of their eyes are closed. His hands rest on their unborn child, and the moment steals the breath from my lungs. I force myself to look away to give them some time. Scanning the room, I find Orrin holding Jade close as they watch the scene before them. Same with Alyssa and Sterling. My eyes land on Brooks, and he's holding Palmer, and they, too, are watching Declan and Kennedy soaking up the moment. My eyes survey the room again, looking for Crosby. Orrin said she was here when he dropped Jade off. I don't see her anywhere, so I step into the kitchen and stop at what I see. Crosby has Remi in her arms, gently rocking her back and forth as she feeds her a bottle. I stay just outside the doorway so she can't see me, but I can see and hear her.

"You're about to have a new baby cousin," she tells Remi. "I have no doubt Blakely is going to take you both under her wing and show you the ropes." She laughs softly to herself. "You're lucky, little one. You have such a big family and so many people who love you. Never take that for granted," she says, emotion filling her voice.

The thought of her being upset twists me up inside, so I step into the room. "There you are. I was wondering if you ran off amid all the excitement."

"Nah, just getting this little one away from it all." She smiles down at Remi before pulling her eyes back to me. "Everything okay out there?"

"Yeah." Before I can comment further, Brooks steps into the room.

"There's my girl," he says, moving to stand next to Crosby as she feeds Remi. "Thank you for taking her."

"She's precious," Crosby replies, still smiling down at my niece in her arms.

"What's the plan?" I ask Brooks.

"Orrin and Jade are taking Kennedy and Declan to the hospital. Ramsey and Deacon are dropping Piper off at her house. Sterling and Alyssa are taking Mom to the hospital."

"Ryder went to Mom and Dad's. He's going to stay with Blake. We all know Dad's going to want to be there too."

Brooks nods. "Yeah, he will."

"You going?" I ask him.

"Nah, we don't want to take Rem," he says, looking at his daughter.

"I know you don't know me well, but I'd be happy to watch her for you. I can stay here or go to your place, or mine, or your parents' with Ryder. Whatever makes you the most comfortable. I'm happy to help. In fact, I want to help. Your wife, your family," she corrects, "has welcomed me with open arms. New girl in a new town, all alone, and they've invited me into their lives. It's the least that I can do."

"Well, damn. I was going to volunteer to watch Remi. I know Palmer will want to be at the hospital for Kennedy. You stole my thunder." I smile at Crosby.

"You should be with your family," Crosby insists.

"Remi is my family. Besides, I'm working on being her favorite. That takes time and attention."

"Thank you, Crosby," Brooks says. He looks at me, and I nod. "We'd appreciate that very much."

"I'm going to stay too. Just in case you all need anything. I can take the next shift if needed. Besides, I have a key to your place if we run out of supplies for Remi."

"Could you maybe go there? She does better if she sleeps in her bed, and I don't know how long we'll be and how much formula we have left."

"Sure." Reaching into my pocket, I pull out the keys to my truck and toss them to him. "We'll swap vehicles since I don't have a car seat base in mine. Just a booster for Blake."

"Thanks, man." He turns to Crosby. "Thank you for helping this one watch her." He acts as if I'm not capable, and we all know that I am. However, I'm not mad about it. Whatever it takes to spend a little time with the beautiful Crosby, I'm all for it. She'll find out soon enough that I'm more than capable of watching my niece all on my own.

Palmer walks into the kitchen, and Brooks tells her the plan. She looks at me and winks before she turns to Crosby. "Do you mind riding in the back seat with her? She's sometimes fussy during car rides."

My sister-in-law is up to no good, and I'm all for it. We all know Remi is the best baby. She doesn't get fussy unless she's tired, hungry, or needs her diaper changed. She's helping me out, making sure that Crosby is at my mercy with no way home once we get to her place. I make a mental note to offer my babysitting services again whenever they want or need it. She's earned it. Not that I wouldn't have readily agreed otherwise. Maybe I'll do the dishes or a couple of loads of laundry while I'm there. That will definitely help keep me from trying to seduce my babysitting companion.

"Oh, sure. Is it okay if I leave my car here?" Crosby asks.

Hook. Line. Sinker.

Thank you, Palmer!

"Yeah," Brooks chimes in. "It will be fine here. Thank you for this."

Crosby smiles at my brother and his wife. "I'm happy to help."

Brooks leans down and places a kiss on Remi's forehead. "Daddy loves you," he says softly. Palmer repeats the process, and with a wave and a promise to keep us updated, they're out the door.

"Let me walk through the house and lock up. I'm going to clean up the food and whatnot, and then we can go. Is that all right?"

"Yes, of course. I can help." She's quick to offer.

"No. You go sit on the couch and make sure my niece gets her belly full. It won't take me long to clean up." She glances at all the food on the island. "I got this," I assure her. "Big family, we're used to this kind of thing. Go sit, and relax. Finish feeding her. I'll be done before you know it." She nods and moves toward the living room, and I jump into action.

Twenty minutes later, I have all the food put away, the counter wiped down, and the dishwasher running. I make my way through the house, checking all the candles are blown out and the back door is locked before I stop next to Crosby, who's watching Remi sleep in her arms.

"She's so peaceful," she whispers.

"She trusts you." I don't know why I say it, but it has to be true, right? Babies can sense things, and the way that Remi is sleeping away in Crosby's arms tells me she's happy and content.

"Are you ready?" she asks.

"I am. Do you want me to take her?"

"No, I can get it." She stands carefully, and as if she's done it a million times, she settles Remi into her car seat with ease.

"You're good with her. Lots of experience with babies?" I ask.

"Yeah, you could say that. I—" She stops and peers up at me. I can see war waging behind her eyes, and when she speaks again, it feels as though I've been punched in the chest. "I grew up in foster care. I was moved around a lot, and many of the families had babies and smaller kids. They would take on foster kids for the income while on maternity leave or whatever and then send us on our way once they were done with us."

"Fuck." I hiss under my breath.

"Can we just forget that I just blurted that out?"

"No. No, we can't forget that you just blurted that out. However, we can table it. For now, let's get this place locked up and get this little one at home and in bed." She seems grateful for the pause in the conversation that's sure to happen regarding her confession.

She's not the only one. I need some time to wrap my head around what she told me. She didn't say the words, but I read between the lines. She truly is all on her own. Here in this strange town, living by herself. I send up a silent thank-you to whoever is listening that she was brought into my life. Into the lives of my sisters-in-law, who have taken her under their wings.

"Ready?"

She smiles and nods. "Ready."

I grab Remi in her seat, Crosby picks up the diaper bag, and we make our way to Brooks's vehicle after locking the house up. I get Remi situated, and I almost ask Crosby what she's doing when she climbs in the back seat next to her. Thankfully I remembered Palmer's request and bite down on my cheek to keep my smile at bay.

I don't know what it is about this woman, but I've been trying to get her alone since the moment we met. Not because I want to fuck her, although I've thought about that too. There's something intriguing about her. Hopefully, the time we spend together tonight will pacify my curiosity, and I can stop spending so much time thinking about her. Because I do think about her. More than I care to admit.

Willow River
Georgia

WILLOW RIVER, GA · HOME OF THE KINCAID BROTHERS · WILLOW RIVER, GA · HOME OF THE KINCAID BROTHERS · WILLOW RIVER, GA · HOME OF THE KINCAID BROTHERS

WWW.KAYLEERYAN.COM

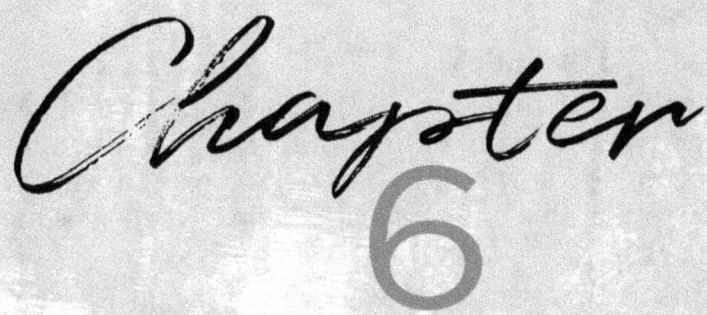

Chapter 6

CROSBY

THE DRIVE IS QUIET. I spend my time watching Remi as she drifts off to sleep, and Rushton remains quiet in the front seat.

I don't know why but that surprises me. I guess I assumed he'd be his chatty self during the drive. I most definitely did not expect his silence. When we pull into the driveway, he pushes the button for the garage door and drives inside as if this is his house. I guess since it's his brother's, he knows the ins and outs.

"I'll grab Rem if you can get her bag," he says as he exits the vehicle.

It's not until now that I realize what I've gotten myself into. I agreed to babysit with a man I barely know. Sure, my gut tells me I can trust him, but this isn't the smartest decision I've ever made. I should have insisted that I could watch her on my own, but then they were in the same boat as I am currently. They don't know me that well, either.

"Sure," I reply, grabbing the diaper bag that's next to me on the seat, and climbing out of the SUV. I follow Rushton into the house. He leads us to the living room, where he places Remi's seat on the couch, and he quickly unfastens her and lifts her to his chest.

"You can make yourself at home. I'm going to change her diaper and get her into some jammies."

"Do you want me to do that?"

"Nah, that's why I'm the favorite uncle." He kisses the baby on her forehead.

"Do you hold that title?"

He chuckles. "I think we all do. Blake plays us like a damn fiddle, and we love every minute of it. But this little angel, she's still too young to know how to play us, so yeah, tonight, while I'm the one here, I'm this one's favorite uncle." He flashes me a wide, endearing grin.

He turns on his heel and heads toward what I assume is her bedroom, and I find myself following along behind him. I tell myself it's because I promised Palmer and Brooks I would help him watch her, but if I'm being honest, I just want to see Uncle Rushton in action. I have no doubts that this man could have handled this adorable baby girl all on his own. He didn't need my help, but he orchestrated this—me being here. He took my offer and turned it into his own, one he shared with me.

He moves expertly around her adorable princess bedroom, gathering pajamas before placing her on the changing table. He changes her diaper as if he's done that very thing thousands of times.

"All right, little miss. Let's get through this as cleanly as possible," he tells the baby. In no time at all, she has a fresh diaper, and he gets her wiggling arms and legs into her sleeper and lifts her into his arms. "I think she's ready to party," he tells me as he smiles down at his niece in his arms.

"What time is she usually in bed?" I ask.

"Not for another hour and a half or so. Wanna watch a movie?" he asks me.

I shrug. "Sure." I mean, what else are we going to do?

"Here." He hands me the baby. "I'll make popcorn and get drinks. Water? Tea? I'm sure they have other options, but I know for a fact they have those two."

"Water is fine." I cradle Remi in my arms, and she just stares up at me.

"I'll get the TV set, and you can pick a movie while I gather the snacks." His grin is not only boyish, but it's infectious. I find myself smiling right along with him as I follow him back to the main living area of the house.

Gingerly, I sit on the couch, still holding Remi in my arms. She's content, and I'll admit I don't want to put her down yet. I don't get baby snuggles often, and I'm not ready to give them up just yet.

Rushton grabs the remote, presses a few buttons, and hands it to me. "Pick anything you want. I'm not picky."

"Really? So, you're good with a sappy love story?" I place the remote next to me on the couch. I don't really care what we watch, either.

He shrugs. "I have a mom who loves them, a cousin who is just like her, and two and a half sisters-in-law. I'm used to it."

"Half?"

"Yeah, Alyssa and Sterling are engaged, so she's the half."

"You're too much." I shake my head. He just grins and makes his way into the kitchen. "He's silly, huh, Remi?" I offer her my finger. She latches on and grins. "You're such a cutie," I coo down at her. That's exactly how Rushton finds us when he enters the room with a big bowl of yummy-smelling popcorn and two bottles of water.

He plops down next to me, waters and bowl of popcorn still in his hands. "Shit, can you grab that?" he asks. He leans to the right, and I glance down to see the remote he just sat on. I quickly grab it, and he settles back on his seat as if I didn't just have my hand close to his ass.

"What are we watching?"

"Remi."

He laughs, and the sound washes over me. "Other than this cutie?" he replies, leaning into me and bopping Remi gently on the nose, making her coo at him.

"I didn't look," I confess. "You pick. I'm not picky."

"Nope. That is not going to happen. You have to choose. That's the rule."

"Rule? Since when are there rules?"

"Since now. You have to pick so I can learn what you like if I'm ever going to convince you to have dinner or, hell, even drinks with me."

"Language," I scold him even though Remi doesn't know what he's saying.

"Sorry, baby girl," he tells Remi. "Now, how about we choose together?" he offers.

"Fine," I concede, already knowing that I'm going to go along with whatever he suggests.

"How about this one?" He points to a movie on the screen.

"I've never seen it."

"How is that possible? You've seriously never seen *Road House*?"

"Nope."

"Oh, we are so fixing that." He hits Play and tosses the remote beside him. "Do you want me to take her?" he asks.

"No, she's fine."

"Here." He opens my bottle of water for me and hands it to me to take a drink before taking it back, replacing the cap. Leaning forward, he places it on the coffee table before settling in beside me. Every part of him is pressed up to my right side, and the heat of his body seeps beneath the layers of clothing I'm wearing, causing goose bumps to break out against my skin.

Rushton places the bowl of popcorn mostly on his thigh but a little on mine. He grabs a handful and settles in to watch the movie. I do the same, only eating a few handfuls of popcorn while he devours most of the bowl.

He's right. This is an older movie, but I quickly get lost in it. However, when the intimate scenes come on the screen, I feel my face flush. Why? I don't know. I'm not a prude or a virgin, but something about watching *that* with Rushton sends the heat rushing to my cheeks as if I were both.

We make it through with me hiding my flaming cheeks. By the time the credits start to roll, Remi is getting fussy.

"I'll make her a bottle. Be right back." Rushton stands from his seat next to me and disappears into the kitchen, taking the now-empty bowl of popcorn with him.

"Let's go change your diaper, and then we'll get you fed and in bed. How's that?" I ask Remi. I stand and make my way to her room and quickly go through the process of a diaper change. She's fussing, and when I pick her up, I bounce her in my arms. We enter the living room at the same time.

"I changed her," I tell Rushton. "That way, if she falls asleep, which I'm sure that she will, we won't have to risk waking her to do it."

"I was going to suggest that. Thank you." He sits and holds out his arms.

"You want me to do it?" I offer.

"Nah, you hogged her the entire movie."

"She was snuggly and dozing off. I thought maybe she might go down for the night."

"She for sure will after this." He raises the bottle in his hands as his phone rings. He quickly digs it out of his pocket and hands it to me. "Answer that and I'll feed her."

I place the baby in his arms, glance at the phone, and see *Brooks* on the screen. "Hello."

"Crosby?"

"Yes. Sorry, Rushton just settled on the couch to give Remi her bottle."

"How is she?"

"Perfect. She's been an angel all night long."

He sighs. "Thank you for watching her for us."

"I think Rushton would have done just fine on his own."

"We know he would have, but he wanted you there." I don't know what to say to that, so I remain quiet. "Kennedy is still in labor. Do you need us to come home?" Brooks asks, breaking the quiet on the line.

"He says that Kennedy is still in labor and wants to know if you want him to come home?" I relay to Rushton.

"Nah, we're all set. Just tell him to keep me updated."

"He said he's all set, but to keep him updated."

"We can do that. I'm going to call back so we can say goodnight to Rem." With that, the call ends but immediately rings again, this time with a video call. I accept and turn the phone so that Brooks and Palmer can see their daughter.

"Hey, baby girl," Brooks says softly. Remi immediately stops eating and turns toward the phone. She smiles as she searches for her daddy. Talk about pulling at your heartstrings.

"Are you being a good girl for Uncle Rush?" Palmer asks. Remi's smile grows wider, if that's even possible. They say their goodnights, thank us again, with a promise to keep us up to date, and the call ends.

"You're good to stay, right?" Rushton finally asks.

"Yes." I don't know why I am. I should feel uncomfortable, but I don't. I barely know this man, but I'm not worried at all about being alone with him. In fact, I react to him. Well, my body reacts to him in ways that it shouldn't. The chemistry between us is unlike anything I've ever felt before, but his cousin and sisters-in-law are my friends. At least, I'm hoping that they are. I don't want to mess that up. For the first time in my life, I have people who spend time with me for reasons other than stabbing me in the back or floating the rent for them.

I'm standing on my own two feet, and the idea that I have a group of women in my corner, well, it's something I want more than to see how hot the chemistry between Rushton and me burns between the sheets.

"Good. I'll get this little one fed and asleep, and we can watch another movie. Any suggestions? You need to pick this time."

"I really don't watch a lot of TV. I spend most of my spare time, if I have it, reading."

"We really need to change that. There are some classics that you're missing out on."

"I can guarantee you most of them are based on books and that the books are better."

I expect him to argue, but he just grins. "In my limited experience, I find that you're right. I don't do a lot of reading, but the books I have read that have movie adaptations, the books are by far better."

"Thank you." I nod, and we both laugh. "Should I mark this day down on my calendar? The day that Rushton Kincaid admits that I'm right?" I tease.

"Nah, I'm all about giving credit where it's due."

"She's out," I whisper as I point to the sleeping baby in his arms. "Want me to take her?" I offer.

"I've got her." He sets the bottle on the end table, stands without waking her, and carries her to her room. I follow after him quietly and watch as he kisses her forehead before placing her in her crib. "Night, sweet girl. Mommy and Daddy will be here when you wake up. Uncle Rush loves you."

My heart squeezes in my chest. I've never met a man who so openly shows affection for those he loves. And the way he took care of Remi tonight... as if she were his daughter. This man is unlike any I've ever met before.

"Hey." He smiles when he finds me standing outside Remi's bedroom door in the hallway. "You okay?"

"I'm good." I grin to reassure him. "I was just making sure you didn't need my help."

"She's out." He nods toward the bedroom door that's not completely closed. I assume it's so that we can hear her if she wakes.

"Come on. It's time for another movie." I'm shocked when he grabs my hand, entwining his fingers through mine, and leads me back to the living room. "Want some more popcorn?" he asks. "Or another water?"

"No. I'm set. Thanks, though."

"Have a seat." He points to the couch, and I take the same seat that I had earlier. He moves to turn on the lamp beside the couch, shutting off the overhead light. This leaves the room in a soft, romantic glow. I start to remind him I'm not going there, but he takes a seat on the couch, leaving a little space between us. I'm both relieved and disappointed at the space.

"How about *The Notebook*?"

"You want to watch a romance?"

"It's a classic. Gets me every time."

"You mean you've seen it?"

"Lots of times. Mother, cousin, and sisters, remember?"

I smile when he leaves the in-law off sisters this time. He really does think of them all as his sisters. "What do you mean 'it gets you every time'?"

"Tears, Crosby. I'm secure enough in my manhood to admit that the movie gets me all up in my feels."

"And you want to watch it with me?" I ask him.

"Sure, if you want. You've seen it, right? I'm sure you've already read the book."

"Actually, no. I've never read the book or seen the movie." I shrug. It's a first for me.

"Oh, we are most definitely watching it. But I have to grab supplies. Be right back." He jumps from the couch and bolts out of the room. A few minutes later, he's back. He's carrying two more bottles of water, a pack of chocolate chip cookies, a blanket that looks super soft, and a box of tissues. "We won't need these until later," he says, shaking the tissue box in his hand before setting it on the end table.

He's a fury of activity as he takes a seat next to me on the couch, closer this time, and spreads the blanket over us. He then hands me a bottle of water, sets the cookies between us, and hits Play.

For the next two hours, we sit in silence as we're both engrossed in the movie. My gaze is glued to the screen, and as I wipe the tears from my eyes, I can't help but wonder how good the book would be if the movie touched me like this.

"I can't stop crying," I say, burying my face in my hands, hiding my embarrassment.

"Come here." He pulls me into his chest and wraps his arms around me. I don't know why I can't stop crying. I'm a mess, and this man, this gentle, gorgeous soul, is consoling me as if I just lost a loved one. It was a movie, but it got to me.

To have a love like that... to have that kind of connection with someone, it's unheard of, and at the same time, I yearn for it. To know that I had one person in the world who would love me against all odds, at all costs, until we took our last breaths.

After a few minutes, I get myself under control, but I don't pull away from Rushton like I know I should. Instead, I allow myself to pretend that this man is all of that for me. I pretend that I've known it for years and that this is just another night at home for us. I allow myself a very rare instance of make-believe and wish for things that were never meant for me. My eyes feel heavy as I drift off to sleep, feeling safe and, dare I say, wanted.

"Hey." I hear a groggy voice. "How is everyone?" Rushton's sleep-laced voice asks. I know I should open my eyes, but his arms are still wrapped around me, and I'm comfortable. Not to mention, I'm kind of freaking out about his family. I'm assuming Brooks and Palmer both see me lying on his chest on their couch.

"Everyone is doing great. Healthy baby boy. Kennedy was a rock star." I hear Brooks say.

"We're going to bed. You two are welcome to take the spare bedroom."

"It's not like that," Rushton is quick to explain as he runs his hand up and down my back. "We were watching a movie. We fell asleep."

I swallow hard, still trying to pretend like I'm sleeping, but I can't help the way I stiffen, and his reaction is to hold me tighter with his other arm that's wrapped around me.

"We like her, Rush. Don't scare her away." This comes from Palmer.

"I like her too. I'm not scaring her away. We were watching a movie and fell asleep."

"Well, the room is there if you want it. I'm going to check in on my daughter and take my wife to bed." I hear their footsteps as they leave the room.

"They're gone," Rushton says softly.

I open my eyes to find his waiting for me. "You want to stay or go? It's up to you."

"What time is it?" I ask him.

"Just before three in the morning."

"I guess we should stay."

"Okay." He closes his eyes and wraps his arms around me.

"Um, I can sleep here. You can go to bed. I know this can't be comfortable for you."

"Are you going to come with me?"

"No. I'll sleep here."

"I'm good."

"Rushton—" I stop because I don't even know what I want to say. That we shouldn't finish out the night sleeping wrapped around each other on his brother's couch? Was I going to ask him to stay? Beg him to hold me in his arms the rest of the night. My ex didn't like to cuddle, and I'm embarrassed to admit that this is my first time, and if I'm being honest with myself, I don't want it to end.

"Shh, go back to sleep."

It's on the tip of my tongue to argue, but I can't. I don't want to. Instead, I do as he says. I close my eyes and allow my body to relax into this man who has gained more trust from me than any other in a very long time, and allow myself to drift back to sleep.

Willow River
Georgia

WWW.KAYLEERYAN.COM

Chapter 7

RUSHTON

WE'VE ALL BEEN PITCHING IN to help Declan and Kennedy since baby Beckham arrived a week ago. Today is my day.

It's Friday, and I took a vacation day from work. My boss at Harris Steel is easygoing, and when I told him about my new nephew, he approved my time off without issue. I love being a machinist. I skipped out on college and went to the vocational school for machine trades. Right out of high school, I started working at Harris Steel, and I love it.

Pulling into my brother's driveway, I park but keep my truck running. I told Blakely we could go grab breakfast at Dorothy's Diner in town before I drop her off at school. Since her new baby brother arrived, I want her to know that we all still love her and want to spend time with her. I know that Kennedy was worried about how Blakely would be once the baby arrived, but she's been a little rock-star mother hen helping her mom and dad with her baby brother.

I lightly knock on the door but don't wait for a reply as I turn the handle and walk inside. They know I'm coming, so I'm not too concerned about finding a situation I shouldn't be walking into. "Morning," I tell a sleepy-eyed Declan. He's sitting in the rocking chair, holding Beckham. His eyes may be sleepy, but they're still shining with love for his new son.

"Hey, buddy, look who's here?" he says softly.

I waste no time taking Beckham from his arms. "I'm off all day," I tell him. "Why don't I come back and take care of him while you and Kennedy get some rest?"

"I think Jade was going to come over," he tells me. "And Mom offered as well."

"Jade is ready to pop. Cancel. I'll take care of Mom. I took the day off work. The only plans I have is breakfast with my first niece, dropping her off, and picking her up from school. Other than that, I'm all yours. I can watch him while you nap or run errands or whatever you need."

"You sure?"

"Positive. You need to lean on us."

"It's different this time," he says softly. "When Blake was born, I was here alone at night when I had her, and now I have Kens, and it's just... I fucking love her, man. More than I ever thought possible."

"It's a good thing she married you then," I tease. I hear Blakely's footsteps, so I know she's close. I kiss my nephew on the cheek and give him back to his daddy. "I'll be back in an hour."

"Thanks, Rush."

"Anytime. Blakey, you ready for some of Dorothy's famous pancakes?"

"Yes!" she whisper-shouts. "I don't want to wake up my brother," she tells me when I give her a confused look.

This little girl. She's so damn smart and loving. I love all of my nieces and nephews, even those still cooking, but Blakely was the only one for five years, and there will always be a special little sliver of my heart that's only for her.

"Come here, sweetie." Kennedy opens her arms, and Blakely rushes to her, giving her a big hug.

"Love you, Mommy."

Not gonna lie. That gets me. Every single time I see the way that Kennedy loves Blake, the way that Declan loves Beckham, what they've all been through, bringing them to this point in their lives.

Everyone is happy and healthy, and they have a beautiful family. It gets me all up in my feels.

It seems as though I've had a lot of that lately. Specifically last weekend with Crosby and watching *The Notebook*. I fought against it, but I still teared up at the end of the movie, just like I knew I would. That shit hits you right in the chest, and Crosby, well, I didn't choose that particular movie, hoping I'd get to console her, but I'm not mad about how that night turned out.

Somehow, I managed to convince her to let me hold her for the rest of the night. We woke early the next morning and slipped out before Brooks, Palmer, and Remi woke up. I dropped her off at Declan's to her car and haven't seen or heard a word from her since. I've contemplated sending her a text several times, but I never follow through, and I can't pinpoint exactly why I haven't.

But I can't seem to stop thinking about her. I'm forcing myself to stay away. From the little that I know about her past, she needs someone who's all in, and right now, I'm just not sure that's me.

I want more out of life, but is she the one? I can't possibly know that without getting to know her better, but if I keep deleting the messages I type and she keeps turning me down at every turn, I'm not sure how I'm ever going to get the chance to find out.

"Bye, Daddy." Blakely leans over the side of the chair and gives Declan a hug and a kiss on the cheek. "Bye, baby brother Beckham," she whispers, kissing the top of her brother's head. "Ready, Uncle Rush." She bounces over to me, and I lift her into my arms. Pretty soon, she's going to be too big for any of us to hold her like this.

"I'll be back in an hour or so," I tell my brother and his wife, and we're out the door. Blakely chats away about school and her teacher Miss Crosby Greene as she likes to call her when she's not at school, and how much she loves being a big sister and a big cousin. She continues on as we eat our pancakes at Dorothy's. She's soaking up having all of my attention, and I willingly give it to her.

She drops nuggets of information about school that I hold on to like a starving man, and I ignore my subconscious telling me that there is a reason Crosby is different and instead focus on what I'm learning about the dark-haired beauty that has my niece enamored with her.

"Oh, and Miss Greene, her favorite color is teal green. Isn't that cool?" Blakely asks. "It matches her name, Uncle Rush."

"So cool," I agree, filing yet another small piece of information about the woman in my mind.

Thirty minutes later, we're pulling into the parking lot of Willow River Elementary school. I help Blakely out of her seat, and hand in hand, we walk into the school.

"I'm a big girl, Uncle Rush. You don't have to walk me to my class. I know where I'm going," she says, smiling up at me.

"You are such a big girl," I tell her. "But I want to see your classroom." *And your teacher.*

"I sit by Jacob. He talks a lot, and Miss Crosby G—I mean, Miss Greene has to shush him a whole lot."

"You need to make sure you're minding Miss Greene," I tell her.

"That's what I tell Jacob too," she fires back, and I don't bother hiding my grin as she pulls me by the hand into her classroom.

"Good morning, Miss Greene. Look, my uncle Rush brought me today."

Crosby smiles at my niece. "Good morning, Blakely. I can see that. Why don't you put your things away and take your seat?"

"Okay. Bye, Uncle Rush. I love you." She hugs my legs, and I'm barely able to pat her on the back before she races off.

"I love you too." I watch as she does exactly as she was told, hangs her light jacket up in her cubby, and skips to her seat. Once she's seated, I raise my gaze to Crosby, who is watching me. "Good to see you, Crosby," I say the words softly to ensure none of her students overhear us.

"You too. How's baby boy Kincaid?" she inquires.

"Beckham. They named him Beckham, and he's perfect. I took the day off. I'm going back once I leave here and letting them get some sleep."

"Someone new has dropped her off every day this week."

"Have they all walked her in?"

"Yes, much to her annoyance. She claims she's a big girl and can make it here on her own." She laughs softly.

"Yeah, she tried that with me too, but I had a lot of motive to walk her to her room."

"Really?"

"Of course. How can I keep my favorite uncle title if I don't get to see her classroom or where she sits? Besides, I wanted to see you."

"You wanted to see me?" she repeats my words as if she can't comprehend what they mean, and I know that's not the case.

"I was hoping to hear from you this week."

"Was I supposed to reach out?" There's a glint of mischief in her eyes.

"Yeah, I think you were. You should make it up to me."

"You think so?"

"Yep. We should have dinner tonight." I shoot my shot once again, hoping like hell this is the time that she finally says yes.

"I have plans. I'm sorry."

"With who?" The question is out there, much more forcefully than I intended. "I mean, what are you doing?" I ask in a calmer tone.

"Alyssa, actually. She's taking me to this bookstore she frequents in Harris. I guess Sterling was the one to find it and take her there."

"Is Sterling going?"

"Not that I'm aware of. Is Alyssa not capable of taking a trip to Harris that's what, twenty minutes from Willow River on her own?"

"No. I mean, yes, of course, she can. I just thought that if Sterling were going, I'd tag along to keep you from feeling like a third wheel. My brothers are needy assholes," I whisper, "when it comes to their wives."

"They're not married yet," she counters.

"You know what I mean."

"It's just the two of us, so no, I'm sorry, Rushton, but I can't have dinner with you."

"Uncle Rush, why are you still here?" I look down to find Blakely staring up at me.

"I was just talking to Miss Greene." I kneel so we're at eye level. "Have a good day, squirt. I'll be here to pick you up after school."

"Okay." She gives me a big hug and once again skips off to find her seat.

I stand and smile at Crosby. "Tomorrow night?"

"I can't. I have… papers to grade."

"You teach kindergarten."

"And?"

"You have to grade papers?"

"Yes. I am teaching the young minds of this community. Grading papers is part of my job description as a teacher."

"No. That's not what I meant. I just thought maybe you'd have time for dinner. You have to eat, right?"

"Thank you for the offer, Rushton, but I really can't." With that, she walks to the front of her class and commands the room.

I realize I'm just standing here like the wounded soul that I am from her turning me down yet again. I wave at Blakely and hightail it out of there. Once back in my truck, I can't stop myself from sending a message this time.

Me: If you change your mind, you know how to reach me.

I hit Send before I can think better of it and point the truck toward Declan's. I have nephew snuggles to cash in on.

"How was your day, sweetie?" Kennedy asks Blakely.

We're sitting at their dining room table, having pizza that I picked up for dinner on my way home from picking Blakely up from school.

"It was fun. Jacob talked a lot, and Miss Crosby Greene had to put him in time out."

"Oh, that's not good." Kennedy gives their daughter her undivided attention as if she's invested in Jacob's time out.

"I know. Then when he got to come back, he was being stubborn and wouldn't talk at all." Blakely sighs dramatically, and I look across the table at Declan. His grin matches my own.

"Well, he was just doing the right thing. Maybe his time out taught him a lesson?" Kennedy suggests.

"Maybe. Oh, know what else happened?" she asks.

"What?" all three adults say in the room at the same time. How can you not with this kid's enthusiasm for life?

"Uncle Rush asked Miss Crosby Greene to dinner two days, and she said no." Blakely gasps as if she can't understand how Crosby could have said no. She has no idea. She just threw good old Uncle Rush to the wolves.

"Oh, he did, huh?" Declan asks.

"Yep." Blakely is so damn proud of herself that I can't even be mad about her outing me. She's not lying. I did ask her for two different days, and I was shot down.

"All done." Blakely shoves the last bite of pizza into her mouth.

"All right, you can go play. Wash your hands," Declan calls after her. He waits until she's out of earshot before addressing me. "Is there something going on with you and Crosby?"

"Nope."

"She's sweet," Kennedy speaks up.

"She seems to be," I agree.

"Let's try this another way. What do you want to be going on with you and Crosby?"

Pushing my plate away from the table, I rest my elbows in its place, thankful our mom isn't here to scold me, and bury my face in my hands. "I don't know." It's the truth, and that irritates the hell out of me.

"Explain that."

"She's gorgeous. The day I met her, I thought immediately that she was one of if not the most beautiful woman I've ever seen. She's sweet as hell, and she's a freaking kindergarten teacher, man. She's one of those kinds of women you take home and introduce to Mom." It's not because she's a kindergarten teacher, but she's just so damn genuine, and what little I do know about her, I know that she's someone you wife up, not hit and quit.

"Is that what you want? To introduce Crosby to Mom?" Declan asks. He's not being an asshole. He's genuinely trying to help me out here.

"I don't know her."

"But you want to?" Kennedy asks with hope in her voice.

I point at my sister-in-law, and she grins. "Don't go getting any ideas in that pretty head of yours, Kennedy Kincaid. And don't you dare rally the Kincaid ladies and try to set me up. From what I know of Crosby, she's cool as hell. Her life hasn't been easy, not that I know much, but what I do know is I think she's skittish. Afraid to lower her walls."

"Do you want her to lower them?" Kennedy asks in a sugary-sweet voice.

"I'd like to get to know her better." I've said all along I'm not against falling in love and settling down, but I need to know with absolute certainty that the woman I choose is the right one. We need to fit like two missing pieces of a puzzle. Do I think that's Crosby? I don't know, and I won't unless I can convince the woman to spend time with me.

"Palmer might have mentioned the two of you cuddled up on her couch."

"Yeah, we were, but we fell asleep watching a movie. We just... ended up that way." Not the complete truth, but not a lie either. It feels wrong to tell them she was sobbing, because I'm almost certain her tears were caused by more than just the sappy movie.

"She also said the two of you snuck out early the next morning," Kennedy comments.

"We did. We decided to stay since it was the early morning hours when they got in. We were both up, so we left so I could drop her here to get her car and not interfere with Brooks and Palmer's family time with Remi."

That's bullshit. I knew from the way that Crosby was acting that she was ready to get home. She was embarrassed about our night together, so I did what any gentleman would do. I took the lady to her car and thanked her for her help with my niece.

I lean back in my chair, waiting for the rest of my interrogation. Thankfully, it never comes. "I should get going," I tell them. I stand and take care of the trash and place our glasses in the dishwasher.

"Thanks for today, Rush," Declan says from the doorway of the kitchen. "It was nice to get a few hours of steady sleep."

"Anytime you need me, you call."

"Thanks. I'm going back to work on Monday, so I can handle dropping Blake off at school. Alyssa is going to pick her up each day, and she's going to let her hang out with her until I'm ready to leave."

"Sounds like a plan. You got my number." I walk toward him and pull him into a hug. "You have a beautiful family, Dec."

"Thank you." He's smiling. "I want this for you and for Archer, Ryder, and the twins." He places his hand over his heart. "I know this is going to sound sappy, but I want you all to get to feel this kind of love, Rush. It's unlike anything I've ever felt."

"I think Ryder is there."

"Yeah. I really hope that Jordyn comes home when she's finished with her program, and they can work things out."

"Only time will tell." I hope she does too. Ryder has been miserable since she's been gone.

"You'll find her."

"Find who? Jordyn?"

"You'll find your Kennedy, your Jade, your Palmer, hell, your Ramsey. You'll find her. When you do, you'll know."

"Is Dad passing the words of wisdom baton down to you? I would have thought that Orrin would have gotten that gig since he's the oldest."

"Shut it, asshat." He shoves at my arm.

"There's my big brother." I laugh. "See ya later, man."

"Love you, brother. Drive safe."

I drive home in silence. I don't bother turning on the radio, instead letting my mind drift to Crosby. She's not playing hard to get, and I know from the flare of heat in her eyes that she's interested. Maybe she's just shy, and I need to give her time. I'll keep asking her to dinner, and maybe one day she'll say yes.

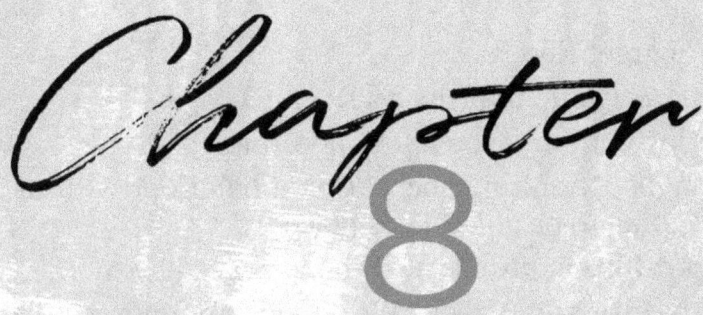

Chapter 8

CROSBY

IF YOU CHANGE YOUR MIND, you know how to reach me. I don't need to open my phone to read Rushton's text message. I have it memorized. He has no idea how hard it is to keep turning him down. I wish that I could be a carefree twenty-five-year-old. I have to focus on my career right now. I have a year to prove to the Willow Elementary school board that taking a chance on a young teacher with only substitute experience was a good idea. So good, in fact, they decide to renew my contract. If not, well, then I need to plan my next step. It's just me, myself, and I, and no matter how badly I want to say yes to Rushton, I know I can't.

Rushton is... magnetic. He's full of life, and those blue eyes and his abundance of muscles are hell on my resolve, but I learned a long time ago there's no one in this world that will look out for me but me. I need to remain focused, and once I get a contract extension and know that Willow River will be my home, I can relax a little. I'll be able to let go of the reins and start building a life here. Until then, I'm on pins and needles until the spring, when contract negotiations begin.

I've cleaned my entire house from top to bottom, and I'm just finishing up my last load of laundry when my cell rings. I race down the hall to answer, and I stop to look at the screen, hoping, even though I know it's wrong, that it's Rushton. I just literally convinced myself that staying strong for the school year is best, but my traitorous heart skips a beat, thinking it might be him.

It's not.

"Hey," I greet Alyssa.

"What are you up to?" she asks.

"Cleaning, laundry, you know, adulting."

She laughs. "Adulting sucks. Come hang out with us tonight. We're all going to be at Declan's place."

My heart flips in my chest. "Who is all?"

"Just the girls and Blakely. We do a girls' night with Blakely that looks a lot different from the ones we have at the Tavern."

"Got ya. I don't want to intrude."

"You're not."

"She's my student."

"And she talks about you and school all the time. Come on, Crosby, it will be fun. We don't do anything crazy. We do our hair and makeup. Well, most of the time, we let Blake work on us, but we help. We snack, and there's no alcohol, so you'll be completely sober with no regrets the next day."

"Are you sure the others won't mind?"

"Nope. Kennedy actually asked me to reach out to you. Text me your address, and I can swing by and pick you up so that you're not coming over by yourself."

"What can I bring?"

"Snacks. Anything works. I think Kens said she had Declan pick up a fruit tray and a veggie tray. Palmer was making buffalo dip, and other than that, I don't know."

"What are you making?"

"Brownies, maybe cookies if I can keep Sterling out of the kitchen long enough not to burn them."

"What time?"

"I'll be at your place at six."

"Okay. Thank you for inviting me. Please thank Kennedy for me too."

"I will, but you can do it yourself when we get there. Oh, and the dress is super casual, jammies, leggings, etc. It's a chill night. No need to fancy yourself up."

"This night keeps sounding better and better."

"Right? And I've managed to convince Palmer to bring Remi, and Kens is keeping Beckham at home, so we get baby snuggles on top of it all."

"Sold," I tell her, making her laugh again.

"Text me your address."

The line goes dead, and I fire off a text of my address.

Alyssa:	That's where you live?
Me:	Yes. Why, is this house haunted or something? I hope not. I signed a one-year rental agreement.
Alyssa:	No. Not haunted. I used to live on that street before I moved in with Sterling.
Me:	Small world.
Alyssa:	Indeed. See you at six.
Me:	See you then.

Opening the cabinets, I look for what I might have on hand to bring, but nothing stands out to me. Pulling up my phone, I search for ideas, and when I see cheddar sausage balls, I know that's what I'm making. It requires a trip to the grocery store, but it will be worth it. They sound so good right now.

Rushing to my room, I take a quick shower, throw on a pair of leggings and a long-sleeved T-shirt, and pull my hair up into a messy bun. It's not like I need to impress anyone. Slipping my feet into one of my many pairs of Hey Dude shoes, I grab my purse and phone, and I'm out the door.

"Hey, neighbor!" I hear called out.

I stop and turn to look and see two guys walking my way. As they get closer, I recognize them. The Kincaid twins. Maverick and Merrick. My mind races with what the girls told me about them. Which one is taller? Maverick, I think.

"Wait. I know you. Crosby, right?" the shorter of the two asks.

"Yes."

"This is Blake's teacher, and we met her at the Tavern with the girls," he tells his brother. He reaches his hand out to me. "Maverick Kincaid."

"Crosby Greene." I don't know why I say my name. They already know who I am. And yes, Maverick is the taller one. Not by much, and I would have missed it had Kennedy not pointed it out. I make a mental note to thank her.

"How did we not realize you were our new neighbor?" Maverick asks.

"I was busy settling in and getting my classroom ready the week I moved." That sounds better than I'm a loner. However, since moving here, I don't feel as alone. I have a great group of ladies to thank for that.

"Where you headed?" Merrick asks.

"Oh, to the grocery store. I'm going to Declan and Kennedy's tonight, and I'm going to make snacks."

"I like snacks." Maverick winks at me.

I can't hide my chuckle. "I'll keep that in mind. See you both later," I say, moving to my car. I climb inside and refuse to look their way until I'm out of the driveway. I beep my horn and wave. A quick glance shows them watching me drive away, both with their arms in the air with a wave.

I've just finished pulling the second batch of sausage balls from the oven. A quick glance at the clock tells me I have twenty minutes before Alyssa gets here to pick me up. Moving the still-hot treats to a plastic container, I slap the lid on it and head next door. There are two trucks in the driveway, so I assume that means the twins are home. I knock on the door, and a shirtless Kincaid brother, I don't know which twin it is, answers the door.

"Crosby, hey." He looks down at my hands. "Whatcha got there?" He leans over to get a better look at the container.

"Who is it?" Another appears, and a slow, sexy smile tilts his lips. "Looks like our girl brought us treats."

The door-opening twin turns and smacks him lightly on the chest before standing to his full height. "Chill, Mav," he tells his brother.

That clears up the confusion. I should have known since they did tell me Maverick was the more outgoing twin. I clear my throat. "I made a second batch for the two of you."

"You did?" Merrick's eyes light up.

"You said you like snacks, right?"

"Yes," they say in unison.

"Well, here you go. I hope you like them."

Maverick reaches for the bowl, pulls off the lid, and pops an entire sausage ball into his mouth. "So good," he says after swallowing and reaching for another one.

"Thank you, Crosby," Merrick says politely before reaching in and grabbing one for himself. He, too, shoves the entire thing into his mouth.

"You're welcome. I need to go. Alyssa should be here any time to pick me up."

"Just tell her to pick you up here. This is her place, after all."

"What?"

"This house. We're renting it from Alyssa. When she moved in with Sterling, they were debating on selling, but we convinced them to rent it to us instead," Maverick explains.

"I didn't know that. She did mention when I sent her my address that she used to live on this street."

A car pulls into my driveway, and I turn to see Alyssa roll down her window. "What are the chances," she calls over.

I smile, wave, and turn back to the twins. "Enjoy."

I'm shocked when Maverick, I think it's Maverick, steps out onto the porch when I turn to wave to Alyssa and gives me a hug. "Thanks, Crosby."

"These are great. We appreciate it." Merrick follows his brother's lead and pulls me into a hug.

"You're welcome. I'll see you later." I wave and rush next door to grab the other container, my purse, and at the last minute, I grab a flannel shirt just in case it gets cool tonight. I don't know what I'm getting myself into.

When I get back outside, the twins are standing by the driver's side of Alyssa's car, and they're chatting. I slide into the passenger seat, shuffling everything to the floorboard between my feet.

"I can't believe y'all didn't catch that you were neighbors."

"We've seen her but never got a good look at her face, and we didn't know what she drove," one of them explains.

"Well, now that we know, we can keep an eye out." One of them, I can't tell which, leans down to peer at me through the window.

"Thank you, but I've been taking care of myself for a long time." I offer him a kind smile.

"Maybe." He shrugs. "But with Mav and me living next door, you won't have to."

Instead of arguing with him, I just nod and smile. Many say they're going to reach out or look out for you, but in my experience, they're just being nice. Never do they follow through. I keep that thought to myself.

"We need to get going. You two behave."

"Always," they say at the same time.

"Keep that brother of ours in line, will you?" Maverick says.

"You know that no one keeps Sterling in line." Alyssa chuckles.

"You do," they say at once. She waves them off, rolls up her window, and we're on the road. "If they bother the hell out of you now, just let me know. I can have Sterling talk to them."

"Oh, they're fine. I met them earlier on the way to the grocery store, and they hinted that they liked snacks, so I made a double batch."

"A double batch of what? Whatever it is, it smells incredible."

"Sausage balls."

"Tell me more."

"They're super easy to make. I brown sausage, I usually do hot, but I wasn't sure what everyone liked, so I did mild this time, add a box of cheddar biscuit mix and lots of cheddar cheese. They're so good."

"My mouth is watering," she says.

"Right? So, I made a double batch, and that's what I was doing. Dropping them off with the twins."

"You know Rush is going to be all kinds of jealous, right?"

"What? Why would he be jealous? I was just being neighborly."

"To his little brothers. And you live next door to them. Rumor has it that you've been shooting down his requests for dinner."

"Wow. Word travels fast in the Kincaid clan."

"You know it. But this time, it was the little Kincaid who spilled the beans. I guess Blake heard him ask, and you tell him no."

"Ugh. I really need to watch what I say around my students. I'm trying to get them to renew and extend my contract, not get fired for fraternizing with a student's uncle."

"That's a lot to unpack." Alyssa chuckles. "First of all, you did nothing wrong. If there's anyone to blame here, it's Rush asking you while your students, even if it was just our niece, were within earshot. Second, this is a small town, Crosby. You're going to be hard-pressed to find a man who's not connected to one of your students in some way, shape, or form. Don't stress. It's all going to work out," she says, pulling into Kennedy and Declan's driveway.

Together, we grab our things and head inside. As soon as I step in the door, Blakely shrieks.

"Miss Crosby Greene!" She comes rushing toward me, and I barely have time to brace before she's barreling into my legs and hugging them tightly.

"Blake, let her go. She has her hands full," Kennedy tells her daughter.

"I'm so happy you came to my girls' night." Blakely smiles up at me.

"I'm happy to be here. Thank you for inviting me."

"This is going to be the best!" She skips off and disappears down the hallway.

"Sorry about that," Kennedy says with a kind smile. "She really likes you."

"She's a sweet girl."

"Come on in. Kick your shoes off and relax. Can I take that?" She nods to the bowl in my hands.

"Sure, it's sausage balls."

Kennedy lifts the lid and peeks in. "They smell amazing."

The next ten minutes or so is a flurry of activity and shrieks from Blakely as each guest arrives. Finally, Declan comes into the room and hands Beckham to his wife. "You sure you don't want me to take him?"

"Back off, daddy-o." Ramsey points at him. "We're getting all the baby-loving in this evening while Blakely does our hair. So be gone." She waves her hand, dismissing him.

"You are aware that this is my house, right?" Declan raises his eyebrows at his cousin.

"But this, my dear cousin, is Blakely's girls' night. No boys allowed."

"Yeah, Daddy. No boys allowed," Blakely chimes in.

"Fine. I'm going. We're all at Deacon and Ramsey's tonight, well, those of us who have wives that are here at least. Call us if you need us, and we'll be here to drive everyone home."

"Thanks, babe. Love you." Kennedy leans in for a kiss that Declan seems all too happy to provide.

"They do that a lot." Blakely sighs. "Mommy says that when I fall in love, I'll want to kiss a handsome man all the time too."

"Are you corrupting our daughter?" Declan asks his wife.

"Nope." Kennedy grins, passes Beckham off to Ramsey, and hugs Blakely to her side. "Us Kincaid ladies need to stick together."

"Oh, and Setty and Greene ladies too, right, Momma?"

"Right, sweetheart. You know you're too smart for your own good."

"I know. Miss Crosby Greene tells me I'm smart 'cause I get A's on my papers."

"You are very smart," I reassure her.

"Can Daddy get a hug?" Declan asks his daughter.

"Only if you go, Daddy. No boys allowed."

Declan chuckles. "A hug and a kiss, and you've got a deal." Blakely keeps her end of the bargain, giving her dad a hug and a kiss. One more peck for Kennedy and one for Beckham, and he's off.

"Well, Blake, how about we eat first?" Palmer suggests.

"We have to wait."

"Everyone is here," Kennedy tells her.

"Nope." Blake grins and rushes off when there's a knock at the door.

"Wait for an adult!" every female but me calls out to her.

"Goodness, what a welcome," an unfamiliar voice filters into the room.

"That's our mother-in-law, Carol Kincaid," Palmer tells me.

"Hello, ladies."

"Aunt Carol, I didn't know you were coming tonight?"

"I don't normally, but I thought I could help with the little ones while you all had your girl time with Blakely."

"Girls' night is really fun," Blakely tells her grandma.

"Then let's get to it."

The next several hours end up being the best night I've had in a really long time. Blakely was the star of the evening, and Remi and Beckham came in as close seconds. There were lots of laughs and being silly, and I can't help but think that this is the kind of thing I missed when I was growing up. There were no inviting friends over to the foster homes I lived in. Not that I had many to invite over. I kept to myself. This is what I imagine a normal childhood would be like. My heart aches for what I missed, but it's soaring for Blakely and the other kids who get this kind of love and attention day in and day out.

"Thank you for a fun night," I tell Kennedy.

"I'm so glad you came. We've all exchanged numbers, so you're a permanent member from here on out," she tells me.

"Thank you."

"Crosby, it was a pleasure to meet you," Carol says, pulling me into a hug. "What are your plans tomorrow late afternoon?"

"Nothing that I can think of. Is there something I can help you with?"

Her eyes sparkle. "As a matter of fact, there is. You can be at my place at five for Sunday dinner."

"W-What?"

"You heard me. I won't take no for an answer. I have enough to feed my small army and then some." She laughs. "We'd love to have you, and I know Blakely will be thrilled."

"I don't want to impose on your family time." Lesson learned. Fake plans or uncertainty until you know what is being asked of you. Rookie mistake. My high from the night of fun has me slipping up.

"You might as well say yes. When she finds out you live next to the twins, she's just going to have them coerce you into going."

"Oh. You live next to Mav and Mer?" she asks.

"Right next door." Alyssa smiles.

"Traitor," I grumble good-naturedly, making them both smile. "Thank you for the invitation. I'd love to come. What can I bring?"

"Nothing!" is the chorused reply from all the ladies.

"She never lets us bring anything." Alyssa rolls her eyes and smiles.

"Just you and your appetite. I'll just tell the boys to stop and pick you up."

"No. I can drive."

"Nonsense. Them being your ride ensures they stay out of trouble and make it on time." She looks at the room. "I'll see everyone tomorrow. Thank you all. It's been a great night."

We all tell her goodbye with another round of hugs, and then Alyssa and I go through the process all over again as we leave as well.

"Thanks for inviting me," I tell Alyssa once we pull into my driveway.

"It was fun. I'm glad you came. I should warn you since they all have your number, you're more than likely going to be added to the family group chat."

"I'm not family." *I'm no one's family.*

She shrugs. "You are now."

I shake my head and climb out of the car, waving goodbye. I glance over to the twins' place. The lights are all off. I'm sure they're out for the night. Making my way inside, I put the now-empty and washed pan away and load the dishwasher before going to bed. I drift off to sleep, thinking of ways to get out of this dinner tomorrow. It's not that I don't want to go, but Rushton is sure to be there, and I need to distance myself from him if I'm going to keep turning him down. The more I learn about him and his family makes that task harder and harder.

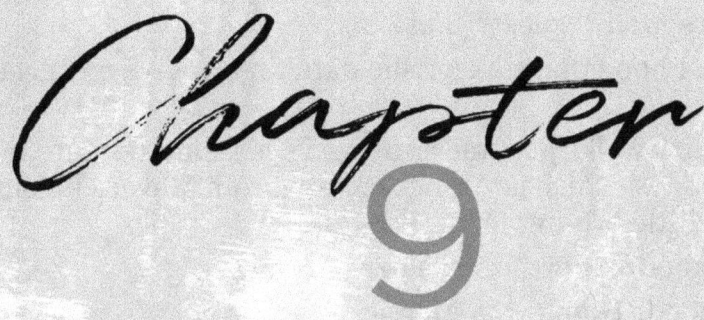

Chapter 9

RUSHTON

"WHERE ARE THE TWINS?" I ask my dad. They're almost always here early. Being the last to move out, they still spend a lot of time at our parents' place, and that includes arriving early for Sunday dinner.

"They're picking someone up for me," Mom answers for him.

"Who?" I glance around the room, and everyone is here except for my two little brothers.

Before Mom gets the chance to reply, the front door opens. "Momma, we're home," Maverick calls out. A smile lights up her face, and if I didn't know she did that each time any of her sons walks through that front door, I might be jealous. Maverick and Merrick are her last babies to fly from the nest. I know that's been hard for her. She spent her entire adult life raising nine rowdy boys, only to be suddenly alone, just her and my dad. They deserve this time together, but I know they miss having a house full of kids.

Curiosity is getting the best of me, so I stand and move to the entryway to see who our guest is today. I'm usually not this nosy, and I can't think of one single reason why I care who the twins picked up, but there's something propelling me to investigate, so that's what I do.

"Kitchen's through there," Merrick says as I round the corner and freeze in my steps.

"Crosby?" I ask, confused.

She gives me a shy smile. "Hey, Rushton."

"You're mom's guest?" I ask her.

"I am. I hope that's okay. She didn't really give me a choice last night."

Maverick walks past me and checks his shoulder into mine. "Be nice," he says, which is strange coming from Maverick. Since when does my little brother lecture anyone?

"You good?" Merrick asks her.

"I'm good. Thank you, Merrick."

He grins down at her. "That didn't take long. You and Kens both learn fast." He gives her a one-armed hug that I don't particularly care for and walks past me down the hall.

"It's good to see you," I say, taking a few steps toward her.

"You too."

"So, how was last night?" I purposely didn't go to Declan's with the rest of them last night. I knew from Sterling that Alyssa picked her up and was taking her home.

"It was fun." Her eyes light up.

"How did you end up with my brothers?"

"We're neighbors."

It takes my brain a few seconds to process what she's just told me. "What? Neighbors?"

"Yep. We found out yesterday."

"You live next door to Alyssa's old place?"

"Yeah, well, Maverick and Merrick's place, now, right?"

"They're renting it from them." I don't know why I'm fixating on the fact that they don't own the house.

"I'm renting too. At least for the next year."

"What happens after a year?" I want any tiny sliver of insight into her life that she'll give me.

"I only signed a one-year contract. If they don't re-sign me, I'll be moving to wherever I can find a job."

Why does the thought of her leaving town cause a stirring in the pit of my stomach? "You'll get hired," I assure her. I know Mom has a couple of close friends on the school board, so I can have her put in a good word for her.

"I hope so. This town is growing on me."

"Just the town?" I ask, stepping into her personal space. We're now standing toe-to-toe, and her head is tilted back, staring up at me.

"I've met some good people."

"That's all you're going to give me, isn't it?" I ask her, laughing.

"Yep." She grins.

"Come on, gorgeous." I offer her my arm, pretending to be the perfect gentleman when what I really want to do is press her up against the wall and kiss the breath from her lungs. Instead, I bury the need to feel her lips against mine and escort her into the kitchen, where my entire family turns to look at us as we enter.

"Crosby." Mom's beaming smile is infectious. "I'm so glad you made it. I hope my sons didn't drive like maniacs."

"Thank you for having me. No, Merrick drove safely."

"I think you've met everyone, but we'll go through it again, just in case." Mom pulls Crosby to the other side of the room, which means she no longer has her arm linked with mine. Disappointment washes over me, followed by confusion. I don't know what the hell is wrong with me. Is it the chase? The fact that this woman keeps turning me down at every turn? Whatever the reason, I need to shake out of this.

"Now, let's eat." Mom claps her hands, and we all form a line around the island and wait our turn to fill our plates.

"You know, Raymond, I was thinking that we're going to need to expand this dining room," Mom says. "Our family is growing."

"Mom, this table is already massive," Maverick chimes in.

"I know, but once you all bring me home a new daughter and eventually grandkids, I'm going to need more room."

"We can just flow into the living room," Archer tells her.

"I guess," Mom says. You can tell from her tone that's not what she has in mind.

"Tell me what you need, dear, and we'll make it happen," my dad says.

"Balls. Vise," Maverick says.

"Maverick!" Mom and my brothers, who have kids, scold him.

"What? I disguised what I was saying." Maverick shrugs and keeps piling food on his plate.

"I want us all to be able to eat together," Mom explains. "We're already eating in the living room, and it's not right. A family should eat together."

"We're all together, Mom. That's what matters," Orrin tries to soothe her.

"I know." She makes eye contact with my dad, and he nods. There's nothing that man wouldn't do for his wife, as long as it's within his power.

By the time we all have our plates, Maverick, Merrick, Ryder, and Archer are set up in the living room. I also see that Ramsey and Deacon are in there as well. I want to sit next to Crosby at the table, but instead, I take a seat on one of the open recliners and kick back before diving into dinner. This way I can watch her without it being obvious to everyone sitting at the table.

There's not much talk as we all stuff our faces. My mom is an amazing cook. Laughter from the dining room catches my attention, and I turn to see Crosby with a smile on her face. She's so damn gorgeous, and when she smiles, her beauty is only intensified.

"What's up with you?" Ryder asks.

I turn to look at him. He's sitting in the other recliner. "Nothing."

"Rush."

"Fine, I don't know, okay. I think about her all the time." I nod toward the dining room.

"Crosby?"

I bob my head.

"Ask her out."

"I have. She keeps turning me down."

"Is it the chase?"

"Honestly, at this point, I'm not sure what it is. She's fucking gorgeous," I tell him.

"That she is."

I bite my tongue because all I want to do is tell him not to look at her. That's irrational, and I know it. Besides, Ryder loves Jordyn, and he's my brother. He'd never go after someone I was interested in.

"Are you interested in her? You know more than just hooking up?"

"That's the million-dollar question. I don't really know her."

"But you want to."

"I do."

He nods. "Then keep after it. You'll wear her down eventually."

"Or cause her to get a restraining order," I retort. It's not that she's telling me no, not really. She's telling me not right now. There's a difference. I know she wants to, but she's holding back.

"What are you two whispering about over there?" Archer asks.

"Nothing. Just talking," I'm quick to answer.

"You heard from her?" he asks.

There's no need for him to clarify. We all know he's asking about Jordyn and if Ryder has heard from her. Jordyn and Ryder were dating when she just up and left for an internship across the pond. Ryder wanted to do long-distance, but Jordyn left before they had the chance to discuss it. She's not taking his calls, but she is reading his text messages. So that's something.

"Yeah, she picked up last night."

"What?" all three of us say too loudly, gaining the attention of everyone in the dining room.

"She answered."

"What did she say?" I ask.

"Not much. Just that she was sorry she left the way that she did. We talked for about an hour. She said she'd pick up the next time I called."

"So you called again today?"

"Nah, she's sleeping right now. The time difference is a challenge."

"That's good news, man."

Ryder nods. "It's definitely a start and more than just random replies to my text messages."

"Are you two working things out?" This comes from Mom. All heads turn to find her standing in the doorway.

"I'm not sure yet. I'm taking what I can get until she's back home where she belongs."

"What if she doesn't come home?" Mom asks. What she doesn't say is that she's worried that Ryder will leave Willow River and go wherever Jordyn decides to live.

Ryder shrugs. "That was never her plan. She always said she was coming home, so that's what I'm holding on to. I'll cross that bridge if we come to it."

Mom walks further into the room, and as if they read each other's minds, Ryder stands and pulls her into a hug. I watch as my brother fights the emotion of the woman he loves moving away and struggling to love her with thousands of miles between them. I don't know why I do it, but I look toward the living room and find Crosby's eyes on me. I hold her stare, trying to see beneath the surface. There's something in her eyes that I can't name, but it looks a hell of a lot like longing.

"You keep loving her harder," Mom tells Ryder. "She feels it." Mom places her hand over her heart, and I'm suddenly swallowing back my own emotions.

"Right. Now, who's up for a game of euchre?" Mom asks.

"We'll pair up." She turns her gaze to me. "You can pair up with Crosby."

"Does she know how to play?" I ask.

"Crosby?"

"I know how to play. I'm just not very good, and there's a good chance I'm going to renege." She shrugs, chuckling.

"I'll grab an extra deck of cards, and we can study while we wait our turn," I tell her.

"Wait, why does he get Crosby?" Archer asks. "What if I wanted her to be my partner?"

"Um, she's our neighbor. We call dibs," Maverick chimes in.

"No one is calling dibs, and I've already put her with Rush. We want her to feel more comfortable with the game, not your game," Mom chastises them.

"Burn!" Brooks says from his spot at the dining room table. "You tell him, Momma." Brooks laughs.

"Raymond, what on earth possessed us to have nine boys? I'm so glad that I now have daughters to even out this testosterone. I need five more before I can really start to feel the shift." She chuckles, turning on her heel and moving to the dining room table.

We all pitch in to clean up, and then the first game begins. Grabbing an extra deck of cards, I motion for Crosby to follow me and make my way down to the basement.

"Will they find us down here when it's our turn?" she asks.

"Trust me, gorgeous, there isn't a single place in this house, hell, on this property, that they won't find us. We've uncovered all the good spots, and all nine of us know them. This will, however, give us a small reprieve from the action to help you refresh your mind before it's time for us to play."

For the next hour or so, we go over the different plays and what each card means, depending on what's trump. "You're a good teacher," she tells me.

"Yeah, I'll leave the teaching to you. I love my nieces and nephews, but I don't know that I could deal with a school full of them."

"You could. I've seen you in action."

"If I had to, but I enjoy what I do."

"What is that?" she asks.

"I'm a machinist. College wasn't my thing, so I went to the vocational school. Learned a trade, and I've been working at the same place in Harris since I graduated. I like working with my hands, and I'm good at it."

"Modest too," she teases.

"If you know, you know." I wink at her. "What about you? Why teaching?"

"Just wanted a stable career. I've always loved kids."

"You can give me more than that," I tell her.

"I didn't have the best life growing up. Foster care, at least in my experience, wasn't a good time. I wanted a career that I knew if I ever got the chance to be a mom, I would have summers and holidays off to spend with them. I never want my child to feel unwanted or unloved."

I reach across the table and place my hand over hers. "I can't imagine what you've been through. The things you've lived through and seen."

"It wasn't all bad, but you're lucky." She lifts her head, and her eyes lock with mine. "Hugs and family dinners weren't things I had growing up. Cherish that. Your parents and your brothers."

Did you hear that? That was my heart cracking in my chest for this woman. I open my mouth to say something, but I don't have words. What can I say? I'm sorry doesn't seem like enough, and I know she doesn't want to hear it anyway. She'll think I pity her, and it's not pity. It's fucking pain, deep in my chest, for what she didn't have. I know how lucky I am. Instead of speaking, I push back in my chair and walk around the table. She peers up at me, and I offer her my hand.

"Is it our turn?" she asks.

"It's your turn." She looks confused but places her hand in mine and allows me to pull her to her feet. I don't step back. Instead, I wrap my arms around her and bury my face in her neck. I hold her as tightly as I can manage without suffocating her. She's stiff in my arms until she isn't. Her arms latch around my waist, and I feel her shudder. That only makes me hug her just a little tighter.

I don't know how long we stand here, just holding onto one another. Thinking about Crosby as a little girl yearning for love and affection and not getting it crushes me. It's a weight sitting on my chest.

"Yo! You're up!" Archer calls down to us.

"Coming!" I call back. I ease my hold on Crosby and, with my index finger beneath her chin, bring her eyes to mine. "You ever need a hug, you call me. I don't care when it is. I'm your guy."

"That's crazy." Her brow furrows as if she can't understand why I would offer this comfort to her. This woman has no idea how incredible she is in every way.

"No, what's crazy is that I can't stop thinking about you, and after holding you twice now...." Her eyes grow wide. We haven't talked about me holding her on Declan's couch. "I think I could grow addicted."

"Such sweet words. I'm still not having dinner with you." Her tone is light and teasing, but her eyes tell me another story. If I'm not mistaken, I see longing.

"I'm good with it," I tell her. "If I get moments like this one... like we had the other night. Just us, I'll take them."

"Actions of circumstance."

"Is that what this is?" I trace my finger over her bottom lip. "I know I was supposed to be comforting you, but damn, gorgeous, you smell so damn good, and you fit just right." I tap my chest. "Right here, like you were made to be in this exact spot. So, no, not actions of circumstance. This is more than that."

"I'm not looking to be involved."

"That's fine. Just remember, when you do need hugs, or something more, you come to me to get it. Not one of my brothers, not some other jackass who won't take care of you. You come to me. Deal?"

"You're something else, Rushton Kincaid."

"Rush. My friends call me Rush."

"Are you playing or not?" Archer calls down the steps.

"We better get up there." I lace her fingers with mine and guide her up the stairs. We reach the top, and it takes herculean effort to drop her hand. I like the feel of her hand in mine. I also like having her in my arms.

I meant what I said, though. If she needs me, I'm dropping everything to be there for her. I don't know why, but I do know that she's never had that in her life. Someone to put her first, and that makes me want to be the man to do it.

I need to unpack what all this means, but right now, I need to focus on kicking ass in euchre and not letting my family figure out that I quite possibly might be falling for the gorgeous teacher.

Chapter 10

CROSBY

I PLOP DOWN ON THE couch with my bowl of macaroni and cheese. It's been an exhausting week, and I don't have the energy for anything more. Besides, it's just me, and there's no need for a huge meal.

My students were in rare form this week. If they weren't extra chatty, they were cranky, and don't get me started on those who are sick. Runny noses and lack of use of tissues were my life. It feels good to be home and just relaxing.

My phone dings just as I take the first bite of my cheesy dinner. Setting the bowl on the end table, I grab my phone and smile when I see Rushton's name on the screen.

Rushton: Dinner?

I smile. If Rushton Kincaid is anything, he's consistent and persistent. I snap a quick picture of my bowl of mac-and-cheese delight and send it to him.

Rushton: Want some company?

Me: I'm going to have to pass. I'm already in my pajamas. It's been a long week.

Rushton:	What kind of pajamas are we talking about?

Another text follows immediately after.

Rushton:	Need a hug?
Me:	Flannel pants and a T-shirt that's way too big for me. And you give the best hugs, but I'm too exhausted to move.
Rushton:	I would do all the work.
Rushton:	That's not an innuendo, but yeah, I'd do all the work for that too.

He sends a string of wide-smiling emojis, and I can't help it; I laugh. Out loud. I'm glad I'm the only one here to witness the insanity. It's as if I become a different person where Rushton is involved. He brings something out in me that others before him have failed to do. Thankfully, there are no witnesses.

I decide to let him sit for a few while I finish my dinner. I should have known he wouldn't let that slide because as I'm shoveling in my last bite, my phone rings. I rush to chew and swallow before answering. "Hey."

"You stopped responding."

"I was finishing my dinner."

"Are you done?"

I take a drink of my sweet tea. "Yep."

"Tell me about your week."

"You already know the kids were not themselves this week," I remind him. We've been texting off and on for the last two weeks. Since I had Sunday dinner with his family. I didn't go last week even though I was invited. I learned to leave my laundry and grocery shopping on Sundays, so I'm not lying when I tell them that I have too much to do to get ready for the coming week.

Last week Maverick and Merrick knocked on my door, wearing matching smiles. When I asked them what they were so happy about, they said that their mom picked them over Rushton to deliver me leftovers. They then proceeded to hand me a container filled with more food than I would ever be able to eat in one sitting.

Asked if I needed anything, and when I said no, they went back to their place.

"Tell me again."

"They were either moody, hyper, or sick. I can only be used as a human tissue so many times."

"You must have an immune system of steel," he replies.

"You probably just jinxed me. If I get sick, I'm blaming you, Kincaid."

"I'll nurse you back to health."

"Nah, I wouldn't want you to get sick."

"You'd be too weak to keep me away."

"Are you always this difficult or just with me?"

He pauses. "Just you."

"I feel special."

"Because you are."

"What are you buttering me up for?" I ask him. There's humor in my voice, but I'm sure he's building up to something.

"Nothing, gorgeous. I'm just keeping it real. You should know by now what you see is what you get with me."

"You're an open book, huh?"

"Not for everyone, but yeah, I'm an open book for you."

"Why?"

"Why not?"

"Come on, Rushton."

"Rush," he corrects me. "We're friends, remember?"

"Rush," I say to pacify him. "Now tell me."

"I want to get to know you better. It's only fair I let you do the same with me."

"I never said I wanted to get to know you."

"Ouch."

"Sorry, that sounded worse out loud than in my head. It's not that I don't want to know you. I just need to stay focused. I need this contract. I like this town."

"Yeah? You want to make Willow River your forever home?" he asks softly.

"I'd really love that. I've never had a forever home."

He mutters fuck, under his breath, but I still hear him.

"How was your week?" I ask to change the subject.

"It was good. I missed you, though. It's been almost two full weeks since I've seen you."

"That's not true. We did a video call last Thursday when I told you I was making cookies for my students."

"That doesn't count."

"You're needy."

"That's a new trait for me. One that only seems to apply to you."

"You know you're wasting all that charm, don't you? I'm pretty set in my ways. I have to be."

"How so?"

I go with honesty. "It's only ever been me, Rush. I had one person who I thought was my best friend, and she slept with my ex."

"What about this ex? Were the two of you not close?"

"No. I mean, at the time I thought that we were, but he claimed he cheated because I was emotionally unavailable, and he's not wrong."

"You're not emotionally unavailable, Crosby."

"I am. I push people away. It's what I do. I don't let them get too close. That way, when they leave, it won't hurt as bad."

"You're building a life here."

"I hope to be. My future lies in the hands of the school board."

"Are you kidding me? Your students love you. There is no way they're not going to renew your contract."

"Until I know for sure, there's no point in me getting involved. I don't know where I might end up."

"Have a little faith, Crosby."

"I'd love to say that I do, but life has taught me that faith is hard to come by." I clear my throat. "So, you see, you're wasting your time and effort. You should move on from whatever it is that has you continuing to ask me to dinner and wanting to get to know me."

"What if I tell you that I'll wait?"

"Wait for what?"

"For you to be ready."

I'm stunned and have to fight against the emotion welling in my throat at the mere thought that he could want something with me that would have him willing to wait until the spring to see what my future holds. "That's not fair to you."

"What's not fair is that I met this gorgeous woman trying to reach some fishing line. Instantly, I was attracted to her. She's hands down the most beautiful woman I've ever seen. Her heart has some scars, but it's enormous. She's got so much love to give, but she's holding herself back. She's got a timeline, and if I want her, I need to abide by it."

"It's October. I won't know until at least May if they're extending my contract."

"Seven months."

"That's a long time for a man like you."

"A man like me?"

"You're... sexy, and I'm sure you have women throwing themselves at you."

"It doesn't matter if it's not the one that I want."

Butterflies take flight in my belly. I need to shut this down. "I should get to bed. I'm exhausted."

"Can I see you this weekend? Breakfast? Lunch? Dinner? Grocery shopping? You tell me when and where, and I'm there."

"It's as if a switch has been flipped. You're coming on a lot stronger the past couple of weeks."

"You let me feel you, Crosby. You let me hold you in my arms while you slept, and I thought maybe it was a fluke, you know? I thought maybe I imagined that it was as good as it was. Then that day at my parents' in the basement, you let me hold you again, and that same feeling washed over me."

"What feeling?"

"The right one."

"What does that mean?"

"Honestly, I don't know. But I liked it enough to do whatever I need to do to find out."

"You're really willing to wait?"

"Can I keep calling you? Texting you? Maybe sharing a meal with you every now and then?"

"I don't know if that's a good idea."

"Tell me why, Crosby."

"Because what if I fall for you?"

"I'll catch you."

"I'm being serious, Rush. I might be leaving Willow River."

"If that happens, we'll talk about it. See where we are when that happens, and decide together."

I think about what that means. He'd have to leave his family, and I'd never do that. I'd never tear them apart. He needs them, and they need him. I'd never pull him from his family. I know what it's like to be on your own, to not have anyone in your corner, and I refuse to be the reason he leaves that behind.

"I should go."

"All right, gorgeous. Sweet dreams."

"Night, Rush." I end the call. Against my greatest efforts, the walls around my heart are being chipped away where Rushton is concerned. That was most definitely not part of the plan.

I jolt out of bed when I hear the shrill ring of my cell phone. Glancing at the alarm clock, I see it's just after one in the morning. Grabbing my phone, I see Rushton's name on the screen, and my heart drops. He never calls this late.

"Rush."

"Gorgeous, we have a baby!" he says excitedly.

"What?"

"Orrin and Jade, she went into labor, and it was fast. They barely made it to the hospital. I'm on my way there. I'm almost to your place."

"What? Rushton, slow down. Why are you coming to my place?"

"To take you with me."

Five words that shouldn't mean anything more to me than he will ever know. My heart feels all gushy just from those five words. They're not declarations of love, but they might as well be.

"You want to take me with you?" I ask, barely getting the words past my lips.

"Damn right, I do. We're going to meet my nephew." His excitement is infectious.

"You should be with your family."

"I will be. And you're going to be with me. I'll be there in five." He ends the call, and it takes me about three seconds to toss off the covers and rush to get ready. I know Rushton well enough now to be sure he's coming, and he's not leaving until I get into his truck with him.

I'm sliding my arms into my coat when there's a loud knock at the door. Grabbing my purse and phone, I pull open the door to find a smiling, disheveled-looking Rushton.

"Crosby." The way he says my name, with so much meaning behind it, has me pausing. He takes advantage and wraps his arms around me, lifting me off my feet. "A new baby Kincaid." He places me back on my feet but doesn't let go of me. "You ready, gorgeous?"

"Yeah, I'm ready. You sure you want me to come with you?"

"Positive." He steps back, gliding his fingers between mine and giving them a gentle squeeze.

"What about the twins?"

"They were on their way home from the club in Harris. They're en route to the hospital now."

I nod. "Are you sure it's okay if I'm there?"

He drops my hand and raises his to cradle my cheek. "My family loves you. Jade and you are friends, and she'd want you there. Besides, I want you there. That's all that matters." He leans in, and I hold my breath, thinking that he's going to kiss me, but his lips land on my forehead. "You got what you need?"

"Yes."

His grin is boyish and contagious. "Let's go meet my nephew." He takes my hand in his and leads me to his truck that's still running in my driveway.

Once we're on the road, he reaches over and grabs my hand, placing our locked fingers on the center console. I know I should pull away, but he's so excited I'm not even sure he realizes what he's doing. It's endearing to see this man excited about becoming an uncle again. My heart squeezes in my chest. I don't know that I'll ever be an aunt or get to experience being a part of a family, let alone one the size of his. I'm honored to be able to share this with them.

The drive to the hospital is quick, probably because I spent the entire time staring at Rushton. The glow from the dash gives me just enough light to make out his features. His smile is permanently etched on his face. We park and head inside with his hand once again locked with mine. I try to pull away, but he just holds on tighter. Hopefully, his family will be too preoccupied with the new baby to notice.

We reach the waiting room, and all eyes turn our way. So much for going unnoticed. "How are they?" he asks, leading us into the room.

"Mom and baby are doing well, and Daddy is beside himself," Carol tells us. She hugs Rushton and then does the same to me. "It's good to see you, Crosby."

"You too. I hope it's okay that I'm here. Rush called and insisted I be here. I don't want to intrude." I'm kind of throwing Rushton under the bus, but it's what happened.

"Oh, we're happy you're here. I'm certain that Orrin and Jade will be as well."

"Where's Brooks and Declan?" Rushton asks.

"They're visiting now. They want to get home to Palmer and Kennedy and the kids."

Rushton nods. "I can relieve them after I meet him if they need me to," he offers.

"Nah, it was a quick delivery. After we all get our turns, they're going to want to get some rest. Palmer and Kennedy have plans to visit in the morning."

"I'm happy to help with the kids," I offer.

"That's so nice of you. I'll be sure to let them know. They might take you up on that, if you're sure."

"Absolutely. Just tell me when and where I can keep all three."

"Are you sure you can handle Beckham and Remi?" Carol asks.

"Definitely. Besides, Blakely is a huge helper. I'll be fine."

Carol nods. "Thank you. You two should go in next so you can get back home and in bed. You'll need your rest if that's the case." She chuckles.

"I can help her," Rushton offers.

"You should be here with your family."

"They'll probably kick us all out. We can be a little overwhelming when we all get together."

"I can see that." I smile at her.

"Damn, he's cute," Brooks says, coming into the waiting room.

"I love that he's going to get to be close with Beck and Remi in age," Declan replies.

Everyone agrees, and Carol tells them about my offer to watch the babies and Blakely tomorrow, which they agree to immediately. It makes my heart happy to know that they trust me with their children outside of the classroom.

It's not just Rushton that I'm in danger of falling for.

"Rush, you two go on in," Raymond tells us.

"You sure, Dad?" Rushton asks.

"Yep. We're going to stay in case they need anything."

"He did that with us too," Brooks says.

"Yep," Declan agrees.

"Okay." Rushton looks at me, and I nod.

We're standing outside the door, and I stop him. "I love your family." I don't know why I say it, but I couldn't stop the words even if I tried. As if they were ready to burst free.

Rushton dips his head and kisses the corner of my mouth. "They love you too, gorgeous." With that, he pushes open the door, still holding my hand.

"Hey," he says softly.

"More family to meet, little man," Orrin says to the baby he's holding in his arms. He stands and kisses Jade before walking to where we stand at the foot of the bed. "Orion, meet your uncle Rush and aunt Crosby."

I choke on a sob. My hand flies to my mouth as I try to mask it. I would give anything to be this little boy's aunt. "Hey, buddy," Rushton says, taking Orion from his daddy. He turns to me. "Say hi to Crosby," he says, keeping his voice low.

Reaching out, I softly trace my knuckle across his cheek. "It's nice to meet you, Orion," I say softly. I raise my gaze to Orrin, who is sitting on the bed next to Jade, cuddling her to his chest. "Congratulations, you two. He's precious."

"Thank you," they reply in unison.

We spend about ten minutes chatting when Rushton turns to me. "You want to hold him?"

"May I?" I turn my question to Orrin and Jade.

"Crosby," Jade scolds me. "Of course, you can."

I nod and allow Rushton to place him in my arms. I stare down at the tiny miracle I'm holding, and a yearning I've never felt before hits me. I've always craved a family of my own, but this... it's as if I can feel the dream in my grip. I close my eyes, and that's when I feel his hot breath next to my ear.

"Are you all right?"

I nod and open my eyes. "Yeah. I'm good," I assure him. We stay about ten more minutes before we give baby Orion back to his parents. We say our goodbyes and do the same to his family in the waiting room before heading back to my place. It's late or early. However, you want to look at it when we pull into my driveway.

"Thank you for letting me be a part of tonight."

Rushton turns to look at me. Reaching over, he tucks my hair behind my ear. "Thank you for being there. I wanted you there with me. You were the first person I thought of when I got the call."

More bricks crumble from the wall around my heart.

"You want to stay?"

"Yeah, gorgeous. I want to stay." He turns off the engine, grabs his keys, and climbs out of the truck. He follows me up the front steps and waits for me to unlock the door. I don't turn on the lights when we step inside. Instead, I make my way in the dark to my bedroom. Rushton places his hands on my hips, blindly following me.

"Just to sleep," I say when we reach my bedroom.

"Okay, baby," he says, bending and kissing my temple. He releases his hold on me, and I walk around the bed. I toss my coat onto the chair in the corner of the room, kick off my shoes, and slide beneath the covers.

I hear rustling, shoes hitting the floor with a thud, and then the bed dips. "Crosby?"

"Yeah?"

"Come here."

I hesitate.

"Let me hold you."

I know it's a bad idea. It's a really bad idea, but I do it anyway. I meet him in the middle of the mattress, and he pulls me into his chest. He makes me feel safe and protected, and in no time at all, I'm falling into a deep sleep.

Chapter 11

RUSHTON

I'VE NEVER REALLY THOUGHT MUCH about what heaven is like. Not until about five minutes ago when I woke up holding Crosby in my arms. She slept curled against me the entire night, and that brings a smile to my face. My arm is numb, and I have to piss, but I'll be damned if I move an inch. Nope, I'm holding out. I don't know how long it will be before I get to do this again, if ever.

Not able to resist the pull, I press my lips to the top of her head as she starts to stir. She lifts her head and peers up at me, and my breath stalls in my lungs. Her eyes are sleepy, and her hair is a mess, but I've never seen her look more beautiful.

"You're here."

"Did you expect me not to be?"

"I'm not sure. I guess I assumed you'd wake and go home."

"No way, gorgeous. We're spending the day together, remember?" Her brows furrow as she deciphers what I'm talking about. "We're babysitting."

"Oh. You don't have to help me. I can do it. You should be with your family."

"I'll be with my family. I got to meet Orion, and now I'm going to spend some time with the rest of my nieces and nephew while their mommas get their turn."

She opens her mouth and quickly closes it, and nods. "Thank you. I'm going to use the restroom, and you can shower. I'll drive and just drop you off here when we're done."

"What time do they need us?"

"If I know Palmer and Kennedy, they're itching to meet him. I'll call and get a plan together while you're in the shower."

"I can meet you there."

Nice try, baby. "Nah, makes just as much sense for us to ride together." I kiss the top of her head and climb out of bed. I make my way into the en suite bathroom and take care of business. Grabbing the toothpaste, I squeeze some onto my finger and do the best that I can until we get to my place so that I can shower. I know I should just head there now, but I want to spend the day with her, and I'm afraid if I let her out of my sight, she'll make up an excuse that she can't help me today, and then I'd spend the day wondering what she's doing. I've done my fair share of that, so yeah, this is the plan.

I stare at my reflection in the mirror, and I don't recognize the man staring back at me. My eyes are lit with something I can't name. I guess I can call it the Crosby effect. She's the only thing in my life that's changed. Sure, we have new babies to welcome to the family, but that wouldn't do this. It wouldn't make me feel... different.

Better.

Happier.

Opening the bathroom door, I find Crosby sitting on the bed. "All yours. I'm going to call my brothers. I assume we'll be at Declan's since he has two of the three kids."

"Okay."

"You all right?"

She nods, and a small smile pulls at her lips. "Yes. This is just... different for us."

My feet carry me to the bed. Lifting her chin so that I have her full attention, I speak freely without thought. "We're a work in progress. You let me know when you're ready to change things up again."

"What does that mean, Rush?"

"It means I want as much of you as you're willing to give me."

"Rush...." Her tone is full of warning and, if I'm not mistaken, regret.

"Shh," I say softly. "When you're ready, gorgeous. Until then, I'm taking all that I can get." I press my lips to her forehead. Bending, I grab my shoes and walk away, shutting the door behind me as I exit her room.

When I reach the living room, I realize I had left my phone in the truck. Cursing myself, I quickly slide into my shoes and jog out to the truck to grab my phone. I don't have any missed calls or messages, which is a relief.

I pull up a text and add Declan and Brooks and start to type.

Me:	What time do you need us today, and whose house?
Declan:	I was getting ready to send a search party. The twins said you didn't come home last night.

Asshole. If the twins told him I didn't come home, then he knew exactly where I was.

Me:	Do you want a sitter today or not?
Declan:	Just saying...
Me:	Well, don't.
Brooks:	Dec, I think you hit a nerve.
Me:	You know what. Never mind. You can find someone else. Crosby and I are out.
Brooks:	Bro, have we taught you nothing? You can't make choices for her. They get pissed about that.
Declan:	He's right. She can make her own choices.

Me:	Sure, let me talk to your wives about that.
Brooks:	My wife will tell you that we decide together.
Declan:	Mine too.
Me:	Whatever.
Me:	When and where?
Brooks:	Declan's place. Give me an hour to get my ladies moving and in the car.
Me:	You better check with your wife.
Brooks:	...
Declan:	...
Me:	That's what I thought.

Sliding my phone back into my pocket, I move to the porch to head inside. I glance over at the house the twins are renting from Sterling and Alyssa, and all is calm. I make a mental note to give them shit for telling everyone where I am. Hell, they probably started a group chat, leaving me out of it. Assholes.

Letting myself back in the house, I head toward the kitchen. Might as well make us some breakfast while Crosby is getting ready. A quick glance in the fridge has me deciding on scrambled eggs and toast.

I'm buttering the toast when she walks into the kitchen. She's wearing a pair of leggings combined with a Willow River Elementary hoodie. Her hair is up in a messy bun, and I hope that I never forget how she looks at this moment. In the last twenty-four hours, I've seen a more relaxed side of her, and I love every moment of it.

"Hey, you hungry?" I nod to the plates on the counter.

"You cooked?"

"Yeah, I mean, it's not gourmet or anything. Just scrambled eggs and toast." I finish buttering the toast and place it on the second plate. Picking them both up, I turn to face her, and she's standing frozen, just watching me. "Crosby?"

"I—No one has ever made me breakfast before." Her confession is soft, and the grit in her voice tells me the confession was hard for her to make.

How is that possible? She must see the question in my eyes. She moves to grab the milk from the fridge and holds the gallon up, and I nod before sitting down. She busies herself by pouring two glasses as she starts to talk.

"My parents died when I was four." She grabs the glasses and places them on the table before walking back to the counter and putting the gallon of milk back in the refrigerator. "I don't remember them, so I guess I can't say never. I know that when I was in foster care, most of the time, we had to fend for ourselves. Many times, it was breakfast at school, lunch, and nothing at home. How some of these families got approved as foster parents, I'm not sure. Don't get me wrong. There were some good families, and they would make sure we had three meals a day, but for me, just me, no one has ever made me breakfast just for me." She looks up from where she's standing next to the counter. "Until you."

I'm frozen in my seat. I want to go to her, but I don't know if she's finished talking, and now that I have her talking, giving me pieces of her past that she holds close to her chest, I'm afraid to even breathe for fear that she'll stop talking.

"I see the look on your face, Rush. It wasn't all bad. In fact, I consider myself lucky. I was safe in all the homes I was in. Sure, there were a few other foster kids, and even biological kids of the family, that tried things. But I used my voice and threatened to tell. That was enough to scare them off. I was lucky. So many who grew up like I did were not." She moves to the table and pulls out her chair.

"Thank you for breakfast," she says, her eyes finally finding mine.

She's done, and I need to hold her. Pushing back in my chair, I'm kneeling beside her in seconds. With shaking hands, I place them on her cheeks, turning her head, so she's looking at me. This beautiful broken girl. She's afraid to love, for fear she won't be loved back. That she'll be left like she's always been. I want to vow to be right beside her for eternity, but I can't do that. I know Crosby well enough to know she doesn't want the words. She wants the actions, and I plan to give them to her.

I don't know how or when, but this woman has quickly become someone who sits at the top of my list as far as importance in my life. I don't know what it means, but I have time to figure that out. She's not ready, and I need to work through these intense feelings I have for her. I need to dissect them and understand them before I give them to her. She deserves that. She deserves my certainty. While I feel certain, I need to take extra caution with her heart.

"Thank you, baby. Thank you for sharing a piece of your past with me." Tears well in her eyes. "I want more of them. More of your firsts. When you're ready to share them with me, I'm ready for them."

"Rush."

"I'm not pushing you. I promise. I listen when you talk, Crosby. I know that you don't want to be attached. I know you're afraid that you might not be here in a year, and that's okay. I can't take those fears from you, but I can be here. Right here. Every day, every laugh, every tear," I say, using my thumbs to wipe the tears that fall from her eyes. "I'm here for them. You set the pace." I give her a gentle smile. "I'll just be over here falling more each day." I wink and lean in. My intention is to place a kiss on the corner of her mouth, but she turns her head just slightly, and our lips connect. I don't move or take the kiss deeper. I just rest my lips against hers. It literally causes a pain deep in my chest to pull away from her, but I won't be that guy. I won't take more than she's willing to give.

Just the insight she's given me this morning tells me she's scared. She's never been able to depend on or rely on anyone, and I'm going to show her that she can. "Eat up. We have to be at Declan's in thirty minutes. Brooks and Palmer are going to drop Remi off."

She nods, picks up her fork, and begins to eat.

When we pull into Declan and Kennedy's driveway, Brooks and Palmer are already there. We're early, so it wouldn't surprise me if they've been here for a while. I'm sure Crosby and I are the topic of conversation. I love my brothers, but sometimes they annoy the hell out of me. They mean well, which is why I'm not going to say anything. I just hope whatever conclusion they came up with during this little pow-wow they've had today, they keep it to themselves or at least don't bring it up in front of Crosby. I'm trying to pull her in, not push her away.

With my hand on the small of her back, I lead Crosby into Declan's house. "Miss Crosby Greene!" Blakely comes running and wraps her arms around Crosby's legs.

"Hey, Blakely. Just Crosby when we're not at school."

"Crosby. Got it. Did you hear that I have a new baby cousin? So many cousins." She smiles up at Crosby.

"I did hear that. You are going to have so much fun teaching them so many things."

Blakely nods. "That's what Mommy says too."

"You got some love for Uncle Rush?" I ask my niece.

"He's so needy," Blakely says, but she releases her clutch on Crosby and holds her arms in the air for me to pick her up, and I do just that. I squeeze her tight, and she giggles.

"Come on in," Kennedy tells Crosby. "I'll show you where everything is. I set up the Pack 'n Play for Remi in Beck's room."

"Blake, I'll be right back. I need to go help Crosby."

"No. It's fine. You stay. I can relay whatever it is." Crosby gives me a reassuring smile and follows Palmer and Kennedy down the hallway with Blakely hot on their heels.

I watch her go, wishing that I was following along behind her. It's not until Brooks starts singing the chorus to "Another One Bites the Dust" that I pull my eyes from Crosby to face my brothers. "Cute," I say, deadpan.

"What's going on there? We didn't expect to see you at the hospital with her this morning."

"I called her. She's gotten close to your wives. I thought she'd want to be there." It's only the partial truth, and we all know it.

"That look." Brooks points to my face. "Tells us that's not all."

"Fine. That's not all, but I don't know what it is. She's had a rough past, and she's scared, and that just makes me want to pull her closer. She's got me at arm's length."

"Is she okay?" Declan asks.

"What do we need to do?" Brooks adds.

"She's good. Now. She's made it to this point in her life all on her own. I don't want to get into it yet, but I will. Not now, when she can walk out at any minute and hear me."

"You know what Dad would say, right?" Declan asks.

"Love her harder," Brooks and I answer.

"Do you love her?" Brooks asks.

"I don't know. What does love feel like? Is it me thinking about her all the time? Is it the fact that when something good, or hell, even something bad happens, she is the first person I want to call? Is it that when I see the pain in her eyes and the tears threatening to fall, I want to tear the fucking world apart to find every fucker in her life that never had the common decency to even give the woman a fucking hug?" I'm breathing heavily, and I know I need to calm the hell down.

"Damn. Okay. Here they come," Declan whispers. "Beers soon. We'll work this out."

I nod and give them both a grateful smile. "Thanks again, man. You too, Crosby," Brooks says, looking over my shoulder. "We won't be gone long. It will be nice not to drag the babies into the hospital."

"We're happy to help," Crosby answers for us, and I grin. She might be pushing me away, but that little slip of the tongue tells me I'm heading in the right direction.

"I made chicken and noodles for dinner last night, and there are leftovers in the fridge. Help yourself to anything you need," Kennedy tells Crosby. She then turns to me. "Make yourselves at home."

"Blake, you be good for Crosby and Uncle Rush," Declan tells his daughter.

"I will, Daddy. I'm going to be the helper. M—Crosby already said I could. I'm the bestest helper, right, Daddy?"

Declan's eyes soften for his daughter. "The best helper ever," he confirms.

I can't help but think about Crosby not having that when she was growing up. No one to tell her she was the best helper, to tell her they love her before leaving, no one to hug her. Fuck. I have to stop thinking about it. That's something I can think about when I have time to empty my head of all she's told me and dissect it when she's not here to witness the array of emotions cross my face.

After a round of hugs, and a baby for me and one for Crosby, with Blakely between us, my brothers and their wives leave with the promise to be back soon.

Blakely immediately grabs Crosby's hand, that's not holding onto Beckham, and guides her to the couch. She begins talking about how much her baby brother sleeps, and Crosby never takes her eyes off my niece. She's giving her the attention she craves, the attention she didn't get as a child.

Actions, I remind myself. This woman needs action. Time to prove she's worthy of someone sticking around. She gives the best fucking hugs, and her heart is huge, even if she's not ready to accept and give love.

Without me telling them, my family is showing her all of that as well. Get ready, baby, Kincaids love hard.

I love hard.

Something I didn't know about myself for anyone outside of my family until I met her.

Until Crosby.

Fuck me. I'm falling in love.

Chapter 12

CROSBY

"HOW ARE PIPER AND BABY Penelope?" I ask Palmer.

Her eyes light up. "They're both doing great. Penelope is adorable. She looks just like her daddy, but I see some Piper in her too. I'm so excited that she and Remi will be so close in age. Beckham and Orion too."

"That will be nice for them to have other kids their age in the family to play with," I agree. I know I would have loved that when I was a kid, but we're not going there tonight.

"I see lots of sleepovers in our future." Kennedy smiles.

"I can't believe we let them talk us into taking all the kids," Palmer says with a pout on her lips.

"Are you worried?"

"No. Not at all. I miss her." She smiles. "If anything, I need to worry about Brooks trying to think of ways to knock me up again." She chuckles. "I know I'm a mess. Right now, I'm taking her to the studio with me, and I'm only working part time. I need to hire another photographer soon. As she gets older, I'm not going to be able to take her to shoots. The days of her sleeping through them are going to come to an end."

"I thought Aunt Carol was going to watch her?" Ramsey asks.

"She is, but Brooks and I talked about it, and if I can find a good photographer to hire, I can cut back. His schedule allows him at least one day a week with her, and I want that too."

"That's definitely a perk of being able to work from home. However, there are times when I know I'll be calling Carol, begging for help as he gets older."

"Can we even call what you do work?" Alyssa laughs. "I have job envy."

"Most of the time, it's great. Then there are the few that come in, and they need a ton of work. Not just grammatical edits but plot holes, and those are a nightmare. It doesn't happen often, but it has happened. I pretty much have the set of authors that I love working with. I'm not taking on anyone new at the moment."

"How's school going?" Ramsey asks me.

"I think they're all ready for a holiday break. They're either super chatty, moody as hell, or sick. I know kids get sick, but at no time during my education did they teach me that I'd become a human tissue."

The ladies grimace. "Seriously?"

"Yeah, but it's not on purpose. They come in to hug me or hug my legs, and they conveniently wipe their faces on my clothes."

"Ick." Alyssa's face twists at my imagery.

"I can't believe I'm getting ready to say this, but I've gotten used to it. I had one with their head in the trash can puking the other day." This time it's me who grimaces. "Sorry, I know we're eating."

Kennedy waves me off. "One of those kids you're talking about is mine. I feel like I should apologize to you."

"No. Not at all. Please don't think that. I was just venting. I'm used to complaining to Rush, and he doesn't get grossed out over anything."

"Speaking of Rush, what's going on there?" Jade asks.

I shrug. "Nothing. He continues to ask me out, and I keep turning him down."

"You have to give us more than that," Alyssa tells me.

"He says he wants to get to know me."

"He's a good guy," Ramsey says.

I sigh. I'm going to have to break down and tell them about my past for them to understand. I don't want them to think that I'm stringing him along. "We're going to need alcohol for this," I tell them.

"Oh, we can all drink!" Jade moves to the refrigerator and snatches two bottles of wine. "I have more in the garage fridge if we need them." She smiles widely.

"We're probably going to need them," I say to her. Jade fills each of us a glass of wine and passes them out.

"Let's go get comfortable in the living room," Jade suggests.

We grab our glasses of wine and follow her to the living room. We each claim a spot, and all eyes look at me expectantly. "When I was four years old, I went into foster care." Their mouths drop open but I forge on. I tell them how my parents overdosed and how I was shuffled from one foster family to another growing up. I don't stop until I've told them about my ex-boyfriend and my ex-best friend, who really was more just a friend. I never confided in her. Not like I have these ladies. "I'm closer to all of you than I was to her, but it still hit me here," I tell them, tapping my hand over my heart.

"Damn," Ramsey mutters. "I don't know what brought you to Willow River, but you have a home here," she tells me. "*We* are your people." She places her wineglass on the table, comes over to where I'm sitting on the chair, and hugs me. "I had a difficult upbringing, but Aunt Carol and Uncle Raymond were there for me. I met Palmer, and we became fast friends and this town." She shakes her head. "This town is almost magical in a way. The minute I rolled into town, my heart shredded. It felt like home." She grabs her wine and takes her seat.

"That's tricky for me," I tell them. "I subbed since I graduated with my teaching degree. This is my first year of having my own classroom."

"How is that tricky?" Kennedy asks. "The kids love you. Trust me. I hear it every day."

"I love them too." I take a hefty sip of my wine.

"Pause." Jade stands and finishes off her glass of wine. "Let me grab another bottle." She disappears into the garage and is back in no time, filling all of our glasses before taking her seat and nodding at me to continue.

"My contract is only for one year. If they don't renew, I have to find another job, which won't be here in Willow River."

"They're going to renew," Kennedy says with confidence.

"I hope so, but there's a chance that I might be moving on. I had a plan. I found a nice rental, and I was going to put all of my focus into being the best teacher I could be. I didn't plan to meet an amazing group of ladies."

"Friends," Alyssa speaks up. "We're your friends, Crosby."

I nod, feeling emotion well in my throat. "Friends," I repeat. "I can't tell you what it means to me that y'all have accepted me into your lives and the lives of your family. I've never had this. A group of people who I truly feel as though I can be myself with."

"We love you," Palmer says, and the next thing I know, they're all gathered around me in a group hug, and we're laughing with tears in our eyes.

When they're finally all back in their seats, it's Palmer who knocks the breath from my lungs with her next question. "So, my brothers-in-law, the single ones." She smirks. "If you had to pick one, who would you pick?"

"W-What?" I sputter.

"Oh, we haven't asked yet, have we?" Ramsey drains the rest of her wine, and right now, that seems like a damn fine idea. I do the same, tilting my head back and emptying my own glass.

"It's kind of our thing," Jade confesses.

"Explain that." So, they do. They tell me how it started and how they've all ended up with the guy they chose for their happily ever after.

"So, you see, you have to pick. Not just to get your happily ever after, but that means you'll get to stay here in Willow River. It's fail-proof. We're prime examples." Kennedy smiles.

"You know that's ludicrous, right?" I ask them.

"I was skeptical too, but they're right," Alyssa admits. "If you pick, it comes true."

I shake my head and reach for my glass, forgetting that I emptied it. "That's not how the world works. At least not for me. If every wish had come true, I would have had a family growing up. Someone there to hug me and love me, and no. This won't work."

"I hear you," Jade chimes in. "I know that unless you've witnessed it that you'd be skeptical, but what's it hurt to just play along and humor us?"

I let her words sink in, and no, it won't hurt anything except maybe my heart. I'm struggling enough as it is. With each passing day, every text message, phone call, or drop-by saying he's been in the neighborhood in the past two weeks is chipping away at the barricade around my heart. It's too risky for me to start believing that all I have to do is tell the universe that Rushton is my pick and I'll get to live happily ever after.

I know that's not how it works. However, my heart, the lazy bitch, lost the memo. "I can't."

"Just humor us," Ramsey says. I look up to find her filling our glasses again. I'm starting to feel the effects, but I ignore that and take a hefty drink.

"So," Kennedy sips her refilled wine. "Rushton, Archer, Ryder, but he's kind of already taken, at least in his heart, so maybe don't pick him. Maverick and Merrick."

"We all know who you're going to pick." Alyssa grins behind the rim of her glass. "However, in order for this to work, you have to say it. You have to put it out there for the universe to hear."

"This is silly."

"You can do it," Ramsey encourages.

My phone pings, and I pull it from my pocket. It's a text from Rushton, and I smile as I open it.

Rushton: Missing you.

It's followed by a picture of him holding Orion.

Me: Looks like you're getting lots of snuggles.

Rushton: These kids are cute as hell.

That's followed by another picture of Blakely, Remi, Beckham, and Orion lying on the floor on a blanket.

Me: Good genes.

Rushton: Add that to my pros column.

Me: ??

Rushton: You know, in case you're making a list. That's a definite pro in my favor. Just look at my brothers' kids. Hell, look at my brothers and me if you need proof. Good genes.

I send back a string of laughing emoji.

Rushton: Laugh it up. I'll remind you of this very conversation after we have our first.

Me: Are you drunk?

Rushton: Tipsy at best.

Rushton: Are you?

Me: Maybe...

Rushton: You know. They say that when you're drunk, you tell the truth.

Me: What is your truth, Rushton Kincaid?

Rushton: I'm falling hard, Crosby Greene.

"Earth to Crosby." Alyssa waves her hand at me. I look up and my face heats. "Pick one." She smirks.

"Rushton." His name is out of my mouth before I can stop. I think about backtracking. About telling them that Alyssa tricked me, but I don't. I would give anything for things to be different, and maybe, just maybe, Willow River will be my chance at happiness. I'll get the offer for an extended contract, and if Rushton is still interested, well, maybe a girl who grew up with no one to love her will finally get someone to call her own.

"See, that wasn't so hard." Palmer grins.

I drain the rest of my wine. "If things were different... if my future plans were not hanging in the balance, I'd pick Rushton. I know without a doubt he'd break my heart, but the way he makes me feel... I'd risk it." I'll regret spilling my innermost thoughts tomorrow, but right now, it feels too good to talk about. To be me and share my true feelings.

"You're falling for him," Jade says softly.

"I can't."

"I don't think you get to decide, sweetie," Alyssa says.

"Maybe in a few months," I tell them my earlier thoughts. "If they renew my contract, I can say yes to dinner and just see where it goes from there."

"It's going straight to pound town," Palmer says dramatically.

Ramsey giggles. "I think we're drunk."

"Quite possibly." Kennedy nods, tipping her wineglass to get every last drop.

"Shit," I mutter. "How am I going to get home?"

"You could call Rushton." Alyssa offers helpfully.

"He's drinking too."

"How do you know?"

I wave my cell phone at her. "He told me."

"Wait. You've been texting him?"

"Yep." I drop my phone on my lap and tilt my head back.

"Deacon, Sterling, Rushton, Ryder, and Archer are drinking. The others are our drivers," Jade offers helpfully.

"You planned this?" Kennedy asks.

"Nah, but I knew we needed to let loose, and you know how our husbands are. They won't touch a drop unless they know we're taken care of. So, those who have kids to tend to and the twins stayed sober. The others got to let loose like we did."

"Maybe I'll organize an Uber." I grab my phone from my lap to open the app, and the ladies start laughing.

"You're in Willow River," they remind me.

"No Ubers," Alyssa says.

"I've got this." Jade dials her phone. "Babe, we're ready," she tells him. She listens and then giggles. "I had a drink," she confesses.

"More than one!" Palmer calls out, and we all start laughing again.

"Does that make me a bad mom?" she asks. Worry lines her features.

I watch as she listens to her husband, and the lines of worry disappear, followed by a slow smile. "Love you." She ends the call. "They're on their way. They just need to load up the babies. Kens, Maverick is going to drop you off since Blakely and Beckham are both sleeping."

"Aw, my babies," Kennedy coos.

"Merrick is taking you, Crosby. Maverick will take Ramsey because they live close to Declan and Kennedy." Jade grins. "I hope I got that right," she says in a fit of laughter, and because when you're tipsy, and your friend laughs, even if it's not funny, you laugh too, we all dissolve into laughter, and ten minutes later that's how the guys find us.

I watch as Orrin goes to Jade, as they peer down at Orion, who's sleeping in his seat. Orrin kisses his wife, and she accepts it with ease. I turn slightly and take in Brooks and Palmer. Remi is wide awake and all smiles at her parents. Brooks kisses the top of Palmer's head, and my heart squeezes in my chest. I'm envious of what they have. My eyes move to Ramsey, who is now sitting on Deacon's lap. He's smiling at her as she talks animatedly. He only has eyes for her.

"Tink!" Sterling comes into the room, walking a little off balance, and heads straight for his fiancée. "I got us a driver," he tells her.

Alyssa giggles, and she, too, accepts the sloppy kiss he presses to her lips.

"You ready, Kens?" Maverick asks. "We have to get these two in the car." He points to Deacon and Ramsey.

I feel hands on my shoulders, and I turn to see Rushton smiling down at me with glassy eyes. "Hey, gorgeous." He beams.

"Rushton."

"I think I'm supposed to kiss you," he says, leaning over the back of my chair.

"You think so?"

"Yep. That's what my brothers did. I feel left out."

"Come on, Romeo," Merrick jokes. "Let's get back in the car. I'll help Crosby."

"No." Rushton shakes his head. "She's my girl. I'll help her to the car."

My heart skips a beat at his words. I open my mouth to tell him I'm not his girl, but then I decide that maybe I can pretend. Just for the car ride home, I can pretend like Willow River is home to me and that Rushton Kincaid is mine.

"Jesus, it's like herding cats," Brooks titters. "Come on. Load it up. We have babies to get to bed."

Rushton steps in front of me and offers me his hand. I accept it, letting him pull me to my feet. He wraps his strong arms around me and nuzzles my neck. "You smell good, baby," he tells me softly.

"Come on, lovebirds." Merrick ushers us outside to his truck. Rushton opens the back door and helps me climb inside. When he tells me to move over and takes a seat next to me, I'm surprised. "You two good back there?" Merrick asks.

"Yep."

"Crosby first," Rushton tells him.

"That's silly. Merrick's my neighbor."

"But then you're alone with my brother."

"He's your brother," I remind him.

"I'm not going to hit on your girl, bro," Merrick assures him.

"Crosby first." Rushton slides his arm around my shoulders and pulls me into his chest. The heat of his skin warms me instantly, and I remember that I'm pretending he's mine for the drive.

"You can stay," I tell him before I have a chance to talk myself out of it. Then again, drunk me is fully on board with this decision.

"Yeah?" Rushton asks. "You going to let me hold you again?"

"That sounds nice," I say, snuggling into him.

"We're both going to her place." I hear him tell Merrick. That's the last thing I remember before my eyes fall closed.

Chapter 13

RUSHTON

MY ARM IS WRAPPED AROUND Crosby as we stumble up her front porch. She was asleep in the truck, and I'm cursing myself for getting drunk. I shouldn't have had to wake her up. I should have been able to let her sleep as I carried her inside. My other option was for Merrick to carry her, and yeah, that's not happening. Lucky for me, she was easy to wake.

She said I could stay, and I can't wait to get her wrapped in my arms. It's been too long since she let me do this. If I'm being honest, I wasn't sure I'd ever have another opportunity. It's been a couple of months of trying to get this girl to take a chance on me. At least she's opened up, and I understand her worries. I just wish I could take them for her. That's going to take time. I need to keep showing up, and that's exactly what I plan to do.

I'm also going to hold on to moments like these with both hands until she knows without a shadow of a doubt that she can always count on me.

"You need some help?" Merrick asks.

"Nope," I say as we take the last step and are both safely on the porch. "Thanks for the lift." I wave over my shoulder as we stumble but quickly regain our footing.

"You sure?" Merrick calls out. I can hear the humor in his voice, even in my inebriated state.

I toss my hand in the air in a wave as Crosby pushes open the front door. I follow her inside, shutting the door and twisting the lock behind me. Just like the last time I found myself in this position, she doesn't turn on the lights. She guides us to her room in the dark, and thankfully, we make it without any major catastrophes.

Inside her room, she stops a few feet from the bed and just stands there. Not able to resist, I wrap my arms around her, aligning her back to my front, and bury my face in her neck. "You okay?" My heart is pounding in my chest. I'm scared as hell she's changed her mind, and my ass is going to end up on the couch, or worse, next door on my twin brothers' couch. Of course, it's her decision, but I'm craving the feeling of her in my arms all night.

The room is bathed in darkness, and the only sound is our breathing. She's still in my arms but relaxed. "Tell me what you want, baby. I'll give you whatever it is." She's second-guessing, and I don't want her to be uncomfortable. I need to show her I'm in this with her and that she's setting the pace.

"I was pretending." Her words are so soft it's as if she didn't mean for me to hear her.

"When were you pretending?"

"Tonight."

"Help me understand, gorgeous."

"When you got there. You came to me, and I pretended that I was yours."

My arms tighten around her as hope swells in my chest. "You don't have to pretend, Crosby. I want you to be mine." I'm not sure if I've ever actually told her that. If I've said the words out loud to her. I've been worried about scaring her away. Apparently, all I needed was to get some alcohol running through my veins to loosen me up and take the risk.

"I can't be yours."

The hope I was feeling crashes as my stomach falls to my toes. "I want you to be. When you're ready." She adjusts her position, and I hold her tighter. "I wish we could stay together just like this. Me holding you in my arms."

She's quiet, and I'm ready to apologize, but her words stop me. "Maybe... maybe we could pretend."

"What?"

Her breaths start to come quicker. In an attempt to calm her down, I press my lips to her neck. She shudders in my arms, and my cock strains against my zipper. "Tell me," I whisper in her ear.

"Tonight. Maybe we can pretend that I'm yours."

"Tell me how you see this going. I need you to be open and honest with me, Crosby."

"I-I see you kissing me. Touching me."

"Where?"

"In my bed."

Fuck me. "What are our limits?"

"Just... holding me and kissing me. I want to feel wanted," she says, her voice cracking.

I turn her in my arms. I can't see her expression, but I need her to be looking at me. I place my hands on either side of her face, and I wish that I could see those big brown eyes of hers, so I could see how she's taking all of this. But something tells me that the darkness of the room, along with the alcohol, is giving her strength to finally ask for what she wants. To finally let herself ask for what she wants.

Me.

"I want you, Crosby. Do you hear me? You are wanted. I want to cherish you, gorgeous girl."

"But we can't. Unless we pretend."

"How drunk are you?" I ask her. I'm suddenly sober. Sure, I've got a buzz going, but I'm not too far gone to know what's at stake here.

"The nap helped," she says, referring to her sleeping on the way here.

"I don't want to be your regret, Crosby. I can't live with that. I'd rather pine for you, dream of what it feels like to kiss and touch you freely than be a regret."

It's her turn to place her hands on my cheeks. "I could never regret you, Rushton Kincaid. You're too good to be true."

"I'm right here. This is me, as real as it gets, and I'm here with you. This is where I want to be. You can tell me I have to sleep on the couch, and I'm still going to be here. You can tell me that all I can do is kiss you goodnight and hold you, and I'd be a happy man. You tell me what you want, and it's yours."

"No regrets?"

"Never. Not with you."

"I want you to sleep next to me. You promised to hold me."

"Done."

"But I want kisses. Lots of kisses."

"Done and done."

She chuckles softly. And the sound lifts the weight from her shoulders. "One more thing."

"Name it."

"You can say no."

"Never. Not to you."

"You sure about that? I could ask you to sleep on your head or something equally as crazy."

"I'd try for you." I'm not feeding her a line of bullshit either. For her, I would try. This woman has me being well... not me. I'm a good guy. I treat women right, but I've never wanted to give them the world. Crosby changed that. Changed me. I'm not sure when or how it happened, but here we are, and I'm all in.

"It's too much to ask."

"Try me."

She shakes her head and tries to pull away. I wrap my arms around her waist and press her body close to mine. Bending, my lips are next to her ear. "Tell me what you need, Crosby."

"Maybe you could take your shirt off? I just—It would be nice to feel your skin."

My hands drop from her waist, and I reach behind my neck, grabbing the collar of my shirt, pulling it over my head, and letting it fall to the floor. I reach out and tug her into my chest. She rests her head there. Her hands wrap around my waist and she grips my bare back.

Damn, this is nice.

"Like I said. Anything."

She's quiet for a long time, and I don't break the silence. I'm content to just hold her, feeling her hot breath against my bare chest. This time when she pulls away, I let her. She moves to the side of the bed that she slept on last time, and I hear her shoes fall to the floor. Knowing she's getting ready for bed, I do the same, kicking off my tennis shoes. I want to strip out of my jeans, but I don't want to push her.

"You can take off your jeans," she says as if she's reading my mind. "I don't have anything for you to sleep in, but you did that last time, and that can't be comfortable. I want you to be comfortable," she rambles.

"I want what you want, Crosby. I don't mind keeping them on."

"Off is fine."

Not needing to be told twice, I pull my phone and my wallet from my pockets and place them on the nightstand before discarding my jeans.

There's a soft glow from the moon shining in her bedroom window, and I can see her shadow as she slides beneath the covers. Her legs are bare, but she's still wearing her long-sleeve T-shirt. Knowing I'm about to kiss her until her lips are swollen or until she tells me to stop, I take my spot beside her in bed. We're both burrowed under the covers, but she's too far away.

"It's okay if you've changed your mind."

"Have you?" she asks.

"Get over here." I open my arms, holding up the blanket, and she moves into my arms where she belongs. "Much better," I say softly. "Can I kiss you now?"

"I'd like that."

Falling to my back, I bring her with me. I slide my hand behind her neck and pull her lips to mine. I don't want her to feel as though she doesn't have a choice with my large body hovering over her. She's nervous, and I know she said she's never been hurt sexually, but that doesn't mean she's never been intimidated. I want her to always feel safe with me.

My lips press to hers in a soft caress. She relaxes into my hold, and her tongue peeks out, swiping at my lips. I nip at her lip, and she opens it for me. I get lost in her taste. In the feel of her tongue sliding against mine. One hand grips her ass, holding her to me. That's when I realize there's nothing between us but a thin piece of cotton. My cock is painfully hard, but I ignore it and keep kissing her. My hand that was gripping her neck now traces up and down her spine while the other kneads her ass. Damn, she has a nice ass. Her nails dig into the bare flesh of my chest, which has me deepening the kiss. I can't get enough of her.

Suddenly she pulls away, and I'm ready to protest, but I realize she's taking off her shirt. With the glow of the moonlight, I watch as she reaches behind her and unhooks her bra. Inwardly I curse the lack of light, knowing that she's bare-chested in front of me.

"You changing the rules on me, baby?"

"Is that all right with you?"

"No complaints."

She burrows back under the covers, and her bare tits press against my chest. "Damn," I mutter as her lips greedily seek mine. This time she's the one in control. Mostly because my brain has short-circuited, feeling her naked body pressed to mine. My calloused hands float over her back, and I don't know that I've ever felt skin so soft.

I can't stop touching her.

I can't stop kissing her.

My cock is so hard that I'm certain I'll have permanent damage.

"Rush...," she says breathily as I trail my lips over her neck. I can't resist rolling to my side and bending my head, pulling a hard nipple into my mouth. The sound that comes from her is one I wish I could bottle and keep forever. It's already going to play over and over in my mind as it is.

My mouth moves from one nipple to the other, giving each equal amounts of attention. Her hands are buried in my hair, and she mumbles incoherent words of encouragement and pleasure.

"Rush... I need...." She trails off when I gently bite down on her neck.

"Tell me, Crosby. What do you need?"

"More."

"More of what, baby? Tell me. You already know that I'll never say no to you."

"You. I want more of you."

"More of this?" I ask, kissing her neck. "Or maybe more of this?" My lips move back to her breasts and suck gently. "Is this what you want?"

She grabs my hand and places it over her pussy.

"Are you aching, baby?"

"Please," she replies.

"Can I touch you here?"

"Yes."

Fuck. My index finger flirts with the waistband of her panties, and she huffs out an irritated breath. "So impatient," I say, kissing her softly.

"I need—"

She doesn't get to finish because my hand slips beneath her panties. My fingers slide through her wetness, making it easy for me to dip one long digit inside her. "This? You need this?"

"Yes. Please. I—That." She nods.

"You're so tight." The sound of her arousal as I pump my finger inside her seems to echo throughout the room. "So wet for me," I praise. I don't wait for her to tell me she needs more. I add another finger, and she moans her approval. My thumb finds her clit easily as I begin to massage gently. Curling my fingers, she cries out, and her pussy squeezes my fingers like a vise. When her body falls to the bed sated, I remove my fingers and bring them to my mouth. Tasting her.

"Did you just lick your fingers?" She's breathless.

"Yep."

"That's... hot."

I chuckle. That's not the reply I was expecting. "You're hot." I lean over and kiss her. She kisses me back, not the least bit deterred that she can taste herself on my tongue. I pull her into my arms and will my cock to relax. It's not happening tonight, but I'm okay with that. I got more of her than I thought that I would.

That's why when she grips my cock through my boxer briefs, I tense. "What are you doing, baby?"

"Can I?"

"You never have to ask permission to touch me." That's the only go-ahead she needs as she slides her hand beneath my boxer briefs and strokes me.

"Can we take these off?"

"This is your show, gorgeous."

She grips the waistband, and I lift, making it easy for her as she slips my boxer briefs down my legs. I kick them, not giving one single fuck where they land. She goes back to stroking me, and I can't ever remember a time being jacked off has ever felt this good.

Just when I think things can't get better, she moves down the bed and takes the tip of my cock into her mouth. "Fuck," I mutter. She's not bothered by my words as she takes as much of me as she can down her throat.

"You don't have to do this," I tell her.

Her head bobs as she takes me over and over again, her tongue sliding along with each pass. I grip the sheets, needing to hold onto something. When she slows and my cock falls from her mouth with an audible pop, I release my hold on the sheets.

"I wonder...." Her words trail off as if she's afraid to ask.

"You wonder what?"

She moves to straddle my hips. She grips my cock, gently stroking. She shocks the hell out of me when she reaches into her panties, runs her fingers through her folds, and uses her cum as lube for my cock. I've never been so fucking glad for the soft glow of moonlight in my life. It would have been a travesty to have missed that.

"That's...." I swallow hard. "Hot as fuck."

"Do you think it would fit?" she asks me.

"What?" My brain is mush with her hands on me, and after what I just witnessed.

"Your cock. Do you think it would fit?" As if I need more description, she rocks her hips forward, holding still when my cock presses against her pussy.

I swallow hard. "It will fit."

"I'm not so sure," she says, rocking her hips again.

I sit up, which has those glorious tits of hers pressing against my chest. "My cock would fit inside you like a glove," I assure her.

"Maybe we should—" She reaches between us and grips my cock, and the next thing I know, her panties are pushed to the side, and she's sliding down. She doesn't stop until I'm fully seated inside her. She's got all of me in more ways than one.

"Like you were made for me," I say against her lips.

"I've never felt so full." My cock twitches inside her, and she moans.

"Wrap your legs around my waist." She does as I ask, locking her legs at the ankles behind me. I grip her panties and tear them from her body, tossing them to the side. She gasps but doesn't reprimand me. Her hands are on my shoulders, and I place mine on her hips. I lift her and then push her back down on my cock.

"Oh, that's nice."

"Nice?"

She laughs. "Sexy. Hot. Life-changing."

"That's better." I kiss her again before lifting her and pushing her back down on my cock. We find a steady rhythm as she begins to bounce on her own. Her legs unlock, and she goes up on her knees as I fall back against the mattress. My hands grip her thighs as she uses her knees as leverage to rise and fall.

I lift my hips as she tumbles, and a deep, throaty, sexy as fuck moan escapes from her lips, and she rocks. Her pussy grows tighter, and I'm two seconds from coming. Knowing I need her with me, my thumb finds her clit, and it takes two passes before she's stilling, her pussy gripping me like a vise as she tumbles over the edge of bliss. I follow along, calling out her name as I find my release.

Crosby drops forward, and I wrap my arms around her. This moment with her has changed me. It's hands down the best sex of my life. It feels as though I gave her a part of me and that she did the same with me. I'm not the same person I was before I felt her from the inside.

We lie in each other's arms for I don't know how long. It's not until she sits up and moves that my cock slips free from her body that I realize we didn't use protection. "Fuck, Crosby. I'm sorry."

"Sorry? You regret it?" I can hear the sorrow in her voice as it cracks.

"Fuck. No. I don't regret it. Never. But, baby, I didn't wear a condom. I was so wrapped up in you that I forgot."

"I'm on the pill."

"I didn't protect you."

"Is there something you should be protecting me from?" she asks.

"Just a little boy or girl with your big brown eyes," I tell her.

"We're good. It's been a long time for me."

"No one for me for a couple of months before I met you, and well, you're all that I can think about."

"You don't have to say that. We're fine."

"Hey." I reach out and press my palm to her cheek. "I'm not just spouting off pretty words. There has been no one for months before you, and you are all I can think about. Just you, Crosby. I want you. I'll take you any way that I can have you."

"We were just pretending." I feel the shift in her immediately.

I'm struggling to find the right words. "You promised me that I could hold you all night. That was the deal." I'm desperate for time with her.

"You still want that?"

"More than anything."

"Let me get cleaned up."

"Let me help you." I move to get out of bed, but her hand on my arms stops me.

"I need a minute. You can clean up once I'm finished." She climbs out of bed, grabs my discarded T-shirt from the floor, and disappears behind the bathroom door.

I lie here staring up at the shadows on the ceiling, wondering where this unexpected turn of events is going to lead us. I remind myself that she's scared, and she's never had anyone stick it out. Actions. My girl needs actions.

Ten minutes later, we're both cleaned up. I'm back in my boxer briefs, and she's in my T-shirt with no panties. Something I fight like hell not to think about as I pull her into my arms, and we drift off to sleep.

Willow River
Georgia

Chapter 14

CROSBY

I'VE BEEN LYING HERE FOR well over an hour, trying like hell not to freak out. As soon as I open my eyes, every single moment of last night comes rushing back. Then there's the feel of his arms wrapped around me. His hold is so tight, it's as if, even in his sleep, he's afraid I'll disappear.

He knows me better than I thought he did.

My first instinct is to somehow escape his hold and flee, but it only takes seconds for me to squash that idea. I've never felt as safe or as protected as I do in his arms. How is it that just the way he holds me while we're sleeping, he makes me feel wanted? Physical affection isn't something I've received a lot of in my life. My ex didn't like to cuddle, kiss, or do anything other than get himself off. One night with Rushton, and I know how selfish my ex was. What's worse is deep down, I knew it all along, but I stayed with him just so I wouldn't be so alone.

I refuse to be that person ever again.

"Morning, gorgeous." Rushton kisses my shoulder. "Sleep well?"

"Morning," I reply. I ignore his question because I have a feeling it's going to be hard for me to keep pushing him away after this, and I don't need to give him any ammunition to use against me.

Somehow, I need to convince him that last night was a mistake. A one-time occurrence that will not be repeated. At least not until I know what my future holds. I'm already so attached to him. I can feel my heart cracking with the thought of telling him last night meant nothing when it meant everything.

His phone rings, and he releases me to reach over and grab it. "Hello?" he answers, his voice gruff and laced with sleep. It's sexy.

"I'm not sure yet." I can hear another male voice on the other end. "I'll let you know." Something else is said before he says goodbye. Dropping his phone onto the bed, he rolls back over and pulls me back into his arms.

Dammit. It was the perfect chance to escape, and I was frozen listening to his raspy, sexy morning voice. "Everything okay?" I ask.

"Yeah, that was Merrick. He was asking if I want him to take me to get my truck."

"Oh, yeah, I forgot that it wasn't here."

"What are your plans for the day?" he asks.

"I have laundry and grocery shopping for the week. Just the normal things I don't have time to get done during the week."

"How about I make us some breakfast? We start on your laundry, head to the store, and then you can go with me to Sunday dinner at my parents'?"

"I really have too much to do." Lies. Sure, I have things to do, but not too much that I can't spare a few hours for dinner. Lines are getting blurred already, and I have to shut this down before they cross completely.

"Come on. I'll make you breakfast." He completely ignores my refusal to go to Sunday dinner with him. He drops a kiss on my cheek before climbing out of bed. I don't move. I stay frozen in place as I hear him getting dressed. The bathroom door closes, and I heave a sigh of relief. Last night, I knew what I was doing was foolish. Nothing good ever comes from pretending.

A couple of minutes later, the bathroom door opens. "Get moving, sleepyhead. We have a big day," Rushton says, with way too much chipper in his voice for this time of the day. My bedroom door opens and closes, and I know he's no longer in the room with me.

Forcing myself to get moving, I grab clothes and lock myself in my bathroom. It's ridiculous after what we did with one another last night to lock him out, but it's not just my bathroom I'm trying to lock him out of. My heart needs to be on lockdown as well. I just need to keep reminding myself of that fact. I seem to forget that when it comes to Rushton Kincaid.

Twenty minutes later, I know it's time to face the music or the man. I head toward the kitchen where I hear him moving around. He looks up when I enter the room, and his smile stalls the breath in my lungs. The Kincaid family's genes really are unfair. Although, to me, Rushton is by far the most handsome of the brothers.

"There she is. I thought I was going to have to drag you out of bed, lazybones." He winks and places two plates of pancakes on the table and heads for me. He wraps me in his arms, and in a moment of weakness, I rest my head against his chest, wrapping my arms around him.

I feel his lips press to the top of my head, and I curse myself for not being stronger. Pulling out of his embrace, I smile up at him. "You didn't have to make breakfast."

He shrugs. "I don't mind. It's kind of our thing." His smile is genuine, and I see nothing sinister lying beneath. All I see is a good man doing right by me, and I still can't let myself give in to this pull between us.

It's not that I don't want him. I do, more than I've ever wanted anyone or anything. Coming from a girl who could hold everything she owned growing up in a single trash bag, who prayed and wished upon every star she could find for a family who loved her, that's huge. I know this, which is why I need to put an end to this.

I can't let myself get any closer.

I can't let *him* get any closer.

If I have to leave Willow River, both of our hearts will be broken, and while I'm used to mine being crushed, the thought of doing that to him causes bile to rise up in my throat. He deserves better. His family deserves better.

"Thank you. It looks great." Grabbing the plate that's next to his, I walk to the other side of the table and sit down. He raises his eyebrows but doesn't comment on my obvious move to put space between us.

"I thought maybe you could drop me off at Declan's to get my truck when we go to the store. I can run home and shower and be back here in time to help you bring it all in and put it away. If we leave right after we eat, we should be back in time for you to get your laundry done and head to my parents' around four."

I set my fork down, take a drink of my water, and force my eyes to meet his. "I'm not going to your parents' with you, Rushton."

"Why?" He looks confused.

"Last night... we were pretending. Remember? That's what we agreed to."

"I wasn't pretending." I can hear the simmering anger and disappointment in his tone.

"We said that we would pretend. For one night, we would pretend."

"That's how it started. You said you wanted to pretend to be mine. You wanted me to hold you and kiss you, and—Fuck!" He pushes back from the table and runs his hands through his hair. He paces back and forth a few times before he stops, grips the back of the chair, and sets his blue gaze on me. "Fuck that, Crosby. I wasn't pretending. Not for one single fucking second. Do you really believe that? That I could fake what you do to me. That I could fake the way you make me feel? Do you really think it's possible for me to pretend that I don't have feelings for you when my cock was buried inside you?"

He pauses, his gaze penetrating. I want to look away, but I can't seem to make myself do it. "No! That's the answer you're looking for, gorgeous. No. I couldn't pretend and wouldn't. Not with you. Never with you." He moves to my side of the table and kneels. His hand rests on my thigh, and the heat of his palm burns through my leggings. "We can do this, Crosby. One day at a time. I'm not asking you to marry me. Just give me a chance to show you."

Hot tears prick my eyes. If he only knew how badly I want to fall into his arms and just take the chance. "You knew," I remind him. I clear my throat. "We said we would pretend. You know why I can't do this." I point at his chest and back at my own. "You know why."

His eyes soften. "I know, baby. I know you're scared, but we can figure it out. There is no way in hell they won't renew your contract. You're incredible with your students, and if they don't, we'll figure it out. Together."

"That's not how my life works, Rushton."

"Rush," he says through gritted teeth. "I'm Rush to you."

"I could never intentionally break both our hearts like that. I could never ask you to leave your family. Open your eyes, *Rush*." I put emphasis on his name. "Do you not see what's surrounding you? You have this big, loud, loving family who would do anything for you. I don't have that. I have me." My hand slaps at my chest as the first tear slides across my cheek. "I have me. I had to learn the hard way that I'm the only one who will have my best interests at heart. I told you if I stay, if they renew my contract, then we could revisit this."

"That was before you let me make love to you."

I scoff. "We fucked, Rushton." I glare at him, daring him to bitch about me using his full name and to debate what happened between us last night.

"You're right. We fucked." He stands and leans over, bringing his face a breath away from mine. "News flash, sweetheart, if my cock is inside of you, I'm making love to you. It might be hard and dirty, or it might be soft and slow. It doesn't matter how it's packaged. If I'm inside of you, I'm loving you."

"W-What?"

"You're a smart woman, Crosby. Read between the lines."

I shake my head as I lose my battle with my tears. Surely, he's not saying what I think he's saying. No. He can't be. No. Just no. I can't do this with him. I can't deal. I swallow past the lump the size of Texas in the back of my throat and square my shoulders. "Leave." My voice is calm and quiet, nothing like the war that's being waged inside my head and, if I'm honest, my heart.

I let Rushton get close. I knew better. I should have stayed away from him, but somehow his life became intertwined with mine. From his niece being my student to his sisters-in-law befriending me. Hell, his brothers are my neighbors. I couldn't escape him, and I can be honest with myself.

I didn't want to escape him.

However, it's all too much. I had a plan. I have to stick to the plan. Maybe in a few months, if he doesn't hate me by then. Shit, what happens if he can never forgive me, and I have to live in this town and watch him with other women? What happens when I have to watch him fall in love with his forever love and witness the happy life they build together every single day?

He's pacing again. "Can we talk about this?" he asks.

"We've said all there is to say. I was honest with you. I can't do this with you. Not yet," I add. "You knew about my reservations before last night. You said you would be here waiting for me. Last night we pretended for a while, and now you're changing your mind."

"I'm not changing my mind!" he roars. "I'm not the one leaving. You're pushing me out the fucking door."

"We were pretending!" I shout back at him.

He stops pacing and opens his arms wide. "Look at me," he pleads. His voice is soft. "Look at what you see. I'm a man standing before you, begging for time with you. I just want you to give us a chance. Last night... last night changed my life." He speaks with so much conviction in his voice, it's impossible not to believe him.

"I believe you," I tell him. "But that doesn't mean I change my plan. I've been what others needed me to be in the past, and I still got shit on. I can't do that this time, Rush. I can't put aside the plan I made for my future and risk breaking both of our hearts." I take a deep breath. "Please, leave. I just... I need you to go."

"The tears that are sliding down your face and the crack inside my chest are proof you've already done that." He strides toward me and bends to press a kiss to the top of my head. "I have to go because I hate seeing your tears, knowing that I'm the cause of them. I'm sorry for yelling. I see everything I've ever wanted slipping through my fingers, and I can't stifle the desperation. You asked me to leave, and I'm going." His index finger pushes up on my chin so that he can look into my eyes. "I'm leaving this house, but I'm not leaving you. I need you to understand that, Crosby. I'm not walking out on you. I'm taking some time to cool off because I hate that I'm making you cry. I hate that I'm raising my voice at you, but know this. I want you. I want us, and you pushing me out that door isn't going to change that."

A sob breaks free from my chest when his soft lips press against mine. "I'll call you later. If you change your mind about dinner, text me, call me, hell, just show up. You're always welcome." He kisses my forehead this time. "I'd love for you to be there with me."

His words hit me. He's not inviting me as a friend of the family. This invitation is more. It's him offering me a piece of himself. "How will you get home?" I ask. "I'll take you."

"No." He stands and shakes his head. "I'll walk next door and have one of the twins take me." He waits for a few heartbeats to see if I'm going to stop him. He begs me with his eyes to ask him to stay. When I don't, he takes a step back.

"I'm sorry," I say, feeling a fresh set of tears building behind my eyes.

"I'm not walking out on you," he reminds me. "Remember that." With that, he turns and leaves the house shirtless. The tears break free when I realize his T-shirt, the very one I slept in last night, is lying in the dirty clothes basket in my bathroom.

Pushing back from the table, I lock my front door and rush down the hall to my bedroom. Sliding under the covers with his smell surrounding me, I sob as the pain of pushing him away hits me like a thousand pounds of bricks.

I'm doing the right thing protecting us both. If my heart is breaking like this after one night with him, how would I feel after months of waking up feeling cherished to know that I have no job prospects and have to leave? I don't really have a home. I never have. It was reckless to pretend that I found that in Rushton, even for one night.

I was lying to myself.

We weren't pretending.

We were falling.

I was falling.

I broke my own rules.

I fell in love with Rushton Kincaid.

Chapter 15

RUSHTON

MY SHOES FEEL AS THOUGH they're filled with lead as I walk across her lawn to the twins' place. I stomp up the steps and rap my knuckles against the front door. My chest feels heavy, and my mind is screaming for me to go back to her. I never want her to think that I'm walking out on her. She asked me to leave.

Twice.

I was yelling, and my anger got the best of me. She deserves better than that. Hell, *I'm* better than that. I wasn't lying when I told her last night changed me. I never understood it before now. I knew my brothers, and hell, even my dad, said that when you know, you know. It's not that I didn't believe them, but until you live it, it's not something you can comprehend.

Now I know.

The door pulls open and Maverick stares at me in confusion. "Where's your shirt?"

I look down. I didn't even remember I wasn't wearing one. "Crosby." He nods as if just saying her name is a good enough answer for him.

"Why are you standing on our front porch if your girl is next door with your shirt?"

"Are you going to let me in or not?"

He steps back, letting me pass.

"Hey, where's Crosby?" Merrick asks.

"At her place."

"With your shirt, I'm guessing?" He laughs.

"Something like that. Can one of you take me to Declan's to get my truck?"

"What's wrong?" Maverick immediately sobers.

"Nothing. I just need to get to my truck."

"No." Merrick shakes his head. "He's right. Something's off."

"I'm fine. Just tired."

"Bullshit," they chorus. Sometimes that freaky twin shit still takes me by surprise.

"She's got a lot going on today."

"Try again," Merrick tells me.

"Can you please just take me to my truck?"

"Not until you tell us what happened."

"Whatever," I mutter. Reaching into my pocket, I grab my cell and dial Ryder's number.

"What's up?" he answers.

"I'm at the twins' place. Can you pick me up and take me to get my truck at Declan's?"

"Why can they not take you?"

"Can you do it or not?" I ask him.

"We've got it!" Maverick calls out.

"You good?" Ryder asks.

I think about his question. "No." If anyone understands what I'm going through, it will be Ryder. The woman he loves up and left the country without telling him she was leaving. He's still fighting for her, even with her living thousands of miles away.

"I'm on my way."

"Thanks." I slip my phone back into my pocket, turn around, and walk out the door. I settle on the top step and wait for Ryder to get here to pick me up.

The door creaks open, and two sets of footsteps sound behind me. Before I know it, I have a brother sitting on either side of me. They both put a hand on my shoulder, and I hate the emotion that swells inside me.

This time they don't try to talk to me. They don't ask me why I'm being an asshole. They don't ask me why I can't walk next door and get my shirt. They don't question why the woman who I spent the night with can't take me to pick up my truck. No, my loud, boisterous baby brothers sit next to me in silence and allow me to lose myself in my thoughts.

When Ryder pulls up, he doesn't bother getting out of his truck. He just sits in the driveway, letting the engine idle. I stand, descend the remaining steps, then turn to face Maverick and Merrick. "I'm sorry for being a dick."

"We're here." Merrick nods.

"Whatever it is, we'll get you through it," Maverick assures me.

I nod to them and make my way to the passenger side of Ryder's truck. I realize that my baby brothers are growing up. Life is moving forward, but for me, I feel as though I'm suspended in time. My world stopped spinning this morning, and I know it will feel like that until she's mine.

Until she admits that she's mine.

"Your truck is at Dec's, right?" Ryder asks.

"Yeah. Left it there last night."

"How did you get here?"

"Merrick."

He nods and doesn't ask for more than that. We drive to Declan's in silence. I open my mouth to tell him what happened on three separate occasions, but all three times, I clamp my mouth shut and decide against it. Not because I don't want to tell him. I really think Ryder, if anyone, will understand, but I'm not ready to unpack it. I'm still reeling from everything that's happened in the last twenty-four hours. How can I tell him when I don't have my head wrapped around it?

He pulls into Declan's, and I reach for the handle. "Thank you for this."

"Any time, brother. When you're ready, call me."

I nod, climb out of his truck, and make my way to mine. I should go inside and see my niece and nephew, but I'm not in the right headspace. Instead, I pull out of the driveway and point my truck toward home.

When I get into the house, I head straight for my bedroom, strip out of my clothes, and start the shower. Finding my phone on the bed, I send Crosby a message.

Me: I miss you.

I hit Send and toss my phone back on the bed. I don't expect a reply from her, but it's important that she understands I'm still here. She needs to know I want her and that even though she asked me to leave, I'm not gone forever. How can I disappear from her life forever when all I want is for us to stay together?

Stepping out of my bedroom, I hear low murmurs, and I sigh. I don't need to keep walking to know who it is. My guess is all eight of my brothers are sitting in my living room. My feet, still feeling as though they're lead weights, carry me toward my living room to face my brothers. I should have known they wouldn't let me stew in peace. That's just now how we do things.

"Please, come in. Make yourselves at home," I say sarcastically.

"Thanks." Archer smirks.

I stomp into the room like a toddler throwing a fit and plop down on the only remaining seat. I cross my arms over my chest and glare at them. Why? I have no idea. It's not their fault I'm in a pissy mood.

Crosby's words about how lucky I am to have a big family filter through my mind, and I find myself relaxing my stare and dropping my hands to my lap. Taking a deep breath, I say the first words that pop into my head. "I'm in love with her."

There's a knock on the door, and in walks Deacon, not bothering to wait for an invitation to enter. "Sorry, I'm late." He moves toward the kitchen and brings back a chair setting it next to Archer and Ryder, who are also sitting in chairs from my kitchen table.

"You didn't miss much. Rush just declared his love for a woman."

"Crosby?" Deacon asks.

"Yeah, Crosby."

"Start from the beginning," Orrin tells me.

So I do. I tell them about the day I met her and how she was easily the most beautiful woman I've ever seen. I continue telling them about each and every interaction with her. I tell them about our text messages and how she's suddenly the first thing I think about when I open my eyes, and she's always my final thought before closing my eyes at night.

"You two seemed good when you left with Merrick last night," Brooks points out.

"I wasn't done with my story," I tell him. I tell them about last night. How I thought all she wanted was for me to hold her, and I was okay with that. "I didn't expect more from her. I didn't expect it to turn into a night that would change who I am."

"Change you?" Archer asks.

"Yeah. I know it sounds insane, but there was just something about being with her, being a part of her, that changed me. I can't explain it." I make eye contact with Deacon and my four older brothers, my eyes finally landing on Ryder's.

"You can't control it," he tells me. "We don't get to choose who we fall in love with."

"That's just it. I'd choose her every damn time," I confess.

"So, what's the plan?" Declan asks.

"Fight for her."

"Love her harder," they all say at the same time. If this were not my future we were talking about, it would be funny.

"Dad would be proud," I tell them.

"That's what I'm doing," Ryder tells me. "I refuse to give up on her. I was willing to do long-distance, and well, I guess I still am. I don't know if she's seeing someone while she's there, but I have to believe that I'm such a big part of her that she won't."

"And if she does?" Sterling asks.

"I just want her to come home to me," Ryder answers.

"So, let's lay this out. You want her, and you've told her that you want her?" Brooks asks for clarification.

"Yes."

"And she's worried about not getting a contract renewal and leaving Willow River and, in turn, leaving you?" Orrin asks.

"She's had a rough life." I pause, debating on what I should tell them. It's not my story to tell, but I trust my brothers with my life, and to be honest, I need help getting the girl. "This stays between us," I tell them. "You can't tell your wives, although my guess is that they already know at least a little of it."

I wait for all of them to agree. "Crosby lost her parents when she was four. She grew up in foster care. She bounced from home to home, never feeling like she had anyone who was hers. She never had someone who was there, no matter what. Her ex-boyfriend and her supposedly best friend slept together, crushing what she thought she was building." I pause. "She said she stayed because she was tired of being lonely. The same with the friend. She knew they were using her, but she just wanted to belong to something more."

"Fuck," Declan curses.

"I understand where she's coming from," Deacon speaks up. "Ramsey didn't want to depend on anyone. She never wanted to feel as though she needed someone else to survive. Crosby is afraid of losing you."

"I know," I tell him. "I understand too, but she won't lose me."

"What happens if her contract isn't renewed?" Archer asks.

"Harris is only twenty minutes away, and there are other surrounding towns."

"But what if it's not even in Georgia? She's going to have to go where her career takes her," Merrick chimes in.

"Would you leave?" Maverick asks.

My eyes find Ryder's. Something flashes in his eyes. He's already said that he would have gone with Jordyn had she given him the option.

"Yeah, I'd do whatever it took to be with her."

"So you told her you were leaving because she asked you to, but that you weren't walking out on her, right?" Brooks asks.

"Yes. I needed her to know I wasn't leaving her. Just leaving her house. Fuck me, I was yelling at her. Well, not at her, but I was yelling. I apologized," I say quickly when I see my brothers' faces change, no doubt getting ready to yell at me for taking my anger out on Crosby.

"I knew that we needed space, but I'm not giving up."

"So you need a plan," Archer says.

"I assumed that's why all of you were here," I tell him.

"You keep showing up," Orrin says.

"Send her flowers," Declan says. "You need to make sure she understands that you're fighting for her and you're sorry for raising your voice."

"We'll keep our ears open," Sterling tells me. "Assuming she still talks to our wives." He grins, calling Alyssa his wife. We don't call him out on the fact that she's his fiancée. Those two are solid. "If we know she's going to be somewhere, we'll tell you."

"Figure out a way to get you in her path," Ryder says. "Let her see that you're still here, and she can push as hard as she wants. You're going to push back."

"She's our neighbor," Maverick reminds us. "We can work on her too. You know, help her carry in groceries, find ways to slip your name into the conversation."

"And we can watch out for her," Merrick adds.

"What if it's not enough?" I ask the question that's been running through my mind since the very second I walked away from her earlier today. "What if she doesn't even give us a chance?"

"She will," Orrin assures me.

"How do you know?"

"Because you love her. You're going to show her. Don't push her too far, but keep nudging her. Let her know that when she's ready, you're there to catch her," Deacon says.

"It's going to take time," Brooks tells me.

"She's scared. She's never had a family. Never had someone in her corner. Look at us," Declan says. "Maverick called, and here we are. You have a support system. You don't know what it's like to have nothing and no one. You need to show her that she has you."

"She has all of us," Archer adds. "We'll do our part to help her see that too."

"He's right," Orrin adds. "And we won't tell our wives what you've told us, but we will tell them that you're in love with her. That you know it's going to take time, but Crosby is yours. They'll understand, and without us asking them to, they're going to do their part too. We're your family, which means if you love her, we're hers too. Besides, they know we're here. We're going to have to give them something."

"No. I'm fine with it. She's gotten close to them, so I'm sure they know a little of her background, but it's her story to tell. There are things I glossed over for you all, but I told you enough for you to understand where her head is at."

"Slow and steady wins the race," Maverick tells me.

"I can do slow and steady." I nod, feeling hope start to build. They're right. She's never had this. I want to give it to her. I want to give her the big, loud, boisterous family she's never had. I want to shower her with so much love and give her all the fucking hugs she's willing to accept.

"Thank you." I don't need to say more. Their nods tell me they get it. I don't have to tell them that I love them or that I couldn't have wrapped my head around the shitshow from this morning without them.

We say our goodbyes with a plan in place. Everyone knows their part, and I'm sure the wives will be on board. With a promise to see them at Mom and Dad's later today, I close the door behind my guests and rush to my room to grab my phone.

As expected, Crosby didn't reply to my message, but that's okay. Slow and steady.

Dinner was good. Mom made this chicken dish with rice, broccoli, and cheese, and it was really good. She offered us all leftovers, and we took them like we always do. However, this time I won't be eating mine.

I pull into her driveway at the same time the twins pull into theirs. Merrick waves and Maverick offers me a thumbs-up before they disappear inside. The lights are on, so I know she's still up. With the container of leftovers in my hand, I make my way up the steps and knock on her door. Her eyes widen in surprise when she opens for me.

"Hey."

"Hi."

I thrust the container out in front of me. "I thought you might be hungry. Mom made this new dish that was really good."

"You brought me leftovers from your mom's?"

"Yeah."

"You didn't have to do that, Rush."

Rush. Not Rushton. Another layer of hope builds inside my heart. "I wanted to. I won't keep you. Honestly, I just wanted to lay eyes on you and make sure you had dinner."

"You don't have to take care of me, Rush." Her voice is soft and cracks with her words.

I step forward. I'm still standing on her porch, but I'm close enough to reach out and lay a hand on her hip. "I never said I felt like I had to. I want to, Crosby. I want you. All of you. That includes me worrying about you."

She shakes her head, and I know it's too soon. I've nudged enough for today. I can't push her over the edge. Just like my brothers said earlier, I have to take it slow and keep showing up. That's how I get the woman I love to admit she loves me too. I know she does. I can see it in her eyes. I can also see the worry and the fear. I'll take care of those as well.

I'll show her it's me and her against the world.

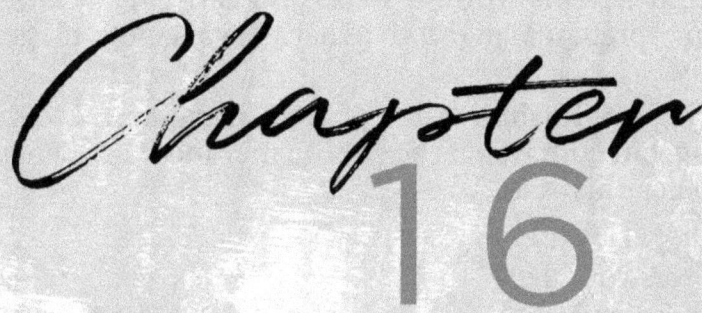

Chapter 16

CROSBY

TODAY WAS HARDER THAN I thought it would be. Blakely was a chatterbox, asking when I was going to come back to her house to see her. She even told me that she would call her uncle Rush when she got home and tell him that's what she wanted. She was confident that it would happen. To have her faith and unwavering security.

Alyssa called and invited me to dinner, but I declined. I assume Rushton has told his family. Something tells me that they don't have secrets. I don't want to lose Alyssa and the other ladies as parts of my life, but it's too soon. I'm still too raw from my night with Rushton. They'll see right through me, and I don't want that. Who am I kidding? I don't think time will keep them from knowing something happened between us. So, yeah, I declined her invitation.

I'm sitting on the couch, trying to read, but I've read the same sentence five times. I turn off my Kindle and place it on the coffee table. Grabbing my phone, I pull up my message thread with Rushton.

Rushton: Goodnight, Gorgeous.

Rushton: Morning, Crosby. Have a great day.

I ignored both messages from last night and this morning. I'm trying like hell to resist him, but he's not making this easy on me. I don't know why I thought that he would. He told me he wasn't walking away. I've heard that before, so I didn't know that when he said it, it was his truth. It's also still early. It's been two days since our "pretend" night together. He's going to get bored eventually.

Speaking of Rushton, my phone rings, and I debate not answering, but guilt weighs heavily on me, and if I'm being honest, I want to hear his voice.

"Hello."

"How was your day?"

"I got it in," I tell him. "It was long," I add. "How was yours?" I'm nervous. Why am I nervous?

"I missed you."

"Rush."

"I'm not going to hide how I feel about you, Crosby. Our night together changed everything. I know that you have rules and a plan, and I respect that. I won't push you, but I'm also not running. Not from you."

"If I knew I was secure here, things would be different." It's important he knows that.

"I know. I can see it in your eyes when you look at me."

"What do you see?" I ask, even though I shouldn't.

"I imagine it's what you see when you look at me."

He's beating around the bush, prompting me to once again read between the lines without telling me to do exactly that. "How was work?" I ask to distract him.

"Good. Same old, but I enjoy what I do, and I like the company I work for. I got a call about twenty minutes ago."

"Yeah?"

"Blakely seems to think we need another pizza date. The three of us."

"Yeah, she told me that today. She was sure that all she had to do was call you and tell you, and you'd make it happen."

"I will. The question is, will you be joining us?"

"I don't think that's a good idea."

"It's a great idea. I get to spend time with you and my niece. It's an excellent idea."

"We can't."

"We can."

"Have you always been this stubborn?"

"Probably. Although, I don't know if I've ever wanted anything or anyone in my life as much as I do you, so maybe not." He pauses a beat. "Just think about it. Can you do that for me?"

"Fine."

"That's all I need. I know it's getting late, and I'm going in early tomorrow, so I need to get in bed. Sweet dreams, Crosby."

"Night, Rush." He ends the call, and I drop my head back against the couch. I want so badly to call him back and ask him to come over, but that's just playing games with both of our hearts, and I refuse to do that. Instead, I lock up, turn off the lights, and head to bed.

Rushton: I miss you more today than I did yesterday. Have a good day.

That's the message that I woke up to today. I've looked at it more times than I'd like to admit. It's just after seven, and I expected him to call by now. Just as I think that, my phone rings. I bite down on my bottom lip and accept the call. "Hi."

"Hey, gorgeous. I can't talk long. I'm on my way to Archer's. He bought some new shelving for his garage and needs help unloading it. We're going to grab dinner after. Do you want to join us? I can bring some by after?" There's hope in his voice.

"I just ate."

"What did you have?" he asks.

"Grilled chicken and asparagus."

"Nice. How was your day?"

"I thought you couldn't talk long?"

"I can't, but I have enough time to ask my girl about her day."

"I'm not your girl, Rush." No matter how badly I wish that weren't true. I overheard a conversation at school earlier this week in the break room. They were talking about contracts, and how some weren't going to be renewed, and my heart dropped to my toes. I don't know if it's me, but I have a feeling that it is. I'm the low man on the totem pole, the new girl, the outsider. There is a damn good chance they were talking about me. Even more reason that even though I want to be his girl, I just can't be. Not until I know for sure.

"You are. We have some time to wait until we can make it official, and I've accepted that. That doesn't change how I feel about you or who you are to me."

I hear Archer say hello. "Talking to Crosby. Give me a second."

"Hi, Crosby!" Archer yells so that I can hear him.

"Tell him I said hello."

"My girl says hello. Now go. I'll be right there." I hear muffled words, and then Rushton is back. "Sorry about that. So, your day?"

"My day was good. Nothing major to report."

"Good. As much as I don't want to, I need to go so we can get this done and go eat. I'm starving."

"Be safe."

"Always, baby. Talk soon."

"Talk soon," I tell him, and the line goes dead. I spend the rest of the night cleaning my kitchen. I wipe down the cabinets, sweep, mop, and even clean out the refrigerator. By the time I get in bed, I'm exhausted, and I hope that means I can fall asleep easily. The past few nights, all I can think about is Rushton while wishing he were here with his arms wrapped around me.

My eyes are closed, and I'm just about to drift off when I get an alert for a new message. Reaching over, I grab my phone and pull up the message.

Rushton: Dream of me.

"Always do," I mutter before placing my phone back on the nightstand and closing my eyes. Just like he asked, I dream of him.

Every morning and every night this week have started and ended with Rushton, and I don't know how I feel about that. He's not doing what I expected. I thought he'd get frustrated and tell me to kiss his ass, but he's done the complete opposite. He tells me he misses me, to have a good day, that he's thinking about me, and he makes sure that it's either a message or his voice that's the last thing I think about or hear before I drift off to sleep each night.

He's made it his mission to stay on my mind, and he's been successful, which is why I'm walking into Pizza Town on Friday night to grab dinner.

This place reminds me of the dinner we had with Blakely, and she's been asking every day, and even though I keep telling them no, I'm still here, letting those memories wash over me as I make my way to the counter to order dinner for one.

I'm not dwelling on that. It's better this way. I smile at a waitress as I make my way toward the counter. I hear my name, and I stop and look around. Crosby isn't a common name, so I'm certain it's someone who knows me. A student, maybe? My eyes scan, and I see Alyssa waving at me. Knowing I can't avoid her forever, I change direction and stop next to their table.

"Hey, guys."

"How are you?" Alyssa asks.

"Doing well. It's been a long week, and I didn't feel like cooking, so pizza it is."

"You should join us," Sterling offers.

"No. I don't want to intrude on date night," I tell them.

Sterling laughs, and it sounds so much like his brother's my breath hitches. "Every night is date night for us. We'd love for you to join us," he tells me. "Have you already ordered?" he asks.

"No. I was going to order and just wait on it," I confess.

"Perfect. We only have our drinks. Sit." He nods, and without being prompted, Alyssa moves over, patting the booth next to her. "Book club is meeting at our place tomorrow. Did you get my text?" Alyssa asks.

"I did. I'm sorry I forgot to reply. I was in the middle of folding laundry the other night when it came through, and I forgot to respond. I'll be there," I tell her. I'm looking forward to seeing everyone.

"We skipped last month. There was too much going on for all of us," she explains. "Have you read the book?"

"Yeah, it was good."

"Good? Girl, he's a dirty talker." Alyssa winks.

"Tink." Sterling's tone is a playful warning.

"What?" she asks him.

"Send me the link."

She nods and blushes. "He's going to read it."

I glance across the table at Sterling. "You read romance?" I ask him.

"When there's a book that makes my girl gush over the guy, then yeah, I'm going to read it."

"He takes notes," Alyssa teases.

"I don't take notes." He mocks and glares at her before turning back to me. "I just like to see what she thinks is so... what's the word I'm looking for here? Swoony. Yeah, swoony. I need to know what's got her all worked up. I will never confirm or deny if I've taken mental notes." He grins and winks at us.

"That's... hot." I shrug, and the three of us crack up laughing.

"Looks like my invite got lost in the mail." I turn to see Rushton standing next to our table. He's got his eyes locked on mine.

"No invites went out until about five minutes ago," Sterling tells him. "Crosby was going to order to go, and we wouldn't take a no from her to join us."

"You want to sit?" Alyssa asks him.

"Crosby?"

"I can go if it makes you uncomfortable. They're your family."

He kneels next to me, right here in the restaurant, for all to see. His big hand rests on my thigh. "I like seeing you with my family, baby. I just don't want you to be uncomfortable."

I can't avoid him forever. "Join us," I tell him. The smile that lights up his face has butterflies taking flight in my belly. This is the first time I've seen him since he showed up at my place with leftovers last Sunday. We've talked and texted, but I've not physically seen him. How is he more handsome?

"We're going to talk about all that," Alyssa says, leaning in and whispering in my ear.

"It's... a lot to talk about," I confess.

"After dinner. Your place?"

"Tonight?"

"Why not? Sterling and I met here, so he can go home or do whatever, and we can catch up."

I hesitate. "Sure. I'd like that." I need to talk to someone about this. Someone other than Rushton. However, she is his family. Grabbing my phone, I send him a quick message.

Me:	Is it okay with you if I talk to Alyssa about what's been going on with us? I know she's your family, and I understand if you'd rather I not.
Rushton:	She already knows.
Me:	What do you mean? You told her?
Rushton:	I told my brothers, and I'm certain they told their wives. I'd tell you.

His text is followed with a shrugging emoji. I glance up, and he shrugs, and I smile.

Me:	It would be nice to be able to talk about it.
Rushton:	You can talk to me. About anything.
Me:	I need to talk about you.
Rushton:	I'm good at talking about me.
Me:	You know what I mean. I have all these feelings, and then there's my contract and what happened between us. I won't tell her that part. That's for us.
Rushton:	Tell her all of it. Some of it. I don't care. I'm not hiding how I feel about you, Crosby. If you need a friend, you'd be hard-pressed to find a better one than Alyssa and the rest of my sisters-in-law. Don't worry about me, baby. In fact, I encourage it. If you're talking about me, you're thinking about me, and that's a win in my book.

I glance up, and he offers me a small smile. It's a private look delivered just for me. I slide my phone back into my purse and join the conversation about what we're going to order. We settle on a large meat lovers, a large veggie, and breadsticks.

"So, the ladies are ditching me after this," Sterling tells Rushton. "You want to head to the Tavern and have a beer?"

"Sure. What are you ladies getting into?" Rushton asks.

"We're going to catch up," Alyssa speaks up. "Book club meets tomorrow, so Crosby is going to help me plan snacks."

"I saw a recipe online for a cheeseball with pickles in it. It looks really good," I tell Alyssa.

"We're adding that to the list."

We spend the next hour talking and laughing and enjoying good food and good company. It's not nearly as awkward as I thought that it would be having dinner with Rushton and his family.

Sterling refuses to let me pay and tells Rush that he can get the next one, and we're all heading to our cars. "I'll meet you at yours," Alyssa says.

"Sounds like a plan."

Rushton falls into step beside me. When we reach my car, he remains silent. It's not until I look up at him that he speaks. "Tonight was nice. When I tell you that I've missed you, I'm not just saying that."

"It was nice. Thank you for walking me to my car." My hands itch to reach out for him, but I refrain.

"Can I have a hug?" he asks. His hands are shoved in his pockets, and he makes no move to give or receive the hug he's asked for. He's waiting on me.

"I could really use one of your hugs right now." The words are barely out of my mouth, and he's wrapping me in his arms and burying his face in my neck. We stand here under the glow of the streetlamp for far too long. Neither one of us is willing to move away, but I know that I need to. Not just because Alyssa will be at my place waiting on me, but because I'm starting to forget why I have to keep him at arm's length.

I pull out of his embrace and peer up at him. "Be safe. If you drink more than one and need a ride home, call me, please. I don't want you driving."

"Are you saying you worry about me?" He tucks my hair behind my ear.

"I'm saying—yeah, I guess I am."

"I'm always safe. I promise you that I'll call you when I get home, and I won't drink more than one."

"Okay."

"It was good to see you. Can we do this again? Soon? Lunch or breakfast or dinner? Hell, I'd settle for a hug on the front porch."

"I'm sure we'll all be together again at some point."

He pulls me into another hug. This one is not as tight. "I'm not going anywhere, Crosby." I feel his lips press to my temple, and then he releases me. "Go have fun. Tell her anything you want. I'm not ashamed of our time together or how I feel about you. I'm glad you have her in your life. You have all of them, and my brothers, my parents. You have so many people who care about you."

"Because of you."

"No, baby, because of you. You're kind and loving. You're fun to be around, and just looking at you steals the breath from my lungs. Trust me when I tell you that if they didn't see those things, they wouldn't go out of their way to see you or invite you to have dinner with them."

I nod because I don't know what to say to that. I might be all of those things, but he brought them into my life. He's the reason they're still there.

"I'll see you soon."

I nod again. "See you soon." He pulls open my door for me and waits until I've clicked the seat belt around me before he closes it. He stands in the parking lot, watching me drive away.

My heart longs for him, but I push the feeling down deep, ignoring the way just being around him has me feeling lighter.

Chapter 17

RUSHTON

I'M THANKFUL THERE ARE NO lights on at the twins' place when I pull into Crosby's driveway. This visit is unannounced, but I was sitting at my place stewing over this week and my girl being alone, and I couldn't take it anymore. So, I grabbed my keys and came straight here. I don't know if I can convince her to come with me tomorrow. I'm not opposed to pulling out the big guns and getting my entire family in on my mission.

I can't let her spend Thanksgiving alone.

Not when she has me and my family who adore her and want to spend time with her. I know she said she needed time. She's scared, but it's the holidays, and I love her, so yeah, I'm not going to take no for an answer, even if I have to play dirty to get a yes.

Making my way up the steps of her front porch, I lift my hand to knock, but the door opens before I get a chance. "Rush. Hi," Crosby says. "I—What are you doing here?"

"I missed you." I can't show all my cards just yet.

"I was actually just running out to grab dinner and pick up a few things."

"How about I drive?" I ask.

"You want to drive me to the grocery store?" The look on her face tells me that she's baffled that I would offer.

"Yes." I don't hesitate with my reply. "I get to spend time with you, so I'm all in. Come on." I step back, and she walks out onto the porch and pulls her door closed.

"You don't have to."

"I want to. Come on. I've been trying to get you to let me buy you a meal for weeks. How about we go to the Tavern for some wings, and then I can take you to the store?"

"I'm sure you have better things to do."

"I'm here." I spread my arms out wide. "My sole purpose this evening was to see you. Come on." I reach for her hand, and I'm shocked when she doesn't pull away and allows me to guide her to the passenger side of my truck.

"How was your week?"

"Short." She laughs. "School's out until Monday, so I spent the day cleaning up my classroom and getting caught up after our staff meeting."

"Short weeks are good weeks. I'm off until Monday as well, but because I took a vacation day."

"You plan to do some holiday shopping?" she asks, teasing in her tone.

"I do most of mine online, but if that's an invitation to go with you, I'm in."

"Right. Like you're willing to get up at the ass crack of dawn to go shopping." I glance over to see her shaking her head at the thought.

"If it gets me time with you, then, yeah. I'm more than willing to get up at the ass crack of dawn to go shopping. I do have gifts to buy, and just because I usually shop online doesn't mean I can't change my ways."

"Well, you're off the hook. I won't be spending my day off at the crowded malls. Besides, it's not like I have a lot of family to buy for."

Fuck. What was a teasing moment has turned heavy. "Fine, new plan. You come to my place on Friday, and we can shop online together."

"You're too much." She chuckles, and I'm glad the heaviness of the moment seems to have eclipsed us.

The parking lot of the Tavern is pretty bare, which doesn't surprise me. With tomorrow being Thanksgiving, I'm sure everyone is prepping for that at home. "How about over here?" I point to a booth in the back that will give us a semblance of privacy. I don't know when or how I'm going to approach her coming to Thanksgiving dinner at my parents' place tomorrow, but if I do it here, we'll have the privacy we need to discuss it.

"What are you getting?" Crosby asks as soon as the waitress leaves to fill our drink orders.

"Boneless wings and onion rings."

She nods. "The broccoli cheddar bites sound good, but so do onion rings."

"We can share. I like them both."

"Are you sure?"

"Definitely. You getting wings?"

"How spicy is the spicy?"

"Hot. If you're not into that, we can get a basket of mild."

"I can handle hot, but I think I'm going to stick with mild this time. You can get hot if you're feeling it." She places her menu back on the table just as our sweet teas are delivered.

"Y'all ready to order?"

I nod to Crosby. "I'll take six boneless wings, mild, and an order of broccoli cheddar bites."

"And for you?" the waitress asks me.

"Give me a dozen hot wings and an order of onion rings."

"Coming right up." The waitress grabs our menus and is off to place our order.

"I got a call from Blakely earlier," I tell her. "She wanted to tell me about the turkey she made yesterday at school with her hand. She was pretty pumped about it."

A smile instantly lights up her face. "They had a blast. You should have seen the way they were concentrating on tracing their hands. I had to help most of them, but they were so laser focused, I've made a mental note to do this activity every year."

Her brow furrows as she says the words, and I hate the stress that she's under. I know I don't make it easier on her, but she's had enough people in her life walk away. I just want her to know that I'm never going to be one of them.

"You'll be here next year. Blakely loves school, and that's because of you. I know for a fact you would never play favoritism because you're close with all of us. I can guarantee that there are several other little minds you're shaping in that classroom, and their families and the school board have taken notice."

"That's kind of you to say. I love my students, and I love what I do. I hope that shines through every single day."

Reaching across the table, I take her hand in mine. "I promise you it does."

She nods. "I'm still scared, you know? I want to be settled. I want to build a life, and if I'm being honest, I could see myself doing that here."

Hope swells in my chest. "You're already building a life here, gorgeous. You have friends who adore you. Students who sing your praises, and you have me." I stare into her eyes, willing her to believe me.

"Here we go." The waitress appears, killing the moment. She delivers our food and promises refills as she skips off.

"I know I'm being irrational. I know that stopping this"—she points from her chest to mine—"whatever this is between us is taking things too far, but I know me. I know how you make me feel, Rush. I know that as it stands at this very moment, my heart will be crushed if I have to leave this town."

"Life is about taking chances. Taking risks. There are no guarantees."

She nods. "I know that. Trust me, if anyone knows that, it's me. I thought that I could just avoid you, and this would all go away." She gives me a rueful smile.

"You can't get rid of me that easily."

"I've never had anyone to stand by me in my lifetime. The thought that I could have it is equally as terrifying as it is exciting. I know I have to open myself up in order for that to happen, and I just don't know if I have it in me to do it. I don't know if I can be that vulnerable. If I can trust that much."

I think about what she's saying. I understand her reasoning, and if I'd lived the life that she had, I'd probably feel that way as well. "I hate that for you, Crosby. I hate that you've never known what it's like to have a solid support system behind you. I hate that you don't wake up every damn day and smile because you know how loved you are. I hate it for you, but at the same time, it's made you who you are. Kind, caring, compassionate. You know what it's like to be without, and you never take anything for granted." I pause, taking a long pull of my sweet tea.

"I don't care if it's tonight, next week, or six months from now. I'm still going to want you." I stare directly into her eyes, willing her to believe me. To trust in me.

"I want to believe you."

I can see the turmoil in her eyes. She wants me, and she wants us, but her past has her scared to death. "I won't stop until you do."

She shakes her head. "I don't deserve that. You deserve better than someone who strings you along."

"What I deserve is someone beautiful, kind, and loving. Someone who will stick by my side through the good times and the bad. Someone to come home to each night after a long day at work. Someone to share my life with. That's what I deserve. That's what we both deserve, and I'm going to give that to us."

"You sure do make it hard for me to resist you."

"Good." I wink. "Now eat up. We have groceries to buy."

She smiles, and we both dig into our food. I still have to find a way to broach the idea of her coming to Thanksgiving dinner tomorrow, but after the conversation we just had, I think I'll be able to convince her.

"Now what?" I ask once we have all her groceries unpacked.

"I was just going to watch some TV before bed."

"Lead the way," I say, motioning with my arm toward the living room.

"You're staying?"

"Are you kicking me out?"

She hesitates and then shakes her head. "No. I'm not kicking you out."

When I nod toward the living room, she leads the way, and I take a seat directly next to her on the couch. "What are we watching?" Not that I really care. I doubt I'll be paying too much attention, if any at all, with her sitting next to me.

"I wasn't really set on anything in particular. Do you have anything in mind?"

"I'm easy."

She scrolls through the channels and stops on an episode of *The Voice*. "Is this okay?"

"Sure." I shrug. She settles back into the couch, and I reach out and put my arm around her, pulling her into my chest.

"What are you doing?" she asks softly.

"Holding you."

"Why?"

"Because I want to. Because it's all I can think about. Because it's my new favorite thing. Because I'm sitting this close to you and can't not hold you."

"You're blurring the lines." While she says the words, she doesn't try to move away.

"Good." I expect her to argue, but she surprises me when her body relaxes into mine. I run my fingers through her hair as we watch *The Voice*. For an entire hour, I hold her, and she lets me. It's the perfect ending to my night, but then I remember our night isn't over. I have something to ask her. When the show ends, she doesn't move her body, but she peers up at me. "What now?"

"I was thinking I could steal a kiss."

"Do you think that's a good idea?"

"Yes. I think it's the best idea I've ever had." Leaning down, I press my lips to the tip of her nose. Her breath hitches, so I lean in again. This time I press my lips to hers. It's a soft caress, testing the waters. She moves to her knees to get closer, and I lift her hips so that she's straddling my lap.

One hand grips her hip, and the other slides behind her neck, pulling into me as I deepen the kiss. She moans, and my cock swells at the throaty sound. She rocks her hips as she pulls out of the kiss.

"We shouldn't."

"We should," I counter as my lips trail down her neck. She tilts her head to the side, giving me full access to her. I drop my hands to her hips and guide her forward and then back again.

Her hands land on my shoulders. "W-What are you doing?"

"Taking care of you." I lift my hips, this time on her forward motion, and her pussy glides over my hard cock. There are layers of clothes between us, but I know she can feel the friction from the sounds she's emitting.

"Rush—"

"Tell me what you need, gorgeous."

"I can't. It's wrong."

"Nothing that ever happens between us is wrong. Tell me."

"More. I need more."

"Can I touch you?" I know she's drawn a line in the sand, and I want to push her, but I don't want to take advantage of her. She needs to tell me that this is okay before we take this further.

"Are we pretending?"

"No." Fuck no. We are not pretending. I should never have gone along with that stupid role-play in the first place. This is real. We are as real as it gets.

"Rush—"

"Tell me I can touch you. I'll give you more. I'll give you everything you need." Not just here tonight on her couch but in life. She'll never be alone again. Not if I have anything to say about it.

"This is the last time. We can't keep doing this."

"Is that a yes?" I don't reply to her comment because we will keep doing this. I'm going to show her that this is where she belongs. In my arms, in this town, in my life. Permanently.

"Yes."

That's all I need. When I stand with her in my arms, she squeals. I lay her down on the couch and kiss her hard. Tearing my lips away, I move to the waistband of her leggings and tug them off.

I'm on my knees on the floor, peering up at her. Her chest is rapidly rising with each labored breath she pulls into her lungs.

She's gorgeous.

After I finally have her free of her leggings and panties, I place one of her legs over each of my shoulders. "Rushton." She doesn't just say my name. She moans it.

"Hands on my head, baby. You're going to want to hold on for this." That's all the warning I give her before I bury my head between her thighs and taste her. My tongue traces through her folds before finding her clit. I suck gently, and her back arches off the couch. I devour her with my mouth as if she's my last meal. She squirms, and I know she needs more. Slowly, I push one long digit inside her.

"Yesss," she hisses.

I pump once, twice, and three times before adding a second digit. Her legs tighten around my neck, and her hands pull on my hair to the point of pain, but it's like gasoline to a fire. She's enjoying this just as much as I am.

Curling my fingers inside her, I make a come-hither motion, and she calls out my name. My mouth is flooded with her release, and I take everything she gives me. I don't stop until she's limp in my arms. Just as slowly as I entered her, I remove my fingers and place a gentle kiss on her clit. She jolts at the contact, and I can't hide my grin.

Kissing her inner thighs, savoring the feel of her soft skin beneath my tongue, I gently remove her legs from my shoulders and take my spot back on the couch, pulling her into my arms and dragging the blanket from the back of the couch over the top of her. We're the only ones here, but I don't want her to feel vulnerable or exposed.

"Can I ask you a favor?"

"Hmm?"

"Come to Thanksgiving dinner with my family tomorrow. Before you say no, you don't have to come as my date or anything. I know that you're not there yet. But I want you there. There's always more than enough food to feed a small army."

"You need to spend the day with your family."

"I want you there."

"I don't think that's a good idea. You can't just drop a last-minute guest on your mom like that."

"You've met my mother, right? She's prepared for half of Willow River to show up tomorrow, and it will just be us."

"Yeah, you and your family. I appreciate you thinking of me, but I can't."

Reaching into my pocket, I dial my mom and put her on speakerphone. "Rush, I was just getting ready to call you."

"Yeah?"

"You should call Crosby and invite her to dinner tomorrow. You know we'll have plenty, and she has no family in town."

I forgot that my mom doesn't know much about Crosby's past. "Funny you should say that. We had dinner tonight, and I was thinking of asking her. I was calling to make sure you were okay with that." Okay, so it's a little white lie, but I want Crosby to see that she's welcome tomorrow. With my family and with me.

"Of course I am. You don't have to call to ask to invite someone to Thanksgiving dinner. If you want her here, she comes. It's that simple. The more, the merrier."

"Thanks, Mom. I'm going to try and convince her."

"You make sure that you do. Love you."

"Love you too." I end the call and toss my phone on the couch next to me. "You heard her."

"It's been a long time since I've had a Thanksgiving dinner."

"When was the last time?"

"I was twelve, I think. The foster family I was with were good to me. They had all their family over, and it was a great day. Lots of food."

"Why didn't you stay with them?"

"The man, his job got relocated, and they had to move. As a ward of the state, I had to stay behind. They weren't interested in adopting me, so on to the next family I went."

"They didn't have big family dinners?"

"No. The next year I was in the children's home, and they had dinner, but it wasn't the same, and in the years following, none of the other two families I was with was bothered with Thanksgiving. They said it was a waste of money on fancy food."

"I want you to spend Thanksgiving with my family and me. I'll come to pick you up, so you're not arriving on your own. We can go early and be the first ones there, or be the last, or arrive in the middle. Whatever will make you the most comfortable. I'll do whatever I need to do to get you there."

"Why?"

"It's a day to reflect on what we're thankful for. You are at the top of my list. I need you to be there."

"Rush."

"Crosby."

"If I say yes, I'm going as a friend of the family. I told you we can't do this. Tonight, it was a lapse in judgment."

"Nope. Tonight was perfect. In my mind, you'll be there for me as my girl. I want you to know that. To my family, we can tell them whatever you want. You and I will know the truth." They will too, but I keep that to myself.

"Are you sure?"

"Never been more certain."

"What time?"

"We eat at one. Everyone usually rolls in around noon and after."

"Can we go early? Earlier than noon? I want to help your mom cook. I'm not the best, but it's the least that I can do for her having me for dinner. And I need to make something."

"Nope. Just ask my sisters-in-law. Mom likes to dote on all of us. She insists we just bring ourselves."

"Well, I'm going to make something."

I smile. "Alyssa did the same thing. Mom thanked her and then scolded her."

"Fine, then. I want to help her as much as I can with the meal."

"Deal. We'll do it together."

"Oh, what are you making?"

"French Toast."

"You know how to make more than eggs and toast," she teases.

"Yes. Carol Kincaid made sure that all her sons could survive on their own. We might not be chefs, but we know enough to get by." I hug her close and bury my face in her neck. "Thank you. I'm excited to spend the day with you and for you to get to spend more time with my family."

"You're sure?"

"I'm sure."

She takes a deep breath and slowly exhales. "Okay."

I hide my smile in her hair. Convincing her was easier than I thought. I'll have to remember to pull Mom aside and thank her for the assist. My girl will be spending Thanksgiving where she belongs. With my family, that hopefully will one day be hers.

Chapter 18

CROSBY

I BARELY SLEPT A WINK last night. If I wasn't replaying my night with Rushton, I was stressing over today. I don't know how I let him talk me into this. I was perfectly fine sitting at home and reading and watching the parade on television. I let him get me relaxed and sated and convince me that this was a good idea.

If I'm being honest, I really want to go. When Carol acted as if it was a given that I be there, my heart swelled in my chest. I'm really excited to see a big family Thanksgiving, but I'm also nervous as hell. I know he told me not to make anything, but I couldn't sleep, so I got up and made mini pumpkin cheesecakes. I just so happened to have the ingredients because I was going to make them for my students for our last day before break and ran out of time.

I've changed my outfit at least three times, and don't get me started with my hair. I decided to add some loose curls and braided my bangs to one side. I'm currently in a pair of black leggings and an oversized burgundy and burnt orange sweater. I plan on wearing my black Hunter boots, and I'm not going to let myself stress over them any longer. Not that I have the choice. It's ten minutes until eleven, and Rushton should be here any minute.

Grabbing my boots from the bottom of my closet, I head to the living room. Taking a seat on the couch, I pull them on and refuse to race back to the bedroom to take another glance in my full-length mirror. Not that I have a chance when there's a knock at the door. I pull it open to find Maverick standing there, grinning.

"Hey, neighbor."

"Hi, Maverick. What can I do for you?"

"Oh, nothing. I was just stopping by to say hello. Do you have any pipes that need tightening or shelves put together?"

"What?" I chuckle at the absurdness of this conversation. "Are you feeling all right?" I ask him.

"Oh, I'm fine."

"Maverick." I pull out my stern teacher's voice. The one where my students know that I mean business.

"Fine. I'm not here for that. Not that I wouldn't be happy to help you, but I'm here for something else."

"And that is what exactly?" I ask him.

"What the hell are you doing here?" I hear a familiar voice behind him. The same voice I spent the majority of the night thinking of its owner.

Maverick doesn't bother turning to address Rushton. Instead, he grins down at me and whispers, "This." He winks and turns, slinging his arm over my shoulders. "Rush, I was just seeing if my neighbor here needed anything. You know, being neighborly."

"She's good," Rushton tells him.

"You sure? She was about to invite me in," Maverick goads him.

"Mav," Rushton growls.

Maverick drops his arm from my shoulders and leans over, placing his hands on his knees. He's laughing so hard he can barely catch his breath. When he finally composes himself, he stands to his full height and pulls his phone from his pocket.

"What in the hell are you doing?" Rushton asks, his irritation evident in his tone.

"Oh, just messaging the group chat." Rushton reaches into his pocket and pulls out his phone, glancing at the screen. "The chat has been quiet since last night."

"Not that one. The one we started without you," Maverick explains.

"Without me?" Rushton honestly looks shocked that there would be a group message that doesn't include him.

"Yep."

Rushton takes the final few steps toward me and wraps an arm around my waist, pulling me into him. "Explain."

Maverick raises his hands in defeat, but his smile is still plastered on his face. "I'll explain later," he tells his brother.

"Tell me now."

"You sure about that?" Maverick asks.

"Start talking, little brother."

Maverick shrugs. "Don't say I didn't warn you. When you texted us all last night to let us know that you convinced Crosby to come to dinner, we all took bets on how long it was going to take for you to confess you wanted her."

Rushton's thumb gently traces circles on my hip. "That's it? That's the secret group chat?"

"Yep."

"And why are you on my girl's doorstep when you knew I was coming to get her at this exact time?" The tension in his body is no longer there as the pieces of the puzzle start to come together.

"Your girl? Bro, are you holding out on us?"

"No. She's mine. She's just not ready to admit it yet."

"Um, hello." I wave my hand in the air. "I'm standing right here."

Rushton surprises me when he presses his lips to my temple. "I see you, baby."

"Well damn." Maverick's grin is wider than before. "The plan was for me to make you jealous to push you into admitting to her that you want her."

"I don't need a push. I know I want her. She knows I want her, and I'm just waiting for her to be ready."

This time it's me that gets the intensity of Maverick's gaze. "He's a good guy, Crosby. Put us all out of our misery. He talks about you all the time, and we thought he was hiding behind his feelings."

"He's not hiding," I tell his brother. "I have some things I'm working through." I glance up at Rushton to find him watching me. "He's been very clear on what he wants with me."

"Is my brother not good enough for you?" Maverick asks. There is no malice in his tone. He's generally curious.

"He's... more than enough. It's me. I—"

"She doesn't need to explain herself to you. I know how she feels. She knows how I feel. We'll work it out."

"I grew up in foster care," I blurt. It's not like his sisters-in-law don't already know. I'm not hiding it; I just don't like to talk about it. "I'm all alone, and my contract here is for a year," I explain. "I refuse to do that to him. I may be leaving Willow River if my contract isn't renewed, and his life is here. His family." I give him a shy smile. "I'm just trying to protect him. To protect both of us."

"Fuck." The next thing I know, I'm being pulled from Rushton's arms and into Maverick's. His hold is tight and comforting. These Kincaid boys really know how to get a girl all up in her feels. "His heart will be broken either way," he whispers before releasing me.

"We should go," Rushton says, reaching for me, but I step back into the house.

"I just need to grab a couple of things."

"You need help?" he asks. The look on his face tells me he's not really asking if I need help. He wants to make sure I'm okay, and much to my surprise, I'm good. The more I talk about my past, the easier it is. That has everything to do with the people in this town. I've never felt more accepted.

Grabbing my jacket and my purse, ensuring I have my phone and keys, I pick up the container of pumpkin cheesecake bites and walk back outside, locking the door and pulling it closed behind me.

"Where's Maverick?" I ask Rushton.

"He went home. I'm sorry. He means well."

I smile. "I know he does. This is all kinds of messy, and I realize that I'm the culprit for that. I hate that my insecurities and my fear are causing issues."

"There are no issues, gorgeous. There is you and me, and that's what matters."

"You're making it really hard for me not to fall for you," I confess.

"Perfect."

"Rushton, you really need to think about this. What if I have to leave? Willow River is a small town with one elementary school."

"There are towns nearby that have elementary schools, and if that doesn't work, we figure it out together."

"You can't leave your family."

"We don't have to talk about this today. We're going to spend the day together with my loud, crazy family. I don't want all the what-ifs to be hanging over our heads. Just be with me today." He swallows hard, and I watch as his throat bobs. "If you have to pretend, do that. Just... be with me today."

I want to argue. To demand that he thinks about what the future would look like if I can't find a teaching position. It's on the tip of my tongue, but the look on his face stops me. He wants this. I see it in his eyes, in the anxious expression. "Okay." I hear myself say before I can think better of it. "Today, but, Rushton, I'm a realist. I know that letting my heart guide me isn't always the best outcome."

He grins and takes the container of mini cheesecakes from my hands before he leans in and presses a kiss to my cheek. "You just told me your heart was involved, baby. We'll figure it out," he says before stepping back. "Now, what is that? I told you Mom will thank you and then remind you that you didn't need to."

I shrug. "I feel better not coming empty-handed."

"I'm sure whatever it is, it will be devoured."

"Mini pumpkin cheesecake bites."

"Perfect." He opens the truck door for me, handing me the container once I'm strapped in. I expect him to close the door, but I should have learned by now Rushton Kincaid never does what I expect him to. He leans in and rests his calloused hand against my cheek. "Thank you for today. I'm thankful for you and the time you're giving me." He grins before stepping back and shutting the door.

He doesn't give me time to reply, and I'm glad because I'm at a loss for words. My heart aches to give in to this connection between us. For once, I want to just let go, and whatever happens will happen, but I can't do that. I can't risk it. But then again, I also know that if I have to leave this town, there will be pain either way.

Willow River feels like home.

Rushton feels like home.

I'm so nervous walking into Rushton's childhood home I don't try to pull away when he grips my hand tightly as we enter. He places the container on a small entryway table and takes my coat and purse, placing them in the closet before grabbing the container, linking our fingers together, and leading me further into the house.

"Well, you two are early. What a nice surprise," Carol Kincaid greets us as we step into the kitchen.

"Hey, Mom." Rushton releases me to kiss his mom on the cheek.

"What's this?" she asks when he hands her the container.

"Crosby made cheesecake." He looks at me and smiles. I know what he's doing. He's including me, and I could kiss him for it.

"Pumpkin cheesecake bites," I clarify.

"You didn't have to bring a thing," Carol tells me. "Just yourself and your appetite. But thank you. These will be gone in no time."

"Told you." Rushton smirks.

"Mrs. Kincaid, can I help with anything?"

"Carol or Mom. Mrs. Kincaid is my mother-in-law. I think I have it all under control. I've got this down to a science after all these years." She chuckles. "What you can do is keep me company."

I nod, because my words are lodged in the back of my throat. I wonder what it would have been like growing up with a mom like Carol Kincaid and a father like Raymond. And the fact that she has so selflessly welcomed me into her home, into their lives, it's bringing out emotions that I try to hide. The ones that are just for me. The one person I know I can always count on.

"Good to see you, son," Raymond Kincaid says, entering the room. "Are you harassing your mother already?" he asks, and I can't hide my giggle.

"Crosby, right?" Raymond asks. "Welcome."

"Thank you."

Rushton sits on a stool at the counter and nods for me to take the one next to him. I do as he suggests and watch as Raymond walks around the counter and wraps his arms around his wife and kisses her cheek.

"What can I do?" he asks her.

"I'm all set," Carol tells him. The smile she gives him is intimate and has me looking away. I glance toward Rushton to find his gaze on me.

"You get used to it," he tells me, not bothering to lower his voice.

"Crosby, if my son doesn't make you feel like a queen, you let me know. There is no other way." His dad winks before kissing the corner of his wife's mouth.

"Thanks for the vote of confidence, Dad. I'm trying to get her to give me a chance, not scare her away," Rushton grumbles.

I feel my face heat and duck my head.

"You two out of my kitchen. Leave us women in peace," Carol scolds.

"I'm not leaving her here alone."

"Alone?" Carol asks. "Am I not standing here in *my* kitchen?" she asks, placing her hands on her hips.

"I love you, Momma, but I want her to feel comfortable."

Carol's eyes soften. "I'm not going to interrogate the poor girl. I'm giving her a break. Go." She waves her hand, and Rushton looks at me. I nod, letting him know I'm a big girl and I'll be okay.

He stands from his stool and places a kiss on my head before leaving the kitchen.

"Now, tell me everything."

"What?" Is she asking me to tell her what's going on with her son and me? Can I do that when I don't really know for sure?

"What's been going on in your life? Read any good books lately?"

My shoulders relax. "I've been exhausted each night after work. I think the kids are ready for an extended break. It's been challenging."

"Bless you. I had nine boys, and I couldn't imagine a classroom full that I can't take TV or toy time away from." She chuckles.

"I have a great class this year, but there are some hard days, that's for sure. Especially since they're all just learning the rules of the school and how it all works."

"Well, my granddaughter loves school. My daughter-in-law tells me we have you to thank for that. Oh, and that turkey she made. She video called all of us. She was so proud of it."

"She's a joy to have in class."

"Come on, now. We all know that our Blakely can be a handful."

I shrug. "They all have their moments, but Blakely's are less than the others."

"That's good to know."

We spend the next half hour or so chatting about anything and everything. Eventually, she gets tired of me asking if I can help and takes pity on me, letting me pull the plates and silverware from the cabinets that we're going to need for today's meal. By the time everyone starts to show up, I don't feel so out of place, and when my eyes meet Rushton's across the room as he holds his nephew Orion, I smile and nod, and that's all it takes for him to understand my meaning.

How is it that he knew what I needed before I did? That's something to dive into another day. Right now, I'm surrounded by a wonderful family who is acting as if I'm a part of them. That I belong here, and that is something that I'm grateful for.

Willow River
Georgia

Chapter 19

RUSHTON

THIS DAY ISN'T AT ALL what I expected it to be.
It's more.

I wanted her here. The thought of her being alone today tore me up inside. What I didn't know was how it would make me feel seeing her fitting in so well with my family. I mean, I knew she got along well with my sisters-in-law and even my mom, but seeing her here, as if she's always been a part of us, that shit hits me deep in my chest.

"You know it takes more than staring at her to get her pregnant." Brooks laughs.

"What?" I tear my gaze away to look at him.

"The way you're looking at your girl holding my daughter is obscene."

"Fuck off," I grumble. He's not wrong, though. How can I not think about what it would be like if that was our baby she was holding? This falling shit is a lot to take on. Sure, I've always envied what my older brothers have been able to find with their wives, but never have I pictured a woman in my life and thought about how it would be to have a family with her.

"You're thinking about it." He smirks.

"So what if I am?" I counter. He and I are sitting in the corner of the living room on our own. The twins, Archer, and Ryder are all in the basement playing pool. Orrin, Deacon, Sterling, and Declan are watching the game with Dad, and the ladies, including my mom, are fussing over the kids. I slipped off in the corner to observe, and of course, my brother would catch on and call me out on my not-so-covert operation. At least it's just the two of us in this conversation. Not that he's not going to share with my brothers. That's just what we do. We meddle in each other's lives, and although it can annoy me, I wouldn't change it. I wouldn't want the alternative.

My eyes go back to Crosby. My hand goes to my chest to try and rub the ache away of what she's lived through. The lack of love and affection she's received in her life makes me want to smother her with it, but I know that's pushing her too far. I sense that I might be wearing her down. Proving to her that I'm in this for the long haul, but she still needs time.

The time I'm going to give her even if it kills me.

"You might want to tell her your plans," Brooks jokes.

"She knows. Well, I mean not that I can see her with our kids. I'm trying to get her to stop fighting our connection, not send her running for the hills."

Brooks shrugs. "I don't hold back. Not anymore. I almost lost Palmer over that shit. I speak what's on my mind regardless. Honesty. Always."

"I've been honest with her."

"You've told her you want to make babies with her?" He raises his eyebrow in question.

"I didn't know that I did until about a minute before you walked up."

He bursts out laughing, which has everyone looking our way.

My eyes meet Crosby's, and she smiles softly before turning her attention back to whatever it is that Ramsey is saying while she remains holding Remi in her arms.

"You know, when you boys were little, if any number of you slipped off and got quiet, that's when your mother and I knew to worry. The quiet is when the mischief happens." Dad laughs, joining us. "What are you two up to?" he asks us.

"This is all you, little brother." Brooks claps me on the shoulder and takes Dad's spot on the couch, joining the others to watch the game.

"What's on your mind, Rush?"

"Just enjoying the day," I tell him.

"You know I raised you, right?" He chuckles. The deep sound is comforting.

"Yeah," I agree. I know he can see through our bullshit. I don't even know why I tried.

"Let's hear it. I'm pretty good at this, you know. You should ask your brothers. The ones that are married anyway." He grins. "That includes Sterling."

I laugh at that because we all know Sterling sees no one but Alyssa. "How much time you got, old man?" I tease.

"As much as you need."

I nod. I should have expected that too. My parents have been there for us every step, good times and bad, no judgment. "She's scared."

"Does she have a reason to be?"

"Not of me, of what we could be."

"Like I said. Should she be?"

"No."

He nods. "Her past?" he asks.

"Yeah." I go on to tell him a little of her background, knowing she's not going to mind. I don't tell him more than she told Maverick this morning on her front porch. "She's scared that she's not going to have her contract renewed, and she's going to have to leave town."

"No way is she not getting renewed."

"That's what I told her, but she's never had the feeling of being secure. From what she's told me, she's never had anyone long-term to stand beside her."

"Is that person going to be you?"

"Yes."

"I assume you've told her that?"

"Yeah, I told her. She's worried that both our hearts will be broken if she has to leave Willow River."

"Too late for that?" Dad guesses.

"Pretty much." I huff out a laugh.

"Told you I was good at this." He smirks.

"Then tell me what to do, Dad. How do I know when to quit or keep fighting? I know she needs time. I can give her time. I've been giving her time, but also not. I'm trying to show her I'll keep showing up. I've told her that whatever happens, we'll figure it out together. She's worried about taking me from my family. She's worried about breaking my heart and hers. She's scared, and it keeps me awake at night. Tell me, Dad. How do I know how long to fight? Forever?"

"Depends. What does forever look like to you? Before you answer that, I want you to picture yourself struggling financially. I want you to think about starting a family. Consider the good times and the bad."

I nod. A lifetime flashes before my eyes, and without him telling me, I know where he's going with this. No matter what scenario I imagine, it's the same outcome. The same pillar of support is standing next to me.

Fuck. I really am in love with her.

"I can see it all over your face, but tell me. Who's with you? Who's weathering the good times and the bad with you, Rushton?"

"Crosby." I whisper her name, my voice gritty. I knew I loved her, but this, it's more. I don't know why, but it feels like more. "We're together, but we're not together," I tell him. "She's mine. I've told her as much. I've told her I'll wait, but she says we need to see how her job turns out."

Dad nods. "You love her harder, son. That's the best advice I can give you. You keep showing up, and you erase every doubt and every insecurity she has. However, to answer your question, you convince her that being together is all that matters. You show her that no matter what life throws at you, staying together is what matters."

I nod. I watch as Crosby laughs at something Palmer is saying, and I know that she's worth the fight. She's worth all the love I have to give her. "I love her." I don't mean for the words to be spoken out loud, but I also don't want to take them back.

"I know you do, son. She might not be able to say the words, but she loves you too. She wouldn't search you out like she is right this moment if she didn't." He pauses. "You never want to ask yourself what if. You don't want that hanging over your head, and you don't want regrets. Show her that love. All will work out as it should."

I turn, and sure enough, Crosby is watching me. She smiles and lifts Remi's hand to wave, and I feel that smile touch something deep inside me that's reserved just for her. "Love her harder," I mutter. Dad grips my arm in a reassuring squeeze before walking away and fussing at Brooks for taking an old man's seat.

It's funny how a short conversation with my father has me seeing clearly. I knew I was willing to go the distance, but there was always worry in the back of my mind that I was pushing her too hard.

A few minutes later, Ramsey steals Remi from Crosby, and she excuses herself to come to me. At least, I assume that's what's going on since she's headed my way where I'm still standing in the corner by the window. As soon as she's within my reach, I snake an arm around her waist and pull her into me.

"Rush," she whispers.

"They all know how I feel about you, Crosby. I don't know if you've figured it out yet, but there's not much you can hide in this family."

"I hear Brooks and Palmer did a pretty good job," she sasses.

I nod. "They did, which is why everyone has been doubling down on getting in the other's business."

She tilts her head back and chuckles. "I think that's just the Kincaid way."

"You're probably right," I confess. I hold her a little closer, and she comes willingly, resting her head on my chest. "I'm really glad you're here."

"Thank you for including me. This has been really nice."

"You know what else would be nice?"

"What's that?"

"For you to be here for every holiday."

"Rush."

"For every Sunday dinner, for every get-together, I'd want you right here."

"In this very spot?" she teases, trying to lighten the moment.

"In my arms. Surrounded by my family."

"Your family is incredible."

I want to tell her that they can be hers too, but I decide against it. I should probably tell her the depths of my feelings for her. Use the words that I confided in my father. She should have been the one to hear them first, but I couldn't stop the admission from falling from my lips.

"You're incredible."

She doesn't reply, but she does let me hold her just a few more minutes until Blakely comes rushing over and drags her away to finger paint. It was on the tip of my tongue to tell Blakely that they're not at school and Crosby has the day off, but the smile on her face when Blakely asked her to join her and Kennedy and the rest of the ladies stops me. She's radiant, sitting around my parents' dining room table, laughing and talking with the ladies in my life as if she's always been there.

"When you know, you know," Orrin says from beside me.

"Was it like that for you?" I ask him.

"Yeah. I'd wanted to ask Jade out forever, and when I finally did, and we had our first date, I knew she was the one for me."

"You make it sound so easy."

"Loving her is easy."

"I think being a dad has made you soft."

"Maybe." He shrugs. "But I'm okay with that. I wasn't unhappy before Jade came into my life. I watched her from afar. I knew I liked her, but after that first night—"

"It all felt different. It changed you," I finish for him.

He points at me. "That's the real deal, Rush. Hold on to it as tight as you can."

"It's hard to do that when she challenges me at every turn."

"No one said it would be easy. Loving them is easy. Sometimes the road we take to get there is longer than others, but the outcome remains the same. You have to work hard and love harder."

"You're Dad," I joke.

We both enjoy a laugh at me teasing him. "I'll take it. Growing up, I knew they had something special. I'd hear kids at school talk about parents fighting and divorce, and it never really occurred to me what I was witnessing. It wasn't until I met Jade that I realized that the main reason I knew how to love her... the reason I know how to show her that love, is that I grew up with a front-row seat watching live-action what love looks like."

"I guess I never put too much thought into that."

"You don't until you fall yourself. Then there are some things in life that to you are nothing but background noise, which is now a clear melody. It means more when you not only know what it looks like, but you feel it. The love of a parent or sibling is different from the love of your wife and kids—" His voice cracks a little. "That little man and his tiny fist have a grip on me so tight—" He shakes his head, overcome with love for his son.

"He's a lucky kid to have you for a father."

"And one day, when it's you, I'll be sure to tell you the same thing."

"One day," I agree.

"Come on. You can't hide in the corner watching your girl all day. Come watch the game with us."

"I'd rather watch her."

"I'd love to give you shit for saying that, but I'm not gonna lie, watching Jade, especially when she's with Orion, is my favorite thing these days."

"Touchdown!" Declan and Deacon are on their feet, fists in the air, gazes glued to the TV.

"Shit, I got money on this game." Orrin stalks off, and I follow along behind him. Only I turn at the last minute and make my way into the dining room.

"You ladies look like you're having a good time." I stop behind the chair that Crosby is sitting in and place my hands on her shoulders. She tilts her head back to look at me.

"It's fun, and you should try it."

"Oh, Uncle Rush paints with me. All my uncles do," Blakely tells her. "It's 'cause they want to be my favorite."

"It's because they love you," Kennedy corrects her.

Blakely shrugs. "That too."

"I'll leave you ladies to it," I say. I give Crosby's shoulders a gentle squeeze before leaving to join the men and watch the game.

We're on the road, just having left my parents' house, and I'm not ready to take her home yet. I've been with her for hours, and yet it's still not enough. At the stop sign at the end of their road, I look behind me. No cars, so I turn to look at Crosby.

"What's wrong?"

"Nothing. I'm just not thrilled about taking you home yet." There is no reason for me to beat around the bush.

"You've been with me all day. I'm sure you're ready for some space," she teases.

"No. It seems like the more time I'm with you, the more that I want."

"That's dangerous," she says. Her tone is light and teasing, but there's a hesitancy there as well.

I glance in the rearview mirror to make sure it's still just us. "I don't think it's dangerous at all."

"You know what I mean."

"I know that I want you to come home with me."

"Rush—" she starts, but I place my index finger to her lips.

"Just tonight. Please, just let me hold you. My family took up all your time and attention today, and I'm feeling neglected." I give her my best puppy-dog eyes.

"We're blurring the lines, Rushton. You agreed you would wait."

"I will wait. But just this one time. I won't ask again. Think of it as an early Christmas gift."

"It's too early for a Christmas gift."

"Not if it's your best gift."

"Just sleeping?"

"A goodnight kiss, but I promise to stop there."

"We've been known to get out of control," she reminds me.

"I promise, gorgeous, and I always keep my promises. Besides, we said we were going to online shop together."

"You're too much."

"If you really don't want to, I'll take you home. I just really want more time with you."

"A goodnight kiss."

"Nothing more than a goodnight kiss and you in my arms."

"This is the last time. We can't keep doing this."

"I'd love to tell you that I'm not going to ask again, but I can't make that promise."

"At least you're honest." She looks down at her hands on her lap. The sun is just starting to set, so I can still make out her features. "After a day with your family, it's going to be hard to go home alone."

"Is that a yes?"

"Just to sleep."

"I promise."

"Yes."

I want to kiss her so fucking bad, but if it's one goodnight kiss I get, it's not going to be a quick peck in my truck. Instead, I reach over the console, take her hand in mine, and bring it to my lips. I rest our hands on the console, look both ways, and pull out on the road. Not the one that leads to her place but the one that leads to mine.

Thirty minutes later, she's dressed in one of my T-shirts and is lying in my arms in my bed. I've already kissed her goodnight. I took my time but didn't push. I kissed her soft and slow and pulled her into my chest. Her body relaxes into mine as we both drift off to sleep.

Chapter 20

CROSBY

"SO, HOW DO Y'ALL HANDLE Christmas?" I ask. I'm sitting in the back seat of Ramsey's SUV. We're a mini two-vehicle caravan on our way to Atlanta to do some Christmas shopping. When Alyssa called me earlier this week and asked me to join them, I tried to get out of it, but she wouldn't take no for an answer.

It wasn't that I didn't want to go. Shopping with a group of friends isn't something I've ever done, and it sounded like a good time. My hang-up was that I didn't really have anyone to buy for. I've been tossing around the idea of getting something for Rushton, but we already blur the lines so much these days I can't determine if it's a good idea or not. At the end of the day, we're friends.

That led me to get something for this amazing group of ladies that I'm spending my day with, and of course, I was going to buy for the kids, and I ordered gifts for all my students. Then that led me to leaving out Rushton's brothers, and that didn't seem fair if their wives and kids were getting gifts, and then his parents and I started to freak out. I don't know what's appropriate. My ex wasn't close to his family, and he was the kind of guy that was like, babe, let's forgo gifts and spend time together. Then he'd blow me off. Yeah, I know I dodged a bullet with that one.

"What do you mean?" Ramsey asks, glancing at me in the rearview mirror.

"There are so many of you. How do you do gifts? Does everyone buy for everyone? Do you draw names?"

"We stopped getting gifts for everyone a couple of years ago. It was getting to the point where we were all just exchanging gift cards. Once the twins turned eighteen, we switched to spoiling Blakely and, of course, Aunt Carol and Uncle Raymond. They buy for all of us, even when we tell them not to. We've also drawn names in the past, but this year, since we have so many new baby Kincaids, we're keeping it to just the kids and my aunt and uncle," she explains.

"There has been the occasional gag gift," Alyssa chimes in. "None of us ever rule that out."

"I can only imagine the gag gifts that the guys come up with."

"There have been some good ones," Ramsey chimes in. "My first Christmas here, I remember Maverick and Merrick bought all the brothers Monkey Butt Powder. They were so certain it was going to be the best gag gift. It backfired because Sterling was excited and said chafing was no joke. The others chimed in with their agreement. The twins were so bummed they pouted the rest of the day."

"I'd like to get something for Carol and Raymond. They've been so good to me, inviting me to Sunday dinners and Thanksgiving. Do you have any ideas?"

"We all went in and got them a week in a cabin at the Smoky Mountains this year. I'm sure Rush will add your name to the card," Alyssa tells me.

"We're not together," I remind her.

They all give me a noncommittal sound, and I sigh. "He makes it impossible for me to resist him," I admit.

"They all do." Kennedy laughs. "It's part of their charm."

"I guess so."

"Are you still worried about your contract not getting renewed?"

"Sort of. I mean, yes, that worries me, but the more time I spend with him, the more times he shows up at my place unannounced with dinner or declaring he's taking me to dinner, the harder it is to remember why I was trying to protect both of our hearts."

"Sweets, it's way past protecting hearts. I'm certain his is already invested, and by the look on your face right now and the conversations we've had, I know yours is as well," Alyssa says gently.

"This was never supposed to happen. I told him we could discuss it more after I found out that my contract was going to be renewed."

"You can't stop love, Crosby," Kennedy says, turning to look at me from the front seat. "I can't even pretend to imagine what you've gone through. What I can tell you is that there are still good people in this world. Good people who know how to love."

"She's right, you know," Ramsey says as we pull into the parking spot beside Palmer and her SUV at the mall. "I had lost my faith in men and people in general. If my own parents couldn't love me, then who would? It wasn't until I made a desperate phone call to Aunt Carol and I started over in Willow River that I learned I could let myself trust and love freely."

"He's so loyal," I say, speaking about the dedication that Rushton has shown me since the day we met. "If I have to move, he's going to want to follow me. That's who he is."

"What's wrong with that?" Alyssa asks.

"His family is here."

"You're right, but we can love him, love both of you from wherever you live. Declan was ready to follow me back to Florida. He was going to take Blakely away from her support group. He asked me to stay, but he was willing to go."

"You didn't let him."

"My grandma was here, and my parents are nomads. They just needed a spot to dock their RV every few weeks and get some baby snuggles before they roll out again. My best friend and her family were in Florida, but my heart was in Georgia. I don't regret my decision for a single second," Kennedy explains. "I know with all that I am, that if that's what happens. If you have to leave and Rushton goes with you, he'll never regret it."

"And before you say it, our family won't hate you for taking him away," Ramsey says. "Love harder is literally the second half of our family motto." She grins as Palmer knocks on her window.

"You ladies ready to shop until we drop?" Palmer asks when Ramsey opens the door.

"Let's do it," we all chorus.

I'm glad that the subject is dropped, but they've given me a lot to think about. I know that I get lost in my own head, and I push people away. I know that part of the reason is that if I keep them at a distance, they don't have a chance to leave me. It doesn't take a shrink to tell me that's what I was doing with Rushton, but he's fought me every step of the way. He's still showing up, and I can deny it all that I want, but my heart didn't stand a chance.

Have I been wrong all this time? Have I wasted months of nights when I could have been curled up in his arms in his bed or mine? Would the risk really be worth the reward this time around? I can't unpack all this today. Instead, I shake out of my thoughts and enjoy the day shopping with my friends.

My friends.

It's not just Rushton that I'll miss if I have to leave Willow River.

Two hours later, we're all bogged down with so many bags we have to make a trip to the cars to unload before we do more shopping.

"Y'all are a bad influence," I tell them on our way back into the mall.

"Hey, we didn't twist your arm," Jade tells me.

"I know, but all the little baby clothes and toys were just so cute. I've never had kids to buy for, and I couldn't resist."

"Well, we appreciate you, but you didn't have to," Jade tells me.

"What she said," Palmer and Kennedy add.

"And the gifts you showed us that you ordered for your students. They're going to love them," Piper speaks up.

"I think so too. They're all so eager to learn. I think giving them all their own book to take home will be a hit. I can't believe I scored them online for two dollars apiece."

"That was a steal," Kennedy agrees.

"I think I'll make them little treat bags to go with them. I'll add some candy. Luckily none of my students this year have food allergies or restrictions, so I'm not limited to what I can get."

"There's a huge candy store on the upper level. We'll make sure we hit that before we leave," Alyssa says.

"Thanks."

We take our time going in and out of almost every store in the mall. I splurge and bought myself some new leggings that were half off and a new sweater. Although they tried to talk me out of it, I bought a Visa gift card for Carol and Raymond to use for whatever they'd like on their trip. I've never been to the Smoky Mountains, and when I googled places to eat, I got overwhelmed and just decided I'd give them a general gift card to use for gas, food, souvenirs, or whatever else they wanted to do with it while on their trip.

"Food," Palmer says dramatically as we exit another store. "I need sustenance."

"Should we make a car drop first?" Piper asks.

"No," Palmer grumbles at her sister, and we all hide our laughs.

"Let's feed the bear, give our feet a rest, and we can drop and start again after," Ramsey suggests.

We make our way to the food court, and we all scatter, going in separate directions for the food we're craving. We meet up at a long table, and to my surprise, we spend the next hour eating, talking, and laughing. I think I've smiled more today than I have in well... ever. I've had the best time with these ladies.

"All right, before we start back, should we figure out what each of us still needs to get?" Kennedy asks.

"Definitely," Jade agrees. "I'd like to be done with my shopping today."

We all go down the line saying who we have left to buy for and what we're thinking as gifts. When they get to me, I shrug. "I'd like to find something for Rush, but I don't really know what I want to get him."

"Is there anything he's mentioned?" Kennedy asks.

"Not that I can think of."

"There's only one thing I can think of that he'd want," Palmer tells me.

"What's that?"

"You."

"Me?"

She nods. "How do I give him me?"

"You take a risk. You don't worry about the what-ifs and just be with him. That's the best gift you could give him," Palmer explains.

"That"—Alyssa points at Palmer—"is genius."

"That's not really a gift," I counter.

"Isn't it?" Jade asks.

"Whose side are you on?" I ask them.

"Both," they all answer.

"Look, it's just an idea. We can all see the sparks between the two of you, and denying yourselves is hurting you both. You're passing up time and precious moments."

"But if I lose him—"

"We all have that fear, Crosby. Just because we're married or engaged and living our lives doesn't mean life can't be cruel and take our loved ones away from us. It could happen at any time, but you can't let that stop you from living and loving," Ramsey says softly. "Just think about it."

"In the meantime, we'll help you find the perfect gift," Alyssa assures me.

"And if you decide to give him you, we'll help with that too." Palmer flashes me a grin.

"I can't believe I'm even going to ask this, but how do you see that going down?"

"Well, you could get naked, tie a red bow around your neck, and invite him over."

"Oh, and you can sing 'Santa Baby' when he walks in the door." Piper cracks up, laughing.

"You could get him something that represents you. Maybe a card with a note or picture frame with a picture of the two of you. You don't have to do anything but tell him I'm yours, and it will be his best gift," Kennedy says.

"I was thinking cologne or a new wallet," I admit, and they all burst into laughter.

"Come on. Let's do a car drop and finish our lists," Ramsey says. We all stand, toss our trash, and head to the cars to drop off our purchases and start again.

Three hours later, we're all exhausted, but we're also completely finished with our shopping. We all met at Palmer and Brooks's house, and when we pull into the driveway, the ladies all smile when they see their husbands' trucks.

"Good, they can do the heavy lifting," Alyssa says.

Sure enough, Sterling and Rushton come out of the house and offer to help us move our bags. The others are in the house with the kids.

"Did you have fun today?" Rushton asks as he places my bags into the trunk of my car. I watch to make sure he doesn't pay too close attention to the bags that hold his gifts. I ended up buying him a pair of Oakley sunglasses, and I remember him saying his were "scratched all to hell"—his words not mine—a hoodie, and some cologne. The idea of giving him me still sits in the back of my mind. The ladies had some good points today, and it's definitely a lot for me to think about, but just like earlier, now is not the time.

"I did actually. It was a good time. They're fun to hang out with. I've never spent an entire day shopping, and I wasn't sure about how it would go, but it wasn't bad at all."

"Do you have time to come in and say hi?" he asks.

It's on the tip of my tongue to say no, but I surprise us both when I say, "Sure." His face lights up, and he pulls me into a hug.

"I've missed you," he says before he steps away.

"You saw me last night when you showed up at my place with Chinese."

"Right? That's been almost twenty-four hours. Too long." He winks and, with his hand on the small of my back, leads me inside.

Everyone spreads out in the living room, and we spend the next couple of hours talking and getting caught up on everyone's day. It's mostly the guys telling us about the babies' adventures. According to Heath, Penelope had a diaper blowout that could have stopped a war or started one. He wasn't sure which angle he was ready to settle.

Blakely was mad that her dad made her wear her wiener pants and that she wasn't allowed to carry her little brother around the house like the big girl that she is.

Brooks claimed that Remi was an angel, despite his T-shirt being his third of the day from her spitting up on him, and Orrin complained that Orion slept the majority of the time.

We laugh at their retelling of the day, and my face actually hurts from smiling.

"I like this on you," Rushton says about twenty minutes later when he walks me to my car that he started for me.

"What? This coat?" I look down at my winter coat.

"This." His thumb traces my lips. "This smile."

His admission only makes my smile grow wider. "I had a really good day."

"You missed me, though, right?" The moonlight shines on his own grin.

"Yeah, I missed you." The confession is easy. I don't stress about what it will mean for us, where it's taking us, or where we might end up. I just gave him my truth.

"You want me to follow you home and help you unload all of this?"

"I didn't buy that much." I laugh.

"Can't blame a man for trying to get an invite from his girl."

"What am I going to do with you?"

"Are you really looking for ideas because I can think of a few things, or fifty." He chuckles.

"I should go," I say. "Thank you for walking me to my car and for warming it up for me."

"You're welcome, baby. Text me when you get home so that I know you made it."

"I'm a big girl," I remind him.

"Yeah, but I'll still worry. Please?"

I nod. "I'll text you. Be safe."

"You too, baby." He leans in, and I'm ready for his lips to press to mine, but they never do. Instead, they land on my forehead before he steps back and gives me room to climb into my car. With a final wave of goodbye, I'm on the road, and this time I don't stop myself when I think of him or try to push him to the back of my mind. That's not been working, so instead, I process everything the girls and I talked about today.

Can I let go of my fear and take a chance? I don't know, but what I do know is that if anyone could change my mind, it's Rushton. After all, he's already made me fall in love with him.

Chapter 21

RUSHTON

IN THE PAST, I MIGHT have been known to give my brothers a hard time about following their ladies to girls' night. It wasn't because I was jealous or because I thought that it was wrong. To be honest, I just wanted to give them shit. We're brothers. That's what we do. However, it never stopped me from joining them as they watched the women they love from the back of a room enjoy themselves.

I didn't understand it.

I supported it, but I never really comprehended what they were doing.

Until now.

When I called Crosby this morning to see if she wanted to go to dinner or maybe see a movie tonight, she informed me she had already made plans. Apparently, Palmer's parents asked to keep Remi and Penelope for the night, to which both couples reluctantly agreed. When I say reluctant, it was my brothers who hesitated. They're big softies when it comes to their wives and kids. Then Blakely asked if she could spend the night with my parents, which prompted them to ask for Beckham and Orion as well.

When the ladies found themselves kid-free for an evening, they declared ladies' night. Something my brothers with kids grumbled about. They don't mind ladies' night, but a kid-free night to them is time alone to practice making more babies, and while I'm sure their wives are on board with that, they also wanted time with their friends.

So, here we are, sitting in the back booth of the Tavern, staring on while our ladies laugh and joke and have a great time, if the sounds from their table and the smiles on their faces are any indication.

"I'm glad they all get along," Declan says, nodding toward the table.

"That would suck if they didn't," Orrin agrees.

"These nights make my wife happy." Deacon shrugs.

"You know that they're over there talking about us, right?" Sterling asks.

"Yeah, about how great we are." Brooks laughs.

"What do you think they're talking about?" I ask.

"I'm not sure I want to know," Orrin admits. "If they're laughing at our manhood—" He nods to where the ladies just start cackling with laughter again. "—I'd rather stay oblivious."

"Facts." Brooks nods.

"Where are the rest of your brothers?" Heath, Piper's husband asks, taking a drink of his pop.

"Ryder didn't want to come out. Something about trying to get a hold of Jordyn. Archer and the twins are all at the club in Harris."

"They go there a lot," Heath comments.

"Not much else to do around here unless you want to drive on to Atlanta."

"This is true," Brooks agrees as his phone rings. "Speaking of our brothers...." He turns so we can see Maverick is video-calling him. "What's up?" he answers.

"Y'all should come down to the club and go back to get the girls later," Maverick tells him. "This place is packed tonight, and the band is pretty good. We saw them here a few weeks ago."

Brooks makes eye contact with all of us, and we each shake our heads. We're not leaving our girls to go clubbing without them. "Nah, we're good," Brooks tells him.

"Let me guess. You're hiding in the back corner, watching them have the time of their lives while you wait for them to be ready to go."

"It's what we do. You'll understand one day." Orrin leans over so Maverick cannot only hear him but see him.

"Can you at least crash girls' night? Why do they get to have all the fun?"

"You just worry about you. Call us if you need a ride," Orrin tells him, still looking over Brooks's shoulder.

"Mer and I are staying sober. We'll take care of Archer. We still aren't legal, remember?"

"When has that stopped you?" Brooks asks.

"Only when our brothers, who are old, decide to get us wasted." Maverick laughs.

He's not wrong. We've let them drink with us way before we should have, but we'd rather let them do it in a controlled environment where we can take care of them and make sure they're safe than to have them doing it at some underage party and try to drive home.

"If you change your mind, shoot me a text, and I'll meet y'all at the door."

"We won't," we all chorus, and he laughs.

"Later," he says, and the call ends.

"You know he's right. We should totally crash girls' night. We're all kid-free, and I want to spend time with my wife, damn it." Brooks drains his bottle of water and stands.

"I'm in." I stand and grab my half-empty glass of tea. "Time to make moves, fellas."

"You're not even married," Declan jokes.

"Doesn't mean I don't want to spend time with her."

"You two together now?" Heath asks.

"Nope, but we'll get there." I turn and walk away. From the shuffle of feet behind me, they're following me. I look up when Brooks claps a hand on my shoulder and advances on Palmer.

She squeals when he sneaks up behind her and tickles her side. "Move over, ladies, we're coming in." That's the only warning they get before we're pulling chairs from surrounding tables and, in Brooks's case, lifting Palmer to sit on his lap.

"What's going on?" Ramsey asks Deacon.

"We're tired of sitting on the sidelines, at least for tonight."

"Kid-free," Orrin says by way of explanation.

"So, what? You're crashing our fun?" Kennedy asks. She turns to look at Declan, and he leans in and kisses her, making her forget her question.

"Yes," we all reply, and they giggle.

I lean into Crosby and lay my arm around the back of her chair. "Missed you," I say softly.

She turns and smiles at me. "Party-crasher."

"Only if it gets me closer to you."

"We need tunes," Deacon announces when the room falls silent. He stands and heads toward the Touch Tunes box hanging on the far wall.

"He can't be trusted to pick the good stuff on his own," Orrin says, standing and following him.

"Um, I love my husband," Ramsey says, watching where Deacon is already at the Touch Tunes, scanning for songs. "But he and Orrin together are not going to pick anything this crowd"—she motions her finger around the bar—"is going to want to hear."

"Luckily, it's not too busy tonight," I tell her. "I'm sure whatever they pick, it will be fine."

Jade points at me. "You remember that when they're queuing up the oldies." She chuckles.

"They're not that old." Alyssa chuckles.

"Doesn't matter, Tink. You know those two will do it just to mess with us."

"Yeah, but some of the oldies are good," Kennedy defends.

Before anyone else can reply, Marvin Gaye's "Let's Get It On" flows through the speakers. "See!" Brooks points at Alyssa and Kennedy. "Told you." He grins.

"This is a good song," Sterling defends. He wags his eyebrows at Alyssa, and she shakes her head and smiles.

"It's baby-making music," Ramsey defends.

"Maybe Deacon is trying to tell you something, Rams," Brooks tells her.

"We're trying," she confesses.

The ladies all nod as if they already knew this information, and I'm sure that they did. I guess that solves a little bit of the mystery of what they talk about when we're not around.

By the time Orrin and Deacon are back at the table, the song changes, and when they pull their wives up to dance, I hold my hand out for Crosby. "Come on, gorgeous, show me what you've got."

"'My Girl'? Really?" Crosby laughs.

"Hey, don't knock The Temptations." Orrin points at her before leading Jade to the small dance floor.

"Come on, ladies." Alyssa stands up. "We might as well embrace the fact that they're crashing our night." She takes Sterling by the hand and leads him in the same direction.

I don't notice if the others join us because Crosby places her hand in mine, and just like anytime I get to touch her, she's all I can see. I swing her around and sing the lyrics to her. She's laughing as I dip her over my arm, only to pull her back up and spin her around. Brooks and Palmer bump into us, and the ladies knock hips before I pull my girl back into my arms and sway my hips against hers.

It's silly and fun, and all because of the woman in my arms. "Is there anything you don't do well?" Crosby asks, smiling up at me.

"There is one thing I'm still trying to master."

"Oh, really? Do tell."

"You sure?" I ask.

"Lay it on me, Kincaid."

"Making you mine," I say, leaning down and kissing the corner of her mouth as the song changes. Al Green's "Let's Stay Together" comes on, and I pull her close and proceed to sway to the beat as I sing every lyric to her.

I hear the guys start to sing, and before you know it, we're all calling out the lyrics while holding our girls in our arms. I don't take my eyes off Crosby's as I do. She's watching me intently, and as the song comes to an end, her eyes well with tears, but her smile, it's radiant. I'm pretty sure these tears are good tears.

This is it.

This is my moment.

I can't keep how I feel about her inside for another minute. I rest my forehead against hers and bring my hands to her face. "Crosby—" My voice is thick. "I love you." Her breath hitches. "I know you want to wait, and I'm okay with that. I'm not pressuring you, but I needed you to know what you mean to me. This is real, Crosby. There is no pretending. I've never pretended one single second of our time together."

A tear slides down her cheek, and I capture it with my thumb. Her hands rest on my wrists. "Rush—" she starts, but I kiss her to keep her from saying anything. It's just a gentle press of my lips to hers, but it's enough to stop whatever it was she was going to say. I know it wasn't that she loves me too, and I don't want nor need to hear how we have to wait. Besides, I don't need her words. Her eyes tell me a story her heart and her head are not ready to admit.

I know she loves me.

I feel it.

"You want to get out of here?"

"Yes."

Dropping my hands, I intertwine ours and turn and see whose gaze I can catch. Sterling looks up, and I point to the door and wave. I bend to whisper in her ear. "You want to say goodbye?"

"No. I'll just text them later. I'm ready." Her eyes bore into mine, and I can't help but wonder if maybe she's trying to tell me something else. That's probably just wishful thinking on my part.

I usher her outside to my truck. I help her inside before making my way to my side. I don't ask her if she wants to go to her place or mine. We're going to mine. Tonight, I'm being selfish, and I want her in my space. If she doesn't want to stay, I can take her home, but I hope she stays.

We're both quiet on the drive, and when I lead her into my house, the silence remains. I turn on the kitchen light and pull two bottles of water from the fridge, passing one to her without asking if she wants one. We both take hefty drinks.

"I didn't tell you to push you or trick you into saying it back. I told you because I had to say it. I couldn't not say it, Crosby. I know you're scared, baby, but I'm here." I tap my hand over my chest. "I'm not leaving you. I'm going to show you what it means to be loved. I'm going to be that person in your corner every day. No matter the issue, the good, the bad, the ugly, I want it all, Crosby."

She doesn't speak as she places her water bottle on the counter and moves to stand in front of me. Her palms land on my chest as she peers up at me. "Show me." Her words are so soft I almost miss them over the thunderous beat of my heart.

"Show you?"

She nods. "Make love to me."

"Baby." I wrap my arms around her. "That's not why I told you either. I'd like to think that I show you every day what you mean to me. I'm not just spouting words of love just to get inside of you again."

"I know that," she assures me. "My head is a mess. It's been a mess for weeks. Since I met you, if I'm being honest. I have so much that I need to work through, but what I know right now, right here at this moment, what I need is for you to make love to me. Please, Rush."

My hands move to the back of her thighs. "Legs around my waist." She doesn't hesitate to do as I ask, and I stalk off toward my bedroom. I place her gently on her feet and start tearing off my clothes. "Clothes off." I ache to feel her, to be a part of her. I'm barely holding onto a thread. She peels off her clothes, painstakingly slow, teasing me as she drops each layer to my bedroom floor.

When we're both naked, I let my eyes roam over every inch of her. My eyes can't seem to get their fill of her. In two small steps, she's standing chest to chest with me, and her hand slides between us, gripping my cock. She lazily strokes me, and I have to stop her.

"You can't do that," I say, pulling her hand from my cock. "I'm teetering on the ledge, gorgeous."

"That's okay."

"You wanted me to make love to you. If you touch me, it's going to be over far too soon. I want to take my time."

"I thought you told me if you were inside me, you were making love to me?" She smiles shyly. "I just want to feel you, Rushton. Fast, slow, hard, soft, it doesn't matter to me. As long as it's you."

"On the bed."

She moves to do as I ask, resting her head on my pillow. I crawl over the top of her, dropping my lips to hers as she opens her legs, making room for me to settle between her thighs. Holding my weight on my elbows on either side of her head, I rock my hips, and my cock slides against her pussy that's soaking and ready for me.

Reaching between them, I align myself at her entrance and hold her gaze as I push inside. "Fuck, baby." I drop my forehead to her shoulder, giving her the time she needs to get used to me. Who am I kidding? I'm giving myself time to talk myself out of coming on the first thrust. She's so tight and wet. Her heat surrounds my cock with a warm embrace, and I could live the rest of my life buried balls deep inside her.

"I'm ready for you, Rushton. I want it all. All of you. Give me everything."

"You don't know what you're asking." I pull back to look into her eyes.

"I know that I want you." There's something in her eyes. I've never seen that look before, but I know she wants this. This isn't just for my benefit because I told her that I'm in love with her.

She needs this.

She needs me.

Slowly, I pull out and push back in. With each thrust, my hips rock a little faster. Her legs are locked at the ankles behind my back, and her nails dig into my shoulders as I do as she asks and give her all of me.

Everything I am.

It's her.

I am hers.

Bracing my hands on the mattress on either side of her head, I lift my weight from her body as I continue to rock into her. Her back arches off the bed, and her pussy goes crazy, gripping me tightly.

"Rush!" she cries out her release. Her head tilts back, exposing her neck, and I bend to kiss her there as I continue to pump inside her while she rides out her orgasm. At least that's the plan, but her orgasm keeps going, and I can't hold off any longer. I call out her name as I spill inside her.

When we're both spent, I pull out, lift her off the bed, carry her into the bathroom, and place her on her feet. I start the water, and once the temperature is right, I climb into the tub and hold my hand out for her. She doesn't hesitate to join me, just as I hoped she wouldn't.

We're both quiet until the tub is full, and I reach over and turn off the water with my foot. I wrap my arms around her as my mind races with ways I can prove to her that this is where she belongs.

Here.

With me.

We soak in the silence, with her cradled in my arms. When the water grows cold, we climb out and get dried off. I don't offer her a shirt to sleep in. I don't want anything between us. Instead, I lead her to my bed and hold up the covers, and she climbs in. This time she snuggles up next to me instantly.

"This is nice," she finally says. Her voice is soft and relaxed.

"This is everything."

She nods and rests her head on my chest. I run my fingers through her damp hair. I should have offered to let her dry it, but I'll keep her warm. When her breathing evens out, I know she's asleep.

I whisper the words one more time. "I love you." I kiss the top of her head and let sleep claim me.

Chapter 22

CROSBY

SCHOOL IS OUT UNTIL THE beginning of the new year for Christmas vacation. Christmas is two days away, and I can't seem to stop my mind from racing. It's been four days since Rushton told me he's in love with me.

Four days since I spent the night in his arms.

Four days of me dissecting every moment between us over the past few months.

Four days of craving the feeling of being in his bed and in his arms again.

I know that I love him too. I also know that I was too afraid to tell him, but I've decided he deserves to hear the words. Rushton has been upfront with me from day one. He's told me over and over again how much he cares and how much he wants us to have a chance.

I want that chance too.

There are still a lot of unknowns, but I'm tired of living with what-ifs. I'm tired of feeling like I don't belong, and if I'm being honest with myself, since the moment I met Rushton Kincaid, I've never felt alone. He made sure of that, and I've been hiding behind my fear. I've been unfair to him. My own insecurities stopped me from giving in to what we have. The love that we've developed for one another.

He's coming over for dinner tonight, and I'm going to tell him that I love him too. I also need to apologize. I was scared. While I'm still scared, I trust in Rushton. He's proven to me time and time again I'm who he wants to spend his life with. I can't worry about what might or might not happen.

All I can do is follow my heart, and it's leading me to Rushton.

Needless to say, I'm nervous. I've never told anyone in my life that I love them. I've never felt this level of love or contentment in my entire life.

I can't sit still, so I'm cleaning my house. Every nook and cranny has been scrubbed and organized, cabinets, refrigerator, closets, you name it. I have one room left, which is the bathroom, and I still have over five hours before he gets off work. Once the bathroom is done, I plan to take a long shower, and maybe I'll run to the grocery store. Even though I'm not looking forward to the pre-holiday crowds, it will be better than sitting here stewing over what I'm going to be doing in a few hours.

Stepping into the bathroom, I glance in the mirror, and the first thing I notice is my smile. I'm all alone, but I can't stop smiling. I'm happy and in love, and I can't wait to tell him. I also see my hair that's in a messy bun, my old college T-shirt, and my threadbare leggings that I refuse to get rid of because they are so damn comfortable. It's a good thing he's not going to be here anytime soon.

I'm a mess.

Getting back to work, I pop my earbuds back into my ears and start with the shower first. Once that's done, I move to the toilet and then the countertop. Dropping to my knees, I pull everything out from beneath the cabinet and wipe it down before putting everything back.

Grabbing the unopened box of Tampons, I place them neatly and close the door. I stand and freeze.

Tampons.

Unopened box.

No.

No.

No.

Digging into the side pocket of my leggings for my phone, I frantically tap at the screen to pull up my calendar.

I'm late.

Two weeks late.

I'm never late, and I've been so preoccupied with trying to pretend as if I wasn't head over heels in love with Rushton to notice. Pulling up the browser on my phone, I search for reasons your period could be late, and stress is one of them. I'm sure that's all that it is. I've been stressing out about what I wanted to do. That's been a lot.

Pulling my earbuds out, I place them on the counter next to my phone and peel out of my clothes. I need a shower. I'm stressing over every little thing. I just need to get ready and wait for Rushton to get here, and everything will be fine.

It's fine.

Except now, I can't turn the idea off. We had unprotected sex. Twice. I'm on the pill to regulate my periods, but crazier things have happened. I finish my shower and get dressed, taking the time to put loose curls in my short hair. The entire time I keep glancing at my flat stomach. I won't be able to stop obsessing until I know.

Glancing at the clock, I still have several hours before Rushton gets off work, so I grab my purse and keys and head to town. Except when I get to town, I keep driving. I can't buy a pregnancy test in Willow River. Everyone knows there's something between Rushton and me, and everyone knows Rushton and his family.

A trip to Harris it is.

I try listening to the radio, but my thoughts are louder, so I complete the drive in silence. When I finally pull into the parking lot of the pharmacy, I'm freaking out. Peering in the rearview mirror, you can't see the internal battle I'm waging inside.

"Just go in and buy the test, Crosby," I whisper to myself. Grabbing my purse and my keys, I head inside. I find the pregnancy tests easy enough, and I'm a little overwhelmed by all of the options, so as any sane person would do, I choose five different ones. Better safe than sorry, and I know myself. One will not be enough to convince me of the outcome.

There's no line at the checkout, and ten minutes later, I'm back on the road and headed toward home. The twenty-minute drive seems to take mere minutes. I'm so lost in thought. I'm lucky I wasn't in an accident or worse with how distracted I am. Clutching the bag, I rush inside and make my way to the bathroom. Dumping the bag out on the counter, I pick a random box, read the directions, and get down to business, taking the first test.

The box says five minutes, so I leave the room and pace back and forth from the living room to the kitchen until my phone alerts me that my time is up. This is it. This is the moment when my life could change forever.

Walking back into the bathroom, I close my eyes and take a calming breath before opening them and reaching for the test. Two pink lines.

I'm pregnant.

Tears immediately prick my eyes as I run to the kitchen, grab a bottle of water, and begin to chug. I should have peed in a damn cup so I could take the rest, or hell, opened them and taken them all at once. Instead, I sit on the bathroom floor, chug the water, and wait until the urge hits me. Within fifteen minutes, I'm taking two more tests and resting them on the counter. I repeat the same process of pacing, but this time I hold the positive test in one hand while the other rests over my flat belly.

Over my baby.

"I'm pregnant," I whisper. I need to say the words out loud for them to sink in.

My phone beeps for the second time, and I rush back to the bathroom to get the results. Flipping over the test, I got two more positives. Three total.

I'm pregnant.

I'm going to be a mom.

Tears instantly coat my cheeks as a sob racks my chest. I can't control my tears. I drop all three tests into the sink and find my way back to the living room. I curl up on the couch, pulling the blanket over me, and let it out.

I cry for all I've lost.

I cry for all I've gained.

I cry for my future, for my baby, and for so many things. I can't stop the tears.

There's a knock at the door, and I wipe at my cheeks, sucking in a deep breath before calling out, "Come in," to whoever it is. It's probably Alyssa. She's the only one who really stops by other than Rush and the twins, but they're all at work, and I know Alyssa was off today.

"Hey, Crosby, can we borrow some sugar?" I hear Maverick ask. "Cliché, but I'm making tea, and we're ou—" He stops when he sees me on the couch. I'm sure my eyes are red and swollen, and no matter how hard I try, I can't stop the tears.

Maverick rushes to me, releasing the measuring cups from his hand as they fall onto the floor as he drops to his knees beside me on the floor. He reaches for my hand. "What's wrong? Are you hurt?" His eyes are wide and panicked, and I know I need to calm down so that I can tell him I'm okay, and then I remember that the stress isn't good for the baby, and I cry harder.

"I don't do good with tears. Here, sis, you're going to have to help me out." He reaches into his pocket and curses. "Fuck, I don't have my phone. Crosby, I need you to answer me. Are you hurt?" His voice is soft and caring, so much like his brother's.

The man I'm in love with.

The father of my baby.

The tears fall harder.

"Yo, Mav, did you get lost? You better not be harassing Crosby. Rush will flip his lid." I hear Merrick call. He stops when he sees us. "What's going on?"

"I don't know, man. I just walked in, and this is how I found her. I can't get her to tell me what's wrong, and she won't stop crying, and I don't know what to do. What do we do with these tears?"

"We were raised with dudes," Merrick says. You can hear the panic in his voice.

Their banter makes me cry harder. This is my baby's family. My baby will have a big, loving family.

Merrick sits on the end of the couch and places his hand on my leg. "Are you hurt?"

I try to answer, but the tears are coming too fast.

"Do you have your phone? Call Rushton. Now!" Maverick yells at his brother, and that makes me cry harder.

Is this what they refer to as pregnancy hormones? Why can't I get a hold of myself? I need to tell them that I'm okay. I open my mouth to do just that, and the only word that comes out is his name. "Rush."

"We're calling him," Maverick tells me.

"Rush, hey, you need to come home or come to Crosby's. I don't know what's wrong. She's crying, and I can't understand her, and we don't know if she's hurt. No, she looks fine, other than the tears, and yeah, Mav and I are here. Okay. I'll tell her. Okay, hold on." Merrick taps the screen and holds the phone closer to me so that I can hear it. "You're on speaker," he tells Rushton.

"Baby?" Rushton's worried voice reaches me, and I sob even harder.

Baby.

"Crosby, I'm on my way to you. Can you hear me? Baby, nod your head if you can hear me."

I manage to nod, and Merrick relays that to Rushton.

"I'm almost there. I was already on my way. I got off work early, and I was coming to you. I'll be there in less than five minutes. You hear me, gorgeous?" His voice cracks. "I'm almost there."

"We'll be here when you get here, man. Just drive safe," Merrick tells him.

"Don't leave her. Don't you dare leave her." Rushton's tone is laced with warning.

"Mav and I are right next to her. I don't think she's hurt, just really upset. The only thing we can get her to say is your name."

"Fuck. I'm almost there." The line goes dead.

For the next two minutes, I try to focus on breathing with the instruction of the twins as they do it with me, trying to calm me down. However, when I hear his truck pull into the drive, and the door slam, then his heavy boots on the front porch, and my front door swinging open, all progress I've made flies out the window.

Rushton races into the room and skids to a stop when he sees me. Maverick moves out of the way, as does Merrick, while Rushton slowly approaches me. His eyes roam over every part of me that he can see before he drops to where Maverick was on his knees, doing the same. He places his palm against my cheek and waits for me to look at him.

"Crosby, baby, I need you to tell me if you're hurt. You're scaring me."

I shake my head, and he instantly relaxes. "Thanks, guys. Can you give us a minute?" he asks his brothers.

"We'll be next door if you need us," Merrick tells him.

Once the front door closes, Rushton stands, sits next to me on the couch, and lifts me onto his lap. He doesn't say a word. He just holds me while I soak his shirt with my tears. His hand runs soothingly up and down my back, and he whispers over and over that he's here for me, and whatever it is that it's all going to be okay.

Eventually, I get my emotions under control, and my tears dry up. I lift my head to look at him. His eyes study me, trying like hell to figure out what caused my tears.

"I love you." My voice is raspy from my tears, but he hears me. "I'm in love with you."

His eyes soften. "I love you too." He wipes at my cheeks with his thumbs. "Why the tears?"

"I got some news today. Some happy news, but before I tell you, I want you to know that I invited you over to tell you that I'm in love with you. I was going to tell you that we can try, and you're worth the risk. I can't stand being away from you, and pushing you away hurts us both."

"You are my everything, Crosby Greene." He kisses me softly. "Now, tell me about this good news that has my girl in uncontrollable tears."

I move to get off his lap, but he tightens his hold. "I'll be right back. I just have to grab something."

Reluctantly, he lets me go. I rush down the hall and grab all three positive tests, and race back to him. I stand before where he sits on the couch with my hands behind my back. "I want this. I want you. I understand if this changes things for you. It wasn't until I started seeing clearly, until I knew that I couldn't keep running from what's between us, that I realized this could even be an option."

"You can tell me anything."

I swallow back my emotions. My palms are sweating and my knees feel as though they might give out at any second. My entire life I've always followed my gut, never allowing myself to lead with my heart, and right now I'm doing both. I'm scared as hell that I've read him wrong, that he's not going to take this news as I have. I'm happy. I hope he's happy too, and this is the start of our life together. No matter what the obstacles, we'll face them. Together.

"Close your eyes and hold out your hand." He does as I ask, and I place all three tests in his palm. "Open."

His eyes pop open, and he stares at his palm. I watch as a shock that is masked by a smile washes over him. He peers up at me. "These are yours?"

"Yes."

"You took them today?"

"Yes."

"This is why you were crying?"

"Yes."

"Happy tears?"

"Very much happy tears."

"We're having a baby?" he asks. His voice cracks as he, too, loses his battle with his emotions.

"We're having a baby."

"And you love me?"

"Very much."

He stands from the couch and crushes me into a hug. "I love you. I love you. I love you," he repeats over and over again. Then he falls to his knees and places his hands over my belly. "I love you too, little one." With his head tilted back, he smiles up at me. "I need to hear you tell me that this is real. That we're going to stay together."

"This is as real as it gets. We're going to stay together. You're stuck with me forever."

"I wouldn't have it any other way."

"You should probably tell the twins I'm not losing my mind," I tell him a few hours later. We're in bed after just making love.

"You're right." He kisses me, kisses my belly, and then climbs out of bed to go in search of his phone. "Hey, yeah, she's good." I hear him say. "She got some good news, and it kind of took her by storm. We're in for the night. Nah, thanks, though."

He walks back into the room and takes his spot beside me in bed. "We have so much to talk about," he tells me.

"We'll take it all one day at a time."

"Who are you and what have you done with my Crosby?" he asks.

"When I finally decided that I was willing to take the risk to be with you, everything just sort of clicked into place. I know that my job is still up in the air, but you're right. I can apply at Harris, or just be a substitute here, or even Harris, maybe? I know that I don't want you to leave your family, so if I have to put teaching on the back burner, then that's what I have to do."

"You love teaching."

She nods. "It's all I've ever had, but now I have you."

"And our baby."

Tears well in my eyes. "And our baby. I love you, and I trust in that love. You've shown me over and over again that I can, that we're stronger together, and I'm so sorry for what I put us through."

"Nothing to be sorry for. You gave me your truth, and I knew you needed time. I was willing to wait forever."

"Now we're forever."

"We were always forever."

Chapter 23

RUSHTON

I DIDN'T KNOW THAT IT was possible to be this happy. My face hurts from smiling. Two days ago, I woke up to a message from Crosby asking me to have dinner at her place after work. Never in my wildest dreams did I imagine that it would be to tell me that she was in love with me.

Even further from my mind is the fact that she found out that same day that we were having a baby.

I'm going to be a dad.

Every damn time I think the words, I get choked up. I can see how my parents were willing to do this nine times, well, eight because of the twins, but the rush of knowing that I created a life with the woman I love is a feeling I can't describe and unlike anything I've ever felt.

My brothers were right. I wouldn't trade this for anything.

We spent the entire day yesterday, Christmas Eve, talking and making plans. Something that we've not been able to do in the past because she was worried about what the future might hold. I stuck to the family motto, took the advice of my dad and my brothers, and I loved the hell out of her, never giving up until she truly felt it. Until she understood she was who I wanted and that I wasn't going anywhere, no matter the timeline she put us under.

The only timeline we have now is when our baby is due. That and when I can convince her to marry me. I'm ready for the happily ever after. Yesterday we decided that she would move in with me. I own my place, and she rents, and she's on a one-year lease. I know the owner, and one phone call was all it took for him to agree to let her out of it. It pays to live in such a small town.

"Hey." I walk into the bedroom just as Crosby is pulling her sweater over her head. "Are you about ready to go?"

"Yes. I just need to find my shoes, and we can load the car."

"I already loaded it."

She smiles. "Thank you."

I walk further into the room and snake my arms around her waist, kissing her softly. "Anything for you. You know that. And you didn't have to buy my family gifts. I thought I told you that I was putting your name on all of mine."

"You did, but I was with the girls and got carried away, and well, it was just another way I was trying to keep myself divided from you."

"No more dividing."

"Never."

"Are you sure you're okay with telling everyone today?"

"Normally, I would say no. There's a rule about these things, but I don't like hiding things from your family. Everyone has been so welcoming to me. But they're your family, so I'll leave that decision up to you. I'm fine with telling them, and I'm fine with waiting until we see a doctor."

"I know there are risks," I say, not wanting to bring it up but feeling as if I need to.

"Whatever happens, we do it together. I'd already made up my mind before I found the unopened box of Tampons."

I lean back, placing my hand on her belly. "Daddy has good swimmers, huh?"

She playfully rolls those big brown eyes. "Come on. We need to go, or we'll be late." She steps out of my hold, grabs her shoes, and disappears down the hallway.

Fifteen minutes later, we're walking into my parents' place. My arms are loaded down with gifts that I refuse to let her carry. She argued that she was barely pregnant, but I didn't care. If I can do it for her, if I can make this pregnancy any easier, I'm going to do it.

I stack the gifts under the tree, take her hand in mine, and stand to face my family. My gaze scans the room to make sure that everyone is here. "Hey." I wave to them, and they all turn to look at me like I've lost my mind.

"Crosby and I exchanged gifts early, and I wanted to tell everyone what I got."

"Nice." Maverick steps forward and gives Crosby a hug, as does Merrick. No one questions why. We're an affectionate family. They don't know that my two youngest brothers stayed with my girl while she cried happy, chest-sobbing tears that she's going to be a mom. Not even the twins. All they know is that once I got there, she calmed down and I haven't left her place since.

"First of all, I'd like to introduce you to my girlfriend." I raise our joined hands. "We're officially official." I grin at my family, and their wide smiles in return tell me they're happy for me. For us.

We're swarmed with hugs and pats on the backs, which I expected. Once everyone is settled and back in their seat, I start again. "That was my first gift, but I got another one. I love them both equally, but one came before the other."

"Would you stop beating around the bush and tell us? Crosby, did you buy him a new PlayStation?" Maverick asks.

She turns to look at me. "No. Did you want one?"

"No, these knuckleheads want one of us to buy one, so they can play it," I tell her.

"Hey, you can't blame us for trying. We're the babies of the family, remember?" Merrick asks. "Besides the one we have is old and getting slow."

"No, Uncle Mer, that's Remi, Beckham, Orion, and me, but now I'm a big girl," Blakely tells him.

"Come here you." Merrick holds his arms out for Blakely, and she rushes to him, giving him a big hug.

"Tell us already," Orrin calls out.

I smile down at Crosby and mouth, "I love you," before facing my family once again. "We found out two days ago that we're having a baby."

I pull Crosby into my arms, her back to my front as our family surrounds us. We're one big group hug, with everyone talking at once, and it's the exact reaction I was expecting. It takes some time for everyone to calm down, but when they do, I keep going.

"She's moving in with me. We just found out, so she hasn't been to the doctor yet, and as soon as I can convince her, she's going to be my wife." I find Sterling's eyes in the room. "You better step up your game, brother. I'll be married before you are."

"Not unless you're planning a spring wedding," Sterling announces.

"You set a date?" Mom asks.

"We did." Alyssa nods.

This time it's my brother and his fiancée who get the praise, and my girl and I are just fine with that. I continue to hold her as we watch everyone laugh and talk.

"Your family is incredible, Rush."

"Our family." I place my hand on her belly. "You and this baby, you're a part of all this now, Crosby. They're just as much yours as they are mine. Don't ever doubt that."

"Is that what happens when two people stay together?" she teases.

"Just us, baby. Just us."

"Is it time for gifts?" Blakely asks.

"Sure is, kiddo," Ryder tells her. "Why don't you go see what you can find under the tree with your name on it?"

Blakely looks to Declan and Kennedy and they nod, giving her permission before she bolts for the family room, with all of us trailing behind her. Our family was already huge, but we're growing, adding wives, fiancées, and babies. We're sitting on every surface, the floor, and the chairs from the dining room table have been brought in so that everyone can be together for opening gifts.

I'm sitting in the recliner with Crosby on my lap. She protested, but once she realized that my brothers and their wives were in similar seating situations, she relaxed against me. We spend the next hour opening gifts, well, mostly, Blakely and the littles get help from Blakely and their parents. It's perfect. It's one of the best Christmases I can remember having since I was old enough to understand there was no Santa Claus. I owe all that to the woman who gave me her heart, the same woman who holds mine.

"Well, that's a wrap," Archer says. He stretches out on the floor surrounded by paper with Remi lying on his chest.

"Not exactly," Mom says. She stands, reaches behind the tree, and grabs an envelope. I glance at my brothers to see if any of them seem to know what she's doing, and they all look as confused as I do. When Mom makes her way to Crosby and me, my brows furrow. "One more." Mom smiles as she hands the envelope to Crosby.

"You've already done too much," Crosby says. "Today has been—everything I ever dreamed it could be. Thank you all for giving me this day with your family." She turns her head to look at me. "Thank you for sharing your family with me."

I lean in and kiss her, which has my brothers cheering me on, and Blakely giggling that I kissed her teacher. The kid and I need to have a chat. Crosby is going to be her aunt, sooner rather than later if I have any say-so.

"This isn't anything we bought for you," Mom tells her. "It's something I know you've been wanting, though." She gives Crosby the same grin she would give us as kids when she knew something that we didn't think she knew. Moms really do have eyes in the backs of their heads.

"Open it," I encourage Crosby.

"Thank you. I don't know what's inside this envelope, and I don't care. You all have given me so much." Her voice cracks. "I couldn't imagine anything that could make this day better than it's been."

"Open it." Mom nods toward the envelope that Crosby now grips in her hands.

Slowly, she slides her finger under the seal and pulls out a stack of papers. Unable to resist, I read over her shoulder, and my eyes snap to my mother's, as Crosby begins to cry. Her shoulders are shaking, and I can see the way her chest is suddenly rising and falling in rapid succession.

"What is it?" Palmer asks.

Crosby shakes her head, before standing and pulling my mom into a hug. "I don't know how you did this. I don't even know what to say. Is it real?"

"Yes, sweetheart, it's real."

"The suspense is killing me," Ramsey calls out, taking away some of the heaviness of the moment.

My mom slides her arm around Crosby's waist and turns to look at the room. "Crosby was offered an extension to her contract. If she chooses to sign, she's going to be the kindergarten teacher at Willow River for the next five years. And before you ask, that's the longest contract they can offer for a teacher. I have no doubt that she's going to hold that position for years to come."

The ladies swarm my mom and Crosby, and there is not a dry eye in the house. I stand, needing to go to her, but I feel a hand land on my shoulder. Looking over, I see my dad standing there. "Your mother...." He shakes his head, his lips tilting into a smile. "Just when I think I can't love that woman any more." He pulls his attention away from my mom to glance at me. "She knew this was what was holding her back. This gift is for you. It's for Crosby and it's for all of us."

"All of you?"

"We get to see you happy. We get to see you become a husband and a father with the woman you love, so yeah. This isn't just for her."

Pulling him into a hug, I quickly release him and head for my girl. I have to shuffle my way through my sisters-in-law, but eventually, I make it to my mom and Crosby. I pull them both into my arms and have to swallow back my own emotions.

"Mom, I love you. Thank you for this. I don't know how you did it, but thank you." I know that we already established that she was here with me regardless of her contract and that we would work it out, but I know Crosby, and this will give her peace and the security she was looking for outside of my love for her.

"I didn't do much. I just happened to mention it to one of the school board members. It was their idea to put it to vote. It happened at the meeting on Monday night. They love you, Crosby, just as much as we do."

Tears coat Crosby's cheeks, and all she can do is nod as words get lodged in her throat. I pull her into my arms and hug her tightly.

When she finally composes herself, she peers up at me. What I see in her eyes, the love that is reflecting back at me almost brings me to my knees. She places her hand over her belly, where our baby is growing inside her. We can't see him or her yet, but we know they are there. And the love... so much love for both of them.

"We're always going to stay together."

"Always, gorgeous." I kiss her temple and guide her back to the chair.

Today couldn't have been any better. It's one I'll remember for the rest of my life.

Epilogue

CROSBY

I CAN'T STOP SMILING. TODAY has been the perfect day, and I'm so happy for Sterling and Alyssa. Every moment of their wedding was beautiful. And the love they share, you can see it every single time they look at one another.

"How are my girls?" Rushton sneaks up behind me and wraps his arms around my waist. He rests our joined hands on my belly, and my heart flutters when I see our own wedding rings.

My husband is a very convincing man, and he didn't want to wait, and to be honest, neither did I. I felt as though I'd been waiting for him, for a family, my entire life, and I was tired of waiting. I was ready to grab life with both hands and hold on for the ride.

With the help of my sisters-in-law, mother-in-law, and Kennedy's grandmother, we were able to plan a small wedding at the Willow Manor the last weekend in February. It was just our family, and it was over just as fast as it began, but I wouldn't change a single thing about our day. Afterward, we all enjoyed cake and great food. Palmer took some incredible pictures for us that we have proudly displayed in our home.

In my wildest imagination, I never dreamed this would be my life. That I would find a man who broke through all of my walls and stands beside me each and every day. I always wanted a family of my own, and that extends past Rushton and our baby. His family is my family. They treat me as such, and I love them all. Every single one of them holds a place in my heart that was once empty but is now overflowing.

"What if it's a boy?"

"It's a girl. I can feel it."

"I wouldn't question him," Palmer says, coming to stand next to us. "Brooks was convinced we were having a girl, and—" She nods to where Brooks is bouncing Remi on his hip as he talks to Orrin and Deacon. "That's what we got."

"Us dads know these things," Rushton says, making us both laugh.

"Stop. Go do manly things," I tell him.

"Oh, I can do many things, gorgeous, but I'm going to need you to come with me."

"Stop." Palmer holds up her hand. "I can't with the two of you." She's grinning. "You're going to make me want to jump my husband, and I'm not ready for baby number two yet."

"Don't tell me you're holding out on him?" I ask, shocked.

"Hell no. You've seen my husband, right? But the way the two of you are all lovey, and then Sterling and Alyssa, and I'm in the frame of mind where I just might let him talk me into it."

Rushton's head falls back in laughter. I can feel the vibration of his chest against my back. "On that note, I'm going to go talk manly things. I'll save the doing for when I get you alone." He kisses my neck, releases his hold on me, and walks away.

"How long do you think until they're pregnant?" Palmer nods to where Sterling and Alyssa are dancing close. They're the only two on the dance floor, but they don't seem to mind.

"Soon, I'd guess. I know they both want kids."

"And Sterling will think he has to keep up since the majority of us are married and have at least one." She reaches over and places her hand on my baby bump.

"Are they really that competitive?"

"Nah, they use it as an excuse. They're all big, lovable teddy bears with hearts of gold. They grew up in a house full of kids, and from what I know from them, they all want that. Even the twins when they decide it's time to settle down."

"I love that. I love that our kids are all going to grow up together and never feel alone."

Palmer places her arm around my shoulders. "Never again, Crosby." I don't ask her to elaborate because I don't need her to.

I'm a Kincaid now.

We are family.

We work hard.

We love harder.

Epilogue

RUSHTON

"What's up?" Brooks asks.

I reach for Remi and she leans out of her dad's arms for me to take her into mine. "Our wives told me to go do manly things."

"You good to watch her?" Brooks asks.

"Yeah, why?"

"I'm going to go find my wife to do manly things." He takes a step, and I crack up laughing.

"I already tried and they still sent me away. Palmer said something about you convincing her to have baby number two."

"Been trying," he confesses.

"Tell Daddy you're not even a year old yet, and that this is your time to be spoiled," I tell Remi.

"She's eight months, so by the time we have another, if we were to get pregnant right away, they'll be almost two years apart."

"I'll confess I see the appeal." My eyes scan to my wife.

"The appeal of what?" Archer asks.

"Keeping our wives knocked up."

Archer chuckles. "I don't know about all that, but I'm not against practicing." He tries to steal Remi from me, but I turn so he can't take her. She giggles, and I kiss the top of her head.

"You got someone you've been practicing with?" Brooks asks.

When Archer doesn't reply, I turn to look at him, only to find his eyes locked on something. Following his gaze, I realize it's not something but someone. "Do you know her?"

"Who?" Archer asks, not bothering to tear his gaze from the redhead holding a camera, snapping what's probably a million photos if she's anything like Palmer.

"The redhead."

"No. No, I don't know her," he replies, his gaze following her every move.

"That's Scarlett," Brooks offers helpfully. "Today is her interview of sorts. Palmer has been looking for help as you know, and Scarlett is her top candidate. She wanted to see her in action before she hired her. She figured what better way than today."

"Scarlett," Archer repeats, testing the newcomer's name on his tongue.

"She's more or less hired. Palmer says her work is good, but she wanted to watch her work." Archer doesn't say anything. Brooks's eyes meet mine and I grin. "She's off limits," Brooks says, barely containing his grin.

"What?" Archer's head whips to face Brooks. "No."

"No?" Brooks raises his brow. He's fucking with him, but Archer is too lost in her to notice.

"She's not off limits. You can't do that."

Brooks shrugs. "Sure, I can. She's my wife's employee, mine by association."

"She's—Nope. Take your off-limits rules and—" He glances at Remi. "—eat them." He pats Brooks on the chest, and walks away. We watch him as he stalks toward Scarlett, and they strike up a conversation.

"You think he's next?" I ask Brooks.

"Hard to tell. Jordyn should be coming home soon, right?"

"Yeah, what's going on there? Has Ryder said anything?"

"Not much. He's still fighting for her."

I nod. "I hope it works out for them."

"Me too, Rush. Me too."

I don't know when the rest of our brothers will find love. I'm confident that they will find that one person who makes them want to be a better man. Ryder has found his; they need to see if they can work their way back to each other. As far as Archer and the twins, who knows. What I do know is that I'll be there for them every step of the way. Besides, I'm a married man and a soon-to-be father. I'll have all kinds of sage advice when the time gets here.

 *Thank* **Y O U**

for taking the time to read ***Stay Together***.

Want more from the Kincaid Brothers?
Look for Archer's story, ***Stay Wild***
releasing August 22, 2023.
Grab your copy at kayleeryan.com/books/stay-wild/

Never miss a new release:
Newsletter Sign-up

Be the first to hear about free content, new releases, cover
reveals, sales, and more. kayleeryan.com/subscribe/

Discover more about Kaylee's books
kayleeryan.com/all-books/

Did you know that Orrin Kincaid has his own story?
Grab ***Stay Always*** for free
kayleeryan.com/books/stay-always/

Start the Riggins Brothers Series for FREE.
Download ***Play by Play*** now
kayleeryan.com/books/play-by-play/

Contact
KAYLEE RYAN

Website
kayleeryan.com

Facebook
facebook.com/KayleeRyanAuthor/

Instagram
instagram.com/kaylee_ryan_author/

Goodreads
goodreads.com/author/show/7060310.Kaylee_Ryan

BookBub
bookbub.com/authors/kaylee-ryan

TikTok
tiktok.com/@kayleeryanauthor

More from KAYLEE RYAN

With You Series:

Anywhere with You | More with You | Everything with You

Soul Serenade Series:

Emphatic | Assured | Definite | Insistent

Southern Heart Series:

Southern Pleasure | Southern Desire
Southern Attraction | Southern Devotion

Unexpected Arrivals Series

Unexpected Reality |Unexpected Fight | Unexpected Fall
Unexpected Bond | Unexpected Odds

Riggins Brothers Series:

Play by Play | Layer by Layer | Piece by Piece
Kiss by Kiss | Touch by Touch | Beat by Beat

Kincaid Brothers Series:

Stay Always | Stay Over | Stay Forever
Stay Tonight | Stay Together

Standalone Titles:

Tempting Tatum | Unwrapping Tatum | Levitate
Just Say When | I Just Want You | Reminding Avery

Hey, Whiskey | Pull You Through | Remedy
The Difference | Trust the Push | Forever After All
Misconception | Never with Me

More from KAYLEE RYAN

Entangled Hearts Duet:
Agony | Bliss

Cocky Hero Club:
Lucky Bastard

Mason Creek Series:
Perfect Embrace

Out of Reach Series:
Beyond the Bases | Beyond the Game
Beyond the Play | Beyond the Team

Co-written with Lacey Black:

Fair Lakes Series:
It's Not Over | Just Getting Started | Can't Fight It

Standalone Titles:
Boy Trouble | Home to You
Beneath the Fallen Stars | Tell Me A Story

Coowriting as Rebel Shaw with Lacey Black:
Royal | Crying Shame

Acknowledgments

To my readers:

Thank you for continuing to show your support with reading each and every release. I cannot tell you what that means to me. Thank you for taking the journey with me.

To my family:

I love you. You hold me up and support me every day. I can't imagine my life without you as my support system. Thank you for believing in me, and being there to celebrate my success.

Sara Eirew:

I've been holding onto this one for a while. Thank you for another great image.

Tami Integrity Formatting:

Thank you for making Stay Together beautiful. You're amazing and I cannot thank you enough for all that you do.

The Book Cover Boutique:

You nailed this series. I rambled about what I wanted, and you came up with something even better. Thank you!

My beta team:

Jamie, Stacy, Lauren, Erica, and Franci I would be lost without you. You read my words as much as I do, and I can't tell you what your input and all the time you give means to me. Countless messages and bouncing ideas, you ladies keep me sane with the characters are being anything but. Thank you from the bottom of my heart for taking this wild ride with me.

My ARC Team:

An amazing group of readers who shout about my books from the rooftops, and I couldn't be more grateful for every single one of you. Thank you for being a part of the team, and a critical part of every single release.

Give Me Books:

With every release, your team works diligently to get my book in the hands of bloggers. I cannot tell you how thankful I am for your services.

Grey's Promotions:

Thank you for your support with this release. I am so grateful for your team.

Deaton Author Services, Editing 4 Indies, Jo Thompson, & Jess Hodge:

Thank you for giving this book a fresh set of eyes. I appreciate each of you helping me make this book the best that it can be.

Becky Johnson:

I could not do this without you. Thank you for pushing me, and making me work for it.

Chasidy Renee:

How did I survive without you? Thank you for making my life so much easier.

Lacey Black:

There isn't much I can say that I have not already, except for I love ya, girl. Your friendship means the world to me. Thank you for being you.

Bloggers:

Thank you doesn't seem like enough. You don't get paid to do what you do. It's from the kindness of your heart and your love of reading that fuels you. Without you, without your pages, your voice, your reviews, spreading the word it would be so much harder, if not impossible, to get my words in reader's hands. I can't tell you how much your never-ending support means to me. Thank you for being you, thank you for all that you do.

To my Kaylee's Crew Members:

You are my people. I love chatting with you. I'm honored to have you on this journey with me. Thank you for reading, sharing, commenting, suggesting, the teasers, the messages all of it. Thank you from the bottom of my heart for all that you do. Your support is everything!

Much love,

Kaylee Ryan
AUTHOR